The Heat Death
of the Universe
and other stories

The Heat Death
of the Universe
and other stories

Pamela
Zoline

McPherson
& Company

ho mitakuya oyasin

Published by McPherson & Company
Box 1126, Kingston, New York 12402
Text and cover design by Bruce R. McPherson.
Typeset by Delmas. Printed on pH neutral paper.
Manufactured in the U.S.A.
Second edition. February 2021.
1 3 5 7 9 8 6 4 2   2021 2022 2023

ISBN-13: 9781620540343
LCCN: 87-31275

NOTE: This edition employs the pages and pagination of the first edition; the only change occurs on page 123, where lyrics (rather than blanks for words) of "The Whiffenpoof Song" are inserted as originally intended by the author. The lyrics are now in the public domain.

Acknowledgement of first publication of four pieces: "The Heat Death of the Universe," *New Worlds*, Michael Moorcock, ed., copyright © 1967; "The Holland of the Mind," *The New SF*, Langdon Jones, ed., London: Hutchinson, copyright © 1969; "Sheep," *Likely Stories*, Bruce McPherson, ed., Treacle Press, copyright © 1981; "Instructions for Exiting this Building in Case of Fire," *Interzone*, copyright © 1985.

CONTENTS

Introduction by Thomas M. Disch   7

The Heat Death of the Universe   13
The Holland of the Mind   29
Instructions for Exiting this Building in Case of Fire   71
Sheep   89
Busy About the Tree of Life   155

The Astonishing Pamela Zoline

by Thomas M. Disch

1. The first painting of Pamela's that I saw was of an angel with the most amazing wings. Gorgeous slapdash wings with a fauvist palette and (if memory serves) lots of gold-leaf. That would have been the fall of 1962, the year Pamela was at Barnard. To be painting like that already at age 21! It didn't occur to me then how utterly unfashionable her painting was. 1962 must have been the nadir for figurative painting in New York. And *angels?* But a successful angel in its nature transcends fashion. Ask Rilke.

2. The first story of Pamela's that I read was "The Heat Death of the Universe." That was in London in spring of '67. It had the same basic out-knocking effect as the angel painting, and then some. At this point Pamela, who had been studying at the Slade School, had produced a small warehouse-full of paintings that confirmed the augery of those gold-leaf wings, paintings at once cerebral and sensuous, quirky and full of the Zeitgeist. And now, here she was, with no visible apprenticeship, producing a short story that out-New-Waved the lot of us, that was the prose equivalent to the wings of that angel.

3. The New Wave. I generally maintain that there never was such a thing. There was a magazine, *New Worlds*, whose editor Mike Moorcock had assembled a small core of SF writers living in and around London, but aside from our propinquity and a general ambition to write science fiction suitable for grown-ups, the nearest thing to a common esthetic would have been Ballard's "mini-novels." These narrative mosaics deliberately fractured the sense of a continuous dramatic scene or even a sustained tone of

7

voice, presenting instead a series of vivid *tableaux vivants* and quick bright bursts of Idea in a raw and indefensible state. These bright ideas characteristically were erotic interpretations of the semes of modern life, i.e., the Consumer Society. Which for Ballard had meant mainly cars, high-rises, and medical technology. (It only now occurs to me that this approach closely parallels the concurrent work of such pop-semiologists across the Channel as Barthes, but there was no direct influence: none of us read French.)

4. The problem with appointing Ballard standard-bearer of the New Wave was that, while his images were trendy and easily (and much) borrowed, his *modus operandi* was inimitable. Except by Pamela, who created, in "The Heat Death of the Universe," the most technically accomplished and humane mosaic fiction produced by the New Wave. A Ballard story for human beings.

5. And I can't even say I kibbitzed! Pamela wrote it while I was away from London for a month, traveling about Ireland in an ecstasy of youthful Weltschmertz. John Sladek was on hand while it was written ("built" might be a better word) and did get to kibbitz and offer moral support and generally play the Muse. But Pamela assured me, after my first gasps of praise and consternation, that she'd intended to knock *me* particularly out. Literary historians, bear that in mind.

6. What I didn't understand about that story, or the others that were to follow, each one so different, each so anomalous in its intention and inspiration, each so neatly balanced between the most rarified artistry and the most sensational emotional assault-and-battery, what I don't understand is this: What makes Pamela write? That's not quite true. I understood it but was disinclined to believe it: everything Pamela writes has been an act of friendship, the written portion of a much larger dialogue she is carrying on with a particular denizen of the world. Other writers may be motivated by the carrot of a lucrative sale or the *reclam* of appearing in an Important magazine. A few may be genuinely obsessive about their writing and would write if theirs were the only eyes in the world. But Pamela writes for an Other.

7. Pamela lived on Camden High Street when she wrote "The Heat Death," in a duplex flat that was already at that time

filled to the rafters with a generous sampling of Everything. Pamela may be particular in her aim as to her audience, but when it comes to her material she is a true Earth Mother. She wants it all, and she wants to *put* it all in her flat, and into her paintings and stories. (Just consider the chutzpah implicit in the title of that first story.) She is a born encyclopedist, and the flat in Camden Town was, in consequence, a depository for several mounds of antiquated children's encyclopedias, which she collected as another sort of paleontologist would collect the bones of dinosaurs. Pamela didn't collect encyclopedias exclusively. She was also fond of English milk bottles, having come to London from a land that had abolished the beauty of glass milk bottles for the disposable drabness of paper cartons. So the flat was full of milk bottles too. And large brass shell casings left over from World War II, which were to be had for a few shillings from the venders in the flea market just outside the entrance to her flat. (Pamela's neighborhood has since replaced Portobello Road as London's main flea market, but she got there first and snapped up most of the real bargains.)

8. It also seems relevant that Pamela is by nature one of the happiest people in existence. It is a fate ordained by biochemistry: she has abnormally high endorphin levels. This doesn't mean that her fictions or paintings are lacking in tenebrous expanses. Indeed, her encyclopedist tendencies would militate against an all-bright emotional spectrum. She celebrates all gamuts she is party to. But when she is dark, she is hugely and energetically dark. Tragedy might interest her, but she's never been one to kvetch about boredom. That's why, whatever may be going on—a crisis or a moonrise—Pamela is fun to be with and to read.

9. One of Pamela's recurrent "themes"—and something we manage to argue about every time we get together—is the realm of the spiritual/supernatural. She believes in it in a way that I don't, but I'm always happy to *visit* it in her company. She is an excellent guide to the realms of the unseen, the supposed, the otherwise apprehended.

10. As a believer in the decimal system, and because it does sort of sum it all up, I must add that I love Pamela. She has that effect on a lot of people. And her stories operate similarly.

The Heat Death
of the Universe
and other stories

The Heat Death of the Universe

1. ONTOLOGY: That branch of metaphysics which concerns itself with the problems of the nature of existence or being.

2. Imagine a pale blue morning sky, almost green, with clouds only at the rims. The earth rolls and the sun appears to mount, mountains erode, fruits decay, the Foraminifera adds another chamber to its shell, babies' fingernails grow as does the hair of the dead in their graves, and in egg timers the sands fall and the eggs cook on.

3. Sarah Boyle thinks of her nose as too large, though several men have cherished it. The nose is generous and performs a well-calculated geometric curve, at the arch of which the skin is drawn very tight and a faint whiteness of bone can be seen showing through, it has much the same architectural tension and sense of mathematical calculation as the day after Thanksgiving breastbone on the carcass of turkey; her maiden name was Sloss, mixed German, English and Irish descent; in grade school she was very bad at playing softball and, besides being chosen last for the team, was always made to play center field, no one could ever hit to center field; she loves music best of all the arts, and of music, Bach, J.S.; she lives in California, though she grew up in Boston and Toledo.

4. BREAKFAST TIME AT THE BOYLES' HOUSE ON LA FLORIDA STREET, ALAMEDA, CALIFORNIA, THE CHILDREN DEMAND SUGAR FROSTED FLAKES.

With some reluctance Sarah Boyle dishes out Sugar Frosted Flakes to her children, already hearing the decay set in upon the little milk-white teeth, the bony whine of the dentist's drill. The dentist is a short, gentle man with a moustache who sometimes reminds Sarah of an uncle who lives in Ohio. One bowl per child.

5. If one can imagine it considered as an abstract object, by members of a totally separate culture, one can see that the cereal box might seem a beautiful thing. The solid rectangle is neatly joined and classical in proportions, on it are squandered wealths of richest colors, virgin blues, crimsons, dense ochres, precious pigments once reserved for sacred paintings and as cosmetics for the blind faces of marble gods. Giant size. Net Weight 16 ounces, 250 grams. "They're tigeriffic!" says Tony the Tiger. The box blatts promises: Energy, Nature's Own Goodness, an endless pubescence. On its back is a mask of William Shakespeare to be cut out, folded, worn by thousands of tiny Shakespeares in Kansas City, Detroit, Tuscon, San Diego, Tampa. He appears at once more kindly and somewhat more vacant than we are used to seeing him. Two or more of the children lay claim to the mask, but Sarah puts off that Solomon's decision until such time as the box is empty.

6. A notice in orange flourishes states that a Surprise Gift is to be found somewhere in the package, nestled amongst the golden flakes. So far it has not been unearthed, and the children request more cereal than they wish to eat, great yellow heaps of it, to hurry the discovery. Even so, at the end of the meal, some layers of flakes remain in the box and the Gift must still be among them.

7. There is even a Special Offer of a secret membership, code and magic ring; these to be obtained by sending in the box top with 50¢.

8. Three offers on one cereal box. To Sarah Boyle this seems to be oversell. Perhaps something is terribly wrong with the cereal and it must be sold quickly, got off the shelves before the

news breaks. Perhaps it causes a special, cruel Cancer in little children. As Sarah Boyle collects the bowls printed with bunnies and baseball statistics, still slopping half full of milk and wilted flakes, she imagines *in her mind's eye* the headlines, "Nation's Small Fry Stricken, Fate's Finger Sugar Coated, Lethal Sweetness Socks Tots."

9. Sarah Boyle is a vivacious and intelligent young wife and mother, educated at a fine Eastern college, proud of her growing family which keeps her busy and happy around the house.

10. BIRTHDAY.
Today is the birthday of one of the children. There will be a party in the late afternoon.

11. CLEANING UP THE HOUSE. ONE.
Cleaning up the kitchen. Sarah Boyle puts the bowls, plates, glasses and silverware into the sink. She scrubs at the stickiness on the yellow-marbled formica table with a blue synthetic sponge, a special blue which we shall see again. There are marks of children's hands in various sizes printed with sugar and grime on all the table's surfaces. The marks catch the light, they appear and disappear according to the position of the observing eye. The floor sweepings include a triangular half of toast spread with grape jelly, bobby pins, a green band-aid, flakes, a doll's eye, dust, dog's hair and a button.

12. Until we reach the statistically likely planet and begin to converse with whatever green-faced, teleporting denizens thereof—considering only this shrunk and communication-ravaged world—can we any more postulate a separate culture? Viewing the metastasis of Western Culture, it seems progressively less likely. Sarah Boyle imagines a whole world which has become like California, all topographical imperfections sanded away with the sweet-smelling burr of the plastic surgeon's cosmetic polisher; a world populace dieting, leisured, similar in pink and mauve hair and rhinestone shades. A land Cunt Pink and Avocado Green, brassiered and girdled by monstrous

complexities of Super Highways, a California endless and unceasing, embracing and transforming the entire globe, California, California!

13. INSERT ONE. ON ENTROPY.

ENTROPY: A quantity introduced in the first place to facilitate the calculations, and to give clear expressions to the results of thermodynamics. Changes of entropy can be calculated only for a reversible process, and may then be defined as the ratio of the amount of heat taken up to the absolute temperature at which the heat is absorbed. Entropy changes for actual irreversible processes are calculated by postulating equivalent theoretical reversible changes. The entropy of a system is a measure of its degree of disorder. The total entropy of any isolated system can never decrease in any change; it must either increase (irreversible process) or remain constant (reversible process). The total entropy of the Universe therefore is increasing, tending toward a maximum, corresponding to complete disorder of the particles in it (assuming that it may be regarded as an isolated system). See *Heat Death of the Universe*.

14. CLEANING UP THE HOUSE. TWO.

Washing the baby's diapers. Sarah Boyle writes notes to herself all over the house; a mazed wild script larded with arrows, diagrams, pictures; graffiti on every available surface in a desperate/heroic attempt to index, record, bluff, invoke, order and placate. On the fluted and flowered white plastic lid of the diaper bin she has written in Blushing Pink Nitetime lipstick a phrase to ward off fumey ammoniac despair: "The nitrogen cycle is the vital round of organic and inorganic exchange on earth. The sweet breath of the Universe." On the wall by the washing machine are Yin and Yang signs, mandalas and the words, "Many young wives feel trapped. It is a contemporary sociological phenomenon which may be explained in part by a gap between changing living patterns and the accommodation of social services to these patterns." Over the stove she had written "Help, Help, Help, Help, Help."

15. Sometimes she numbers or letters the things in a room, writing the assigned character on each object. There are 819 separate moveable objects in the living room, counting books. Sometimes she labels objects with their names, or with false names, thus on her bureau the hair brush is labeled HAIR BRUSH, the cologne, COLOGNE, the hand cream, CAT. She is passionately fond of children's dictionaries, encyclopedias, ABCs and all reference books, transfixed and comforted at their simulacra of a complete listing and ordering.

16. On the door of a bedroom are written two definitions from reference books, "GOD: An object of worship"; "HOMEO-STASIS: Maintenance of constancy of internal environment."

17. Sarah Boyle washes the diapers, washes the linen, Oh Saint Veronica, changes the sheets on the baby's crib. She begins to put away some of the toys, stepping over and around the organizations of playthings which still seem inhabited. There are various vehicles, and articles of medicine, domesticity and war; whole zoos of stuffed animals, bruised and odorous with years of love; hundreds of small figures, plastic animals, cowboys, cars, spacemen, with which the children make sub and supra worlds in their play. One of Sarah's favorite toys is the Baba, the wooden Russian doll which, opened, reveals a smaller but otherwise identical doll which opens to reveal, etc., a lesson in infinity at least to the number of seven dolls.

18. Sarah Boyle's mother has been dead for two years. Sarah Boyle thinks of music as the formal articulation of the passage of time, and of Bach as the most poignant rendering of this. Her eyes are sometimes the color of the aforementioned kitchen sponge. Her hair is natural spaniel brown; months ago on an hysterical day she dyed it red, so now it is two-toned with a stripe in the middle, like the painted walls of slum buildings or old schools.

19. INSERT TWO. HEAT DEATH OF THE UNIVERSE.
The second law of thermodynamics can be interpreted to

mean that the ENTROPY of a closed system tends toward a maximum and that its available ENERGY tends toward a minimum. It has been held that the Universe constitutes a thermo-dynamically closed system, and if this were true it would mean that a time must finally come when the Universe "unwinds" itself, no energy being available for use. This state is referred to as the "heat death of the Universe." It is by no means certain, however, that the Universe can be considered as a closed system in this sense.

20. Sarah Boyle pours out a Coke from the refrigerator and lights a cigarette. The coldness and sweetness of the thick brown liquid make her throat ache and her teeth sting briefly, sweet juice of my youth, her eyes glass with the carbonation, she thinks of the Heat Death of the Universe. A logarithmic of those late summer days, endless as the Irish serpent twisting through jeweled manuscripts forever, tail in mouth, the heat pressing, bloating, doing violence. The Los Angeles sky becomes so filled and bleached with detritus that it loses all color and silvers like a mirror, reflecting back the fricasseeing earth. Everything becoming warmer and warmer, each particle of matter becoming more agitated, more excited until the bonds shatter, the glues fail, the deodorants lose their seals. She imagines the whole of New York City melting like a Dali into a great chocolate mass, a great soup, the Great Soup of New York.

21. CLEANING UP THE HOUSE. THREE.

Beds made. Vacuuming the hall, a carpet of faded flowers, vines and leaves which endlessly wind and twist into each other in a fevered and permanent ecstasy. Suddenly the vacuum blows instead of sucks, spewing marbles, dolls' eyes, dust, crackers. An old trick. "Oh my god," says Sarah. The baby yells on cue for attention/changing/food. Sarah kicks the vacuum cleaner and it retches and begins working again.

22. AT LUNCH ONLY ONE GLASS OF MILK IS SPILLED.

At lunch only one glass of milk is spilled.

23. The plants need watering, Geranium, Hyacinth, Lavender, Avocado, Cyclamen. Feed the fish, happy fish with china castles and mermaids in the bowl. The turtle looks more and more unwell and is probably dying.

24. Sarah Boyle's blue eyes, how blue? Bluer far and of a different quality than the Nature metaphors which were both engine and fuel to so much of precedent literature. A fine, modern, acid, synthetic blue; the shiny cerulean of the skies on postcards sent from lush subtropics, the natives grinning ivory ambivalent grins in their dark faces; the promising, fat, unnatural blue of the heavy tranquillizer capsule; the cool, mean blue of that fake kitchen sponge; the deepest, most unbelievable azure of the tiled and mossless interiors of California swimming pools. The chemists in their kitchens cooked, cooled and distilled this blue from thousands of colorless and wonderfully constructed crystals, each one unique and nonpareil; and now that color hisses, bubbles, burns in Sarah's eyes.

25. INSERT THREE. ON LIGHT.

LIGHT: Name given to the agency by means of which a viewed object influences the observer's eyes. Consists of electromagnetic radiation within the wavelength range 4×10^{-5} cm. to 7×10^{-5} cm. approximately; variations in the wavelength produce different sensations in the eye, corresponding to different colors. See color vision.

26. LIGHT AND CLEANING THE LIVING ROOM.

All the objects (819) and surfaces in the living room are dusty, gray common dust as though this were the den of a giant, molting mouse. Suddenly quantities of waves or particles of very strong sunlight speed in through the window, and everything incandesces, multiple rainbows. Poised in what has become a solid cube of light, like an ancient insect trapped in amber, Sarah Boyle realizes that the dust is indeed the most beautiful stuff in the room, a manna for the eyes. Duchamp, that father of thought, has set with fixative some dust which fell on one of his sculptures, counting it as part of the work. "That way madness lies, says Sarah," says Sarah. The thought of ordering a household on Dada principles balloons again. All the rooms would fill up with objects, newspapers and magazines would compost, the potatoes in the rack, the canned green beans in the garbage can would take new heart and come to life again, reaching out green shoots toward the sun. The plants would grow wild and wind into a jungle around the house, splitting plaster, tearing shingles, the garden would enter in at the door. The goldfish would die, the birds would die, we'd have them stuffed; the dog would die from lack of care, and probably the children—all stuffed and sitting around the house, covered with dust.

27. INSERT FOUR. DADA.

DADA (Fr., hobby-horse) was a nihilistic precursor of Surrealism, invented in Zurich during World War I, a product of hysteria and shock lasting from about 1915 to 1922. It was deliberately anti-art and anti-sense, intended to outrage and scandalize, and its most characteristic production was the reproduction of the *Mona Lisa* decorated with a moustache and the obscene caption LHOOQ (read: *elle a chaud au cul)* "by" Duchamp. Other manifestations included Arp's collages of colored paper cut out at random and shuffled, ready-made objects such as the bottle drier and the bicycle wheel "signed" by Duchamp, Picabia's drawings of bits of machinery with incongruous titles, incoherent poetry, a lecture given by 38 lecturers in unison, and an exhibition in Cologne in 1920, held in an annex to a café lavatory, at which a chopper was provided for spectators to smash the exhibits with—which they did.

28. TIME PIECES AND OTHER MEASURING DEVICES.

In the Boyle house there are four clocks; three watches (one a Mickey Mouse watch which does not work); two calendars and two engagement books; three rulers; a yard stick; a measuring cup; a set of red plastic measuring spoons which includes a tablespoon, a teaspoon, a one-half teaspoon, one-fourth teaspoon and one-eighth teaspoon; an egg timer; an oral thermometer and a rectal thermometer; a Boy Scout compass; a barometer in the shape of a house, in and out of which an old woman and an old man chase each other forever without fulfilment; a bathroom scale; an infant scale; a tape measure which can be pulled out of a stuffed felt strawberry; a wall on which the children's heights are marked; a metronome.

29. Sarah Boyle finds a new line in her face after lunch while cleaning the bathroom. It is as yet hardly visible, running from the midpoint of her forehead to the bridge of her nose. By inward curling of her eyebrows she can etch it clearly as it will come to appear in the future. She marks another mark on the wall where she has drawn out a scoring area. Face Lines and Other Limitations of Mortality, the heading says. There are thirty-two marks, counting this latest one.

30. Sarah Boyle is a vivacious and witty young wife and mother, educated at a fine Eastern college, proud of her growing family which keeps her happy and busy around the house, involved in many hobbies and community activities, and only occasionally given to obsessions concerning Time/Entropy/Chaos and Death.

31. Sarah Boyle is never quite sure how many children she has.

32. Sarah thinks from time to time; Sarah is occasionally visited with this thought; at times this thought comes upon Sarah, that there are things to be hoped for, accomplishments to be desired beyond the mere reproductions, mirror reproduction of one's kind. The babies. Lying in bed at night sometimes the memory of the act of birth, always the hue and texture of red plush theater seats, washes up; the rending which always, at a certain intensity of pain, slipped into landscapes, the sweet breath of the sweating nurse. The wooden Russian doll has bright, perfectly round red spots on her cheeks, she splits in the center to reveal a doll smaller but in all other respects identical with round bright red spots on her cheeks, etc.

33. How fortunate for the species, Sarah muses or is mused, that children are as ingratiating as we know them. Otherwise they would soon be salted off for the leeches they are, and the race would extinguish itself in a fair sweet flowering, the last generations' massive achievement in the arts and pursuits of high civilization. The finest women would have their tubes tied off at the age of twelve, or perhaps refrain altogether from the Act of Love? All interests would be bent to a refining and perfecting of each febrile sense, each fluid hour, with no more cowardly investment in immortality via the patchy and too often disappointing vegetables of one's own womb.

34. INSERT FIVE. LOVE.
LOVE: a typical sentiment involving fondness for, or attachment to, an object, the idea of which is emotionally colored whenever it arises in the mind, and capable, as Shand has pointed out, of evoking any one of a whole gamut of primary emotions, according to the situation in which the object is placed, or represented; often, and by psychoanalysts always, used in the sense of *sex-love* or even *lust* (q.v.).

35. Sarah Boyle has at times felt a unity with her body, at other times a complete separation. The mind/body duality considered. The time/space duality considered. The male/female duality considered. The matter/energy duality considered. Sometimes, at extremes, her Body seems to her an animal on a leash, taken for walks in the park by her Mind. The lamp posts of experience. Her arms are lightly freckled, and when she gets very tired the places under her eyes become violet.

36. Housework is never completed, the chaos always lurks ready to encroach on any area left unweeded, a jungle filled with dirty pans and the roaring of giant stuffed toy animals suddenly turned savage. Terrible glass eyes.

37. SHOPPING FOR THE BIRTHDAY CAKE.
Shopping in the supermarket with the baby in front of the cart and a larger child holding on. The light from the

ice-cube-tray-shaped fluorescent lights is mixed blue and pink and brighter, colder, and cheaper than daylight. The doors swing open just as you reach out your hand for them, Tantalus, moving with a ghastly quiet swing. Hot dogs for the party. Potato chips, gum drops, a paper table cloth with birthday designs, hot dog buns, catsup, mustard, picalilli, balloons, instant coffee Continental style, dog food, frozen peas, ice cream, frozen lima beans, frozen broccoli in butter sauce, paper birthday hats, paper napkins in three colors, a box of Sugar Frosted Flakes with a Wolfgang Amadeus Mozart mask on the back, bread, pizza mix. The notes of a just graspable music filter through the giant store, for the most part bypassing the brain and acting directly on the liver, blood and lymph. The air is delicately scented with aluminum. Half and half cream, tea bags, bacon, sandwich meat, strawberry jam. Sarah is in front of the shelves of cleaning products now, and the baby is beginning to whine. Around her are whole libraries of objects, offering themselves. Some of that same old hysteria that had incarnadined her hair rises up again, and she does not refuse it. There is one moment when she can choose direction, like standing on a chalk drawn X, a hot cross bun, and she does not choose calm and measure. Sarah Boyle begins to pick out, methodically, deliberately and with a careful ecstasy, one of every cleaning product which the store sells. Window Cleaner, Glass Cleaner, Brass Polish, Silver Polish, Steel Wool, eighteen different brands of Detergent, Disinfectant, Toilet Cleanser, Water Softener, Fabric Softener, Drain Cleanser, Spot Remover, Floor Wax, Furniture Wax, Car Wax, Carpet Shampoo, Dog Shampoo, Shampoo for people with dry, oily and normal hair, for people with dandruff, for people with gray hair. Tooth Paste, Tooth Powder, Denture Cleaner, Deodorants, Antiperspirants, Antiseptics, Soaps, Cleansers, Abrasives, Oven Cleansers, Makeup Removers. When the same products appear in different sizes Sarah takes one of each size. For some products she accumulates whole little families of containers: a giant Father bottle of shampoo, a Mother bottle, an Older Sister bottle just smaller than the Mother bottle, and a very tiny Baby Brother bottle. Sarah fills three shopping carts and has to have help wheeling them all down the aisles. At the check-out counter her laughter and hysteria keep threatening to overflow as the pale blonde clerk with no eyebrows like the *Mona Lisa* pretends normality and disinterest. The bill comes to $57.53 and Sarah has to write a check. Driving home, the baby strapped in the drive-a-cot and the paper bags bulging in the back seat, she cries.

38. BEFORE THE PARTY.

Mrs. David Boyle, mother-in-law of Sarah Boyle, is coming to the party of her grandchild. She brings a toy, a yellow wooden duck on a string, made in Austria; the duck quacks as it is pulled along the floor. Sarah is filling paper cups with gum drops and chocolates, and Mrs. David Boyle sits at the kitchen table and talks to her. She is talking about several things, she is talking about her garden which is flourishing except for a plague of rare black beetles, thought to have come from Hong Kong, which are undermining some of the most delicate growths at the roots, and feasting on the leaves of other plants. She is talking about a sale of household linens which she plans to attend on the following Tuesday. She is talking about her neighbor who has cancer and is wasting away. The neighbor is a Catholic woman who had never had a day's illness in her life until the cancer struck, and now she is, apparently, failing with dizzying speed. The doctor says her body's chaos, chaos, cells running wild all over, says Mrs. David Boyle. When I visited her she hardly *knew* me, can hardly *speak,* can't keep herself *clean,* says Mrs. David Boyle.

39. Sometimes Sarah can hardly remember how many cute, chubby little children she has.

40. When she used to stand out in center field far away from the other players, she used to make up songs and sing them to herself.

41. She thinks of the end of the world by ice.

42. She thinks of the end of the world by water.

43. She thinks of the end of the world by nuclear war.

44. There must be more than this, Sarah Boyle thinks, from time to time. What could one do to justify one's passage? Or less ambitiously, to change, even in the motion of the smallest mote, the course and circulation of the world? Sometimes Sarah's dreams are of heroic girth, a new symphony using laboratories of machinery and all invented instruments, at once giant in scope and intelligible to all, to heal the bloody breach; a series of paintings which would transfigure and astonish and calm the frenzied art world in its panting race; a new novel that would refurbish language. Sometimes she considers the mystical, the streaky and random, and it seems that one change, no matter how small, would be enough. Turtles are supposed to live for many years. To carve a name, date and perhaps a word of hope upon a turtle's shell, then set him free to wend the world, surely this one act might cancel out absurdity?

45. Mrs. David Boyle has a faint moustache, like Duchamp's *Mona Lisa*.

46. THE BIRTHDAY PARTY.
Many children, dressed in pastels, sit around the long table. They are exhausted and overexcited from games fiercely played, some are flushed and wet, others unnaturally pale. This general agitation, and the paper party hats they wear, combine to make them appear a dinner party of debauched midgets. It is time for the cake. A huge chocolate cake in the shape of a rocket and launching pad and covered with blue and pink icing is carried in. In the hush the birthday child begins to cry. He stops crying, makes a wish and blows out the candles.

47. One child will not eat hot dogs, ice cream or cake, and asks for cereal. Sarah pours him out a bowl of Sugar Frosted Flakes, and a moment later he chokes. Sarah pounds him on the back and out spits a tiny green plastic snake with red glass eyes, the Surprise Gift. All the children want it.

48. AFTER THE PARTY THE CHILDREN ARE PUT TO BED.
Bath time. Observing the nakedness of children, pink and slippery as seals, squealing as seals, now the splashing, grunting

and smacking of cherry flesh on raspberry flesh reverberate in the pearl tiled steamy cubicle. The nakedness of children is so much more absolute than that of the mature. No musky curling hair to indicate the target points, no knobbly clutch of plane and fat and curvature to ennoble this prince of beasts. All well-fed naked children appear edible, Sarah's teeth hum in her head with memory of bloody feastings, prehistory. Young humans appear too like the young of other species for smugness, and the comparison is not even in their favor, they are much the most peeled and unsupple of those young. Such pinkness, such utter nuded pinkness; the orifices neatly incised, rimmed with a slightly deeper rose, the incessant demands for breast time milks of many sorts.

49. INSERT SIX. WEINER ON ENTROPY.
In Gibbs' Universe order is least probable, chaos most probable. But while the Universe as a whole, if indeed there is a whole Universe, tends to run down, there are local enclaves whose direction seems opposed to that of the Universe at large and in which there is a limited and temporary tendency for organization to increase. Life finds its home in some of these enclaves.

50. Sarah Boyle imagines, in her mind's eye, cleaning and ordering the whole world, even the Universe. Filling the great spaces of Space with a marvelous sweet smelling, deep cleansing foam. Deodorizing rank caves and volcanoes. Scrubbing rocks.

51. INSERT SEVEN. TURTLES.
Many different species of carnivorous Turtles live in the fresh waters of the tropical and temperate zones of various continents. Most Northerly of the European Turtles (extending as far as Holland and Lithuania) is the European Pond Turtle *(Emys orbicularis)*. It is from 8 to 10 inches long and may live a hundred years.

52. CLEANING UP AFTER THE PARTY.
Sarah is cleaning up after the party. Gum drops and melted

ice cream surge off paper plates, making holes in the paper tablecloth through the printed roses. A fly has died a splendid death in a pool of strawberry ice cream. Wet jelly beans stain all they touch, finally becoming themselves colorless, opaque white like flocks of tamed or sleeping maggots. Plastic favors mount half-eaten pieces of blue cake. Strewn about are thin strips of fortune papers from the Japanese poppers. Upon them are printed strangely assorted phrases selected by apparently unilingual Japanese. Crowds of delicate yellow people spending great chunks of their lives in producing these most ephemeral of objects, and inscribing thousands of fine papers with absurd and incomprehensible messages. "The very hairs of your head are all numbered," reads one. Most of the balloons have popped. Someone has planted a hot dog in the daffodil pot. A few of the helium balloons have escaped their owners and now ride the ceiling. Another fortune paper reads, "Emperor's horses meet death worse, numbers, numbers."

53. She is very tired, violet under the eyes, mauve beneath the eyes. Her uncle in Ohio used to get the same marks under his eyes. She goes to the kitchen to lay the table for tomorrow's breakfast, then she sees that in the turtle's bowl the turtle is floating, still, on the surface of the water. Sarah Boyle pokes at it with a pencil but it does not move. She stands for several minutes looking at the dead turtle on the surface of the water. She is crying again.

54. She begins to cry. She goes to the refrigerator and takes out a carton of eggs, white eggs, extra large. She throws them one by one onto the kitchen floor which is patterned with strawberries in squares. They break beautifully. There is a Secret Society of Dentists, all moustached, with Special Code and Magic Rings. She begins to cry. She takes up three bunny dishes and throws them against the refrigerator, they shatter, and then the floor is covered with shards, chunks of partial bunnies, an ear, an eye here, a paw; Stockton, California, Acton, California, Chico, California, Redding, California, Glen Ellen, California, Cadix, California, Angels Camps, California, Half Moon Bay. The total

ENTROPY of the Universe therefore is increasing, tending toward a maximum, corresponding to complete disorder of the particles in it. She is crying, her mouth is open. She throws a jar of grape jelly and it smashes the window over the sink. Her eyes are blue. She begins to open her mouth. It has been held that the Universe constitutes a thermodynamically closed system, and if this were true it would mean that a time must finally come when the Universe "unwinds" itself, no energy being available for use. This state is referred to as the "Heat Death of the Universe." Sarah Boyle begins to cry. She throws a jar of strawberry jam against the stove, enamel chips off and the stove begins to bleed. Bach had twenty children, how many children has Sarah Boyle? Her mouth is open. Her mouth is opening. She turns on the water and fills the sinks with detergent. She writes on the kitchen wall, "William Shakespeare has Cancer and lives in California." She writes, "Sugar Frosted Flakes are the Food of the Gods." The water foams up in the sink, overflowing, bubbling onto the strawberry floor. She is about to begin to cry. Her mouth is opening. She is crying. She cries. How can one ever tell whether there are one or many fish? She begins to break glasses and dishes, she throws cups and cooking pots and jars of food which shatter and break and spread over the kitchen. The sand keeps falling, very quietly, in the egg timer. The old man and woman in the barometer never catch each other. She picks up eggs and throws them into the air. She begins to cry. She opens her mouth. The eggs arch slowly through the kitchen, like a baseball, hit high against the spring sky, seen from far away. They go higher and higher in the stillness, hesitate at the zenith, then begin to fall away slowly, slowly, through the fine, clear air.

The Holland of the Mind

The loss of six hours on the flight from New York to Amsterdam meant that night had rushed to meet them as they moved across and above the Atlantic. The water solid beneath them was a sheet of hammered metal, and the clouds, many-colored and substantial, provided the landscape, seemed the actual ocean. The closed, lighted capsule of the plane's interior, suspended in all that space, was just another of the tiny islands carved out of the ignorant Universe; wrapped in the frailest of membranes against the darkness, like the hairy men around the first fires, wolves calling in the cold air, keeping to the edge of that circle of light.

Graham and Jessica sat, shifting the child occasionally from one lap to the other, her warm limbs loose, asleep. Americans amongst the other Americans filling the plane, the traditional journey away and back. Graham smoked steadily, plane nerves, he said. I can always see the skull beneath the stewardess's smile. They ate food out of the portioned containers, Rachel woke, two spoonfuls of mashed potato, refused the peas and lamb, and fell asleep again. They ate, drinking, feeling out what it meant, now that it was actual, to be leaving home and all the various complicated pieces of their lives, though how much they carried with them, how much and what kind of baggage could not yet be determined.

The bald man in front of Jess had shifted back his seat and was asleep, his mouth open, his naked, gleaming head almost in her lap. It was like a world, that head, continents of freckles on the sea of bright skin. Jess threatened to trace their journey in lipstick on the man's skull. Doris Day flickered through a movie on the multiple multiple screens, still young in soft focus; a time lag produced by some quirk of the mechanism showed the same action taking place a few seconds later on each succeeding screen, making a whole small crowd of pasts and futures visible the length of the airplane. They yawned and slumped with the particular fatigue of sedentary travel, the woman behind them was talking of buying diamonds in Amsterdam, a Texan accent, there was a blurb on Dutch flowers in the chair's pocket; tiny salt and pepper containers, motors, the maps and air sickness bags and postcards of just such silver planes in just such cerulean spaces; all hanging, buzzing, through the great vault of sky.

The land began again beneath them, clumps of light, humps, puddles, and Europe spread out below like a map. The airport suddenly, a game board, they landed on the flat field amidst the red and green lamps. Fluorescent light poured through the airport building, down from the ceiling and up from the polished floors, filling the space through which they and the other travelers moved, stunned, like tired fish through bright water.

CITY ON THE WATER
Amsterdam has been called the "Venice of the North." It is laced by sixty canals, which are crossed by more than 550 bridges, and the city is a composite of ninety islands! The capital's center has grown around a series of concentric canals which were first dug more than 300 years ago and served as a principal means of transportation.

In the coach, moving toward the town, the difference of the place, the look of things, surrounded them. I don't like traveling by plane, Jess said. It's too fast and it out-runs my sense of displacement. I arrival places feeling slightly sick, the way you feel in a fast elevator, my ears popping, my mind blank.

The child pressed her face toward the glass, watching the city, and Graham, watching her, saw its reflection on her smooth skin, the colors gliding over that surface. Your nose is green, he said. We're here, he said.

the toilet dĕ-wee-SEE de W.C.
Where's the toilet? WAAR is-de-wee-SEE? Waar is de W.C.?
It's (to the) right. hĕt-is-RECHTS. Het is rechts.
It's (to the) left. hĕt-is-LINKS. Het is links.
straight ahead. rechTUIT rechtuit
Go straight ahead. ghaa-rech-TUIT. Ga rechtuit.
It's here. hĕt-is-HIER. Het is hier.

Walking through the streets to the hotel, a gray stone, the rough-textured narrow passage ways, the canals repeated the clouded sky, reflecting light and so supplying a luminous horizontal to the city. The meat-faced proprietor, polite, rented them two rooms on the top floor. Carrying, dragging their baggage they climbed the steep stairs, two small rooms and very clean, suddenly, exhausted, they were asleep.

The ground plan of the innermost center of Amsterdam is still the same as it was in the Middle Ages when the town first came into existence.

In the morning he woke first. Jess, buried in pillows and her massive dark hair, holding stubbornly to sleep. The room in the daylight was small, finely proportioned, bare. It took its shape from the necessity of roof fitted onto wall, and the ceiling sloped down over the bed. A single window gave a view of shingled roofs, streets with people going to work. The air had a new taste, fresh, slightly bitter, the light a special quality: it was, without doubt, a different place. She stirred in the bed and he said to her, we're in Holland. Smiling, with her eyes still closed, Amsterdam, she said, do you feel Dutch?

THE INFLECTED FORM IS USED
WHEN THE ADJECTIVE PRECEDES THE NOUN
een grote tuin—a large garden
oude bomen—old trees
de rode daken—the red roofs
het warme continent—the warm continent

The plan was to spend some time in Holland and from there visit Belgium and Italy, but the schedule was undetermined. They had even talked of settling somewhere, not going back, at least not for a while. Graham had some photographic work set up with several magazines, but without particular deadlines. They would feel their way.

After eight years of marriage, Graham found it difficult to look back along the tube of weeks and months and recognize himself at the other end; a tall, gawky young man from Oregon finding New York and New Yorkers aggressive and exciting, trying to put together himself and the city out of the hundreds of photographs he took, going slightly night-blind from hours in the darkroom. He and Jess, Jessica Gebhardt, doing post-graduate work in art history, had gone to the same party one Christmas Eve and had awakened Christmas morning, the bells from the city's churches sounding in their ears, in her apartment, hung over, Jess's red dress a puddle of brilliance on the bare floor, the small Christmas tree, which they had apparently taken to bed with them, odorous and prickly under the sheets.

He was tall, very lean, naked he was awkward, thin, loose-hinged, pale, slightly rounded, a shallow chest and a deep, knotted navel. It was a strangely anonymous body, unmarked by his particular life or character. His experiences seemed concentrated in his head and face, an off-sphere pumpkin, an underinflated balloon, a large, compact globe on a slender neck, webbed already with fine lines, blue eyes, a soft, opaque skin. He wore, at times, large round glasses with fine steel frames. The lenses looked like big, shallow bubbles set on his face. He had pale, blunt hands discolored by photographic chemicals and cigarettes; long, soft feet.

The ground plan of the innermost center

EXPOSURE

The exposure of a film or plate is the combined product of two things:

1. The *amount* of *light* which passes through the lens, and is controlled by the *aperture* used, together with

2. The *period* during which the light passes, known as the *exposure time*.

They spent the first days walking around the town, fucking, eating, visiting museums. Rachel was still of the age at which their presence, and that of a particular stuffed blue pig, were the main signs of continuity she required from the world. Late spring, and the town was already filling with tourists; American, English, German predominating. They all moved through the city, pointing, tasting, peering. Myself, said Graham, after one worthy but deadening guided tour, I always think of Amsterdam as the Venice of the North.

Graham's camera was a more complicated and precise machine eye than theirs, but he and Jess were joined with the other tourists in that peculiar state of pure observation. To tourists everything is to be seen and reflected upon without participation. At whatever level, the cooing at a pair of wooden shoes or a Vermeer, aesthetics take over from the usual exigencies. The real Dutch who lived in the place were like a slightly different species, set apart by jobs, dishwashing, appendicitis.

In a strange city, the foreign country, amidst all the alienness, their bodies were the only familiar territory. The corporeal land-scale, the topology of flesh, was their only point of reference.

The nights were long and dark and had the nature of journeys. In the small bed they slept wrapped close to each other, folded against each other and intertwined. Each was aware of the other's least movement, and they surfaced into consciousness several times during the night. In the mornings, waking, it was as though they had not been separated into personal voyages of sleep, but had traveled together.

Rachel had been born on a rainy day in April; they were staying with Jess's family in St. Paul, and the baby had been two weeks early. Jess came in from the grocery store, her arms full of packages, tears and rain running down her face. She was one of the women who look most beautiful pregnant, the swell of her belly marking a tense, great curve into the air. The baby's hair, blonde at first, had later turned brown, and now she was as dark as *her* mother, *his* wife.

> bread broot brood
> water WAATER
> meat VLEES vlees
> potatoes AARappelen aardappĕlĕn
> coffee KOFFIE koffie
> milk MELK melk
> beer BIER bier
> Do you want coffee? wilt-uu-KOFFIE-drinken? Wilt u koffie drinken?
> How much is it? hoe-veel-is-et? Hoeveel is het?

Dear Mother and Dad, We arrived in Amsterdam safe and well, and although Ray has a little cold now it's nothing serious and we're all fine. This city is splendid, small enough to comprehend, with a coherent, rhythmic structure based on concentric canals. How are you both? Will you be able to get away to the lake early this summer or are you, Dad, going to be teaching summer school again? Have you heard anything from Sally? I've written to her, but no word as yet. I hope Aunt Kate is better soon, have the doctors said what's the matter with her? Is it anything serious? The proprietor of the hotel has taken to Ray and keeps giving her chocolates every time we go out, so we wander around the city always with a smeary faced but happy little girl. There is an immense sense of community here after the facelessness of New York. The people are terrifically nice, clean, the bourgeois virtues uppermost and the marks of former greatness. History is lying around in great lumps everywhere. Graham and Ray join me in sending love. xxx Jess.

THE JEWISH BRIDE
For all its richness and splendor, the *matière* of painting is never an end in itself with Rembrandt, but a means of embodying his innermost thoughts. Such is the case with the *Jewish Bride* in the Rijksmuseum, Amsterdam. After countless attempts to explain this picture, its exact meaning

remains a riddle. The magnificent, old-world garments worn by the couple are oriental in character. Isaac and Rebecca, Jacob and Rachel, Tobias and Sarah have all been suggested as the theme. Perhaps it is simply a double portrait. Yet the posing of the figures in their glittering garments of scarlet and gold against the dim background of an abandoned park, and the ritual gesture of the man, laying his hand on his wife's breast, seem to point to the fulfilment of a biblical destiny. The human element of such a portrait is so deep and universal in significance that living models, contemporaries of the artist, are turned into the timeless heroes of the Old Testament and symbolize eternal spiritual values.

They both smoked too many cigarettes, invites death? Jess's grandparents, the Illinois pair, had both died of cancer. Jess had long hair, dark, wavy, a trap for light. Her face, they recognized her in Titus, was strongly marked, seemed full of experience, and went straight from a near ugliness to an occasional beauty without ever passing through prettiness. She bitched at the weather.

What were the myths that they had learned, as children in America, about Holland? Hans Brinker and the silver skates, cheese, tulips, the boy with his finger in the dyke saving the town, windmills, wooden shoes.

REMBRANDT VAN RIJN
1606–1669 covers with his life the greater part of the period of true magnificence in Dutch painting, and within a half century of his birth falls the birth of almost every other Dutch painter of pre-eminence. His contemporaries and pupils form a galaxy of a brilliance hardly equaled in so short a space of time in any other age or place. Rembrandt Harmenszoon van Rijn was born at Leyden in the house of his father, a well-to-do miller of the lower middle class who encouraged his son's artistic bent by apprenticing him to a local "Italianist" painter, Jacob van Swanenburgh.

By 1631, he was in Amsterdam with an established reputation, and from 1632 dates his first masterpiece, the *Anatomical Lecture*, now at The Hague. In 1634 he married

Saskia van Ulenborch, daughter of the burgomaster of Leeuwarden, and his fortune and happiness seemed secure. Of Saskia's four children, however, only Titus, the youngest, survived childhood; and Saskia herself died in 1642. Meanwhile Rembrandt was the leader of a flourishing and profitable school: in 1639 he bought and partly paid for the house in Jodenbreestraat which now contains a collection of his etchings, and the debt incurred was never fully paid off. Rembrandt's vogue as a fashionable portraitist seems to have begun to wane about 1642, the year of the so-called *Night Watch,* a masterpiece of free portraiture which sacrificed individual likeness to balance of composition and may on that account have given offence. At any rate, in July 1656, he was declared bankrupt and his effects, including the collection of art treasures he had amassed, were sold. However, with the loyal assistance of Titus and of the faithful Hendrickje Stoffels, his model and mistress and perhaps his second wife, Rembrandt continued painting with undiminished skill and ardor until his death in 1669.

Graham sat on the bed talking Rachel to sleep, the room half dark, his cigarette a single point of red. When I was six or seven I learned to swim. In Oregon? Yes. My father took me and my brothers and sister down to a swimming pool, a salt water pool near the ocean. They were older and could all swim already. The water was very warm and blue and for a while we all just played in the water, splashing, ducking each other. The little girl shifted in the bed, her eyes just open, her fine profile and shallow nose dusky against the pillow. Then my father took me down to the deeper end, he was a very big man, taller than I am now, and he showed me how to move my arms and legs. I was frightened, but he held on to me and then, when I understood the movements, he began to back away from me, a foot at a time, talking to me and telling me to swim to him. Every time I would almost reach him, he would move further away. I was scared, I think I was crying, but I swam, he moved away, I swam to get to him, until we reached the other side of the pool. The child was asleep now, her fingers curled, her mouth slightly open. Graham went on to finish the story, talking, softly, to himself. We all played some more before we went home, there was an inflated dragon that floated in the water, a beach ball, and, playing around, I discovered that, big as he was, in the salt water I could lift my father up and carry him around the shallow end of the pool. He pulled the blanket up over the child. We stopped in our wet suits and had ice cream cones on the way home.

> ". . . the Girl in a Turban in The Hague, could take its place beside a Bellini Madonna, the Petrus Christus portrait of a young woman in Berlin, and perhaps even Piero della Francesca. . . . And it comes as no surprise that in recent years an affinity has been repeatedly observed between the visual approach of Vermeer and that of Jan van Eyck: the lenslike vision, the luminous 'positive' color, the calm devoted attitude before still, silent objects—these are qualities common to both artists." Vitale Bloch, *All the Paintings of Jan Vermeer*

Amsterdam had them caught and they stayed on week after week, a little charmed by their own indulgent freedom. Getting to know some people they began to break through the almost complete wrapper of English with which English-speaking visitors to Amsterdam are protected. Dutch fell against their ears plosive and slightly comic. Without the hate memories of German to reinforce its gutturals, and with the surprising double vowels, it seemed sometimes a kind of clown English. A new language unravels metaphors back to their first excitement and reacts back on one's own language so that one examines those natural stones.

They ate, walked. They had endless arguments about painting, talking and talking. Rembrandt, Vermeer. Somehow they set up these two painters in opposition to each other. Rembrandt and the subjective, the emotive, the lover. Vermeer, the cool, the objective, the eye.

Bad news from America. More riots, more public deaths. They read the newspaper with a thrill of guilt, a feeling that St. Louis burning was real, had a claim on them, that this fine city, the paintings, the parks, did not.

spiegeling – reflection
lenig – supple, pliant
goochelkunst – juggling art, prestidigitation
spietsen – spear (fish); pierce (man); impale (criminal)
water – water
sight, vision – gezicht, aanblik; vertoning; bezienswaardig-
heid, merkwaardigheid
fish – vis
storten – spill (milk); shed (tears, blood); shoot, dump
(rubbish); pay in (money)
sex – geschlacht, sekse, kunne; seksualiteit; adj, seksueel
helder – clear, bright, lucid, serene; clean.

Eating oranges in the room, they make love. Oh dearest
darling fat, thin, lovely, love, oh kip, oh sweet wet vork. Breast,
skin, kaas, oh lovely slippery love, wet, mouth, mond, vis,
breathing hard in this room full of oranges, the seeds slide down
the creases of your skin, the juices glaze your silver sides, oh my
fish love, my vis, bubbles rise to the ceiling, burst and break
against the light bulb as you move, puff, pant and sniff the air
from the water.

Graham fell asleep, snoring, a weird musiking. Jess lit a
cigarette, keyed up, unable to relax. A headache was beginning at
the back of her neck, the love-making had, had again, a weird
flavor, a taste of desperation. These rooms were too small, this
city, she and Graham saw each other too much, were too much in
each other's pockets. The feeling of panic, of lemmings to the sea.
She could feel the marriage, that fragile edifice, buckling,
breaking apart under his flailing hands.

Adjusting the light, she read, savoring the quiet, the absence
of reaction and the need to react. A fly circled in the room,
Graham grunting beside her in his sleep. Living with a person,
cleaning ears, borrowing razors and occasionally sharing a
toothbrush, not buying bananas to which he has an allergy. What
fine curly hair full of various directions. When, having embarked
upon a certain course, do the alternatives cease to present
themselves? Who was this beside her in the bed?

The war paint designs used by the American Indian

(illustrated). Their marriage had been a strange beast, with its own queer shape. She had thought that Europe might heal some of the fissures, but instead.

Jess's sister Sally, blue-eyed Sally. Three years younger, she had set up some kind of floating residence centering mainly on the East Coast of the States. Her parents still lived in St. Paul, the yellow house, her father teaching history at the night school. The two of them, her parents, stand side by side on some hill in her memory, mother's arm through father's, staring ahead and smiling like figures on a wedding cake. Having developed this conceit in talking about them to Graham it was so strong that, seeing them again before leaving for Europe, she found herself looking down at their feet to see whether traces of the icing, like snow, still clung to their shoes. Her mother translated Jess's and Sally's affairs, the comings and goings, connections, into the vocabulary of her own time; sweetheart, beau. In this language the dark fumblings and disasters became neat, romantic, very like her own nice world. There were, amongst the people she knew, divorces, car accidents, alcoholics, but these always seemed like aberrations, grave departures from the norm. Here, in these places, with these people, this generation, it was the basic coin, the declared form of things. The personal fallings, the difficult acts, breakings. Her mother, loving them, was now always sad and puzzled that these two daughters, so lovely as little girls, should have become such unhappy homeless creatures. That they were not in their own terms so lost she could not believe. She sent them letters and birthday presents, adored Ray, fussed over their health when they visited her home. She hoped, always, for more grandchildren and some magical suburb. They loved her, but could not explain.

The fly buzzed again, in thrall to the light, diving at her head. The Apache, Van Eyck, Manhattan, Vermeer. New Amsterdam. The Beatles. Lapis lazuli. Damn, have to piss again. Curious how the language of excretion varies from family to family, the private code. Piddle, wee, pee. Tinkle in her childhood. Make water, wash your hands. With Ray they used Graham's word, piss, less coy than most.

A smell of baking bread from the bakers across the street.

Outside the frequency of passing cars began gradually to increase, soon the milk trucks and the first shopkeepers would begin to unlock their various doors and engines, turn switches, push buttons, and like knives to a fallen beast, still warm, to cut away pieces of the failing dark. Jess flexed the muscles of her legs and feet, cramped by curling into Graham's sleeping form. If she did not get to sleep before the first real light and noise, she would not sleep at all. Pulling her legs cautiously away from him, then swinging them from the warm cave of sheets and blankets out into the chilly dark. Her feet are stiff, groping over the cold floor, in the hallway she punches the light button and then, the flood of brilliance painful after the small yellow illumination of the reading lamp, her pupils spasm, she goes shut-eyed the known way to the toilet, the light showing orange through her lids.

The surfaces are cold, and the rush of water sounds enormous in the quiet house. A sense of violating and anti-social noise, Jess creeps back. What she wants is a glass of water, her mouth already musty and sour with near sleep, but she fears that the noise of the taps, more groaning of the plumbing, will finally wake Graham and the child sleeping in the next room. Instead she takes a handful of grapes, the spurt of sweet juice shocking her dry tongue, the gritty teeth. Turning out the light, the window's square of sky turns from black to cobalt.

TRANSLATE

These houses. That story. This garden. Those trees. I have read this book; it is much better than that one. I never smoke those cigars. This house has not been painted. Who is that man? This photograph is good, but those are very bad. These are our children, those people have no children. These books are mine. Do you know these people? Yes, of course, they are my neighbors. Those must be my pens. After that he stood up and went into the room. They looked at this for a long time.

The *View of Delft* is the purest square of pulsing light and air. Breath and absolute tonality. What is the nature of vision?

Amsterdam, the Venice of the North. They moved through the city. Even she, who had no sense of direction, began to learn her way around the streets. They argued, and Rachel grew fretful. Concentric canals.

A WALK ROUND AMSTERDAM

From the *station* (1) cross the bridge and go up the main street, Damrak, alongside the little harbor (2). Further on is the *Exchange* (3) built in 1903 (open 9–5; free admission to the galleries). Continue along Damrak to Dam with the Royal Palace (4) originally built as the town hall in 1648 by Jacob van Campen (open summer 9–4, winter 9–3). Next to it stands the Nieuwe Kerk (4) begun in 1490 but frequently altered since.

In one section of the city prostitutes walked along the streets or sat looking out of large glass windows, tempting pedestrians with what seemed to be the same psychology of plenty as that which filled the bakery and fruit shop displays with pyramids of shining goods in juicy, lavish abundance. Butter, chocolate, crystallized fruits, and these women. A big woman smiled at them a they passed by her window, a pile of golden hair and skin as sweet and fat as cream. Their open, vital presence in the city filled the nostrils, gave to the whole place a smell of sex, a nervous excitation, a flush of general body heat.

They ate herring from the stands in the streets. They went ever day that week to the Rijksmuseum. What, she said, is the nature of vision? Trying not to fight, to break the new bitter habit, they made resolutions, broke them made more. Perversely enough, like separate animals, their bodies were still mated, still sought each other out.

The surfaces of the paintings absorbed her, she returned to them again and again, they were her richest food. At night he explored her body hoping to receive some of that nourishment at one remove. Her fingers smelled of herring; later, her tongue, teeth, the soft cusions and hard furniture of her mouth, of herring, raw fish, the pickled smell mixed with the other smells.

Getting up to piss and rinse his mouth, to take the child to the toilet, the strangeness of the plumbing fixtures, the odd, very shallow Dutch toilet bowl, surprised him each morning. It was as though, during every night, he forgot that he was not at home, in New York, and had to relearn that fact at the beginning of each day. He would return to bed to find Jess flung back into sleep again, deep under the blankets, growling at intrusion. He would begin to rub her back, her sides, reach beneath her to touch her round, soft belly and her breasts, loose in his hands, sweet-tipped. A journey through her hair, the absolute abundance of the flowing waves outspringing from the brow, spreading over skin and sheets. The fine hairs penciled along her arms, rough, half-shaved on the legs and armpits, the warm, musty mound. The small arm hairs, forming his horizon against the light, his chin resting on her belly, flamed and moved like the leapings of light from an eclipsed sun. The very particular shapes of flesh and textures of her skin, the odors rising from her, from him, seemed to him at those times the constituents of the whole physical world. The periodic table of desire and repletion.

The light in that city, that room, at that part of the morning, was particularly clear, not yellow but white and silver, filling the space with a lucid intensity. No shadows and massing, just the clarity of surface and color, and the quiet occupation of space by forms. In the movements, pressing, tonguings, vials of scent opened into the air. They would fall away from each other, grateful, tired, and sometimes sleep again.

DROWNING

Drowning is caused by complete immersion of the nose and mouth in water for a length of time which varies with the individual circumstances.

please – alstublieft
many thanks – dank U wel
good morning – goedemorgen
good night – goedenacht

Holland is one of the smallest countries in Europe, with its area of 13,514 square miles. Its greatest width is about 125 miles. 32 percent of the country is under plough, 36 percent pasturage, 7 percent forest, 9 percent heath and sand-dunes, 3 percent gardens and market-gardens, and finally 13 percent built-up area.

Dear Mother, Jessica, Rachel and I are enjoying Amsterdam very much. We've had some rain, but it is pleasant even then. We visit the museums, of course, and I have been working on a photographic project on Water, water in all shapes and places. Mother, this may seem an odd request, but I should like you, when you write again, to answer several questions for me. (1) What was the name of the spaniel we had when I was about ten? (2) What was the name of that family that lived next door, the ones with red-headed children, when we lived on Dundee Road? (3) Did the large closet in Grandma's big upstairs bedroom *really* have a secret passage? I can remember, with awful clarity, a passage opening at the back of the closet, with stairs extending down the length of the house, but I *cannot* remember whether it was a dream. It may have been a dream, but the details are so fine. Please write and tell me the answers to these things as soon as you can—I'm just trying to get some things straight. Let me know how you are. Give my love to Linda and the others.

LAND UNDER WATER

The story of the Netherlands is one of the most remarkable chapters in all of mankind's history, involving a fierce struggle against nature which is still going on today, and is fascinating to witness.

Centuries ago, most of the Netherlands was either permanently inundated, or periodically swept, by the sea. Yet men determined to live there nevertheless. How? By reclaiming land from the sea itself.

Prehistoric men built huge mounds of earth in the sea, and then placed their homes and farms atop the mounds. Later they learned to wall off the sea by building dykes—first out of earth, centuries later out of stone, and today out of concrete and steel. The areas that were walled off were then drained of their water (originally, by windmill-driven pumps) to create reclaimed land—or *polders* as the Dutch call these once-below-the-sea areas. And the *polders* were then farmed and cultivated to create some of the most incredibly fertile and breath-taking scenery in the world today.

By building such *polders*, the Dutch reclaimed nearly half the land that today comprises the nation. "God created the earth," goes a famous epigram, "but the Dutch built the Netherlands."

The process is still going on. In the early 1930s the Dutch completed their famous nineteen-mile-long "Enclosure Dyke" *(Afsluitdijk)* which sealed off the stormy North Sea from the former Zuider Sea into a peaceful inland lake. Elsewhere, in the western section of the country, the Dutch are presently building their gigantic "Delta Works"—a series of five new dykes that will seal off further large estuaries of the North Sea. And remember, too, that even after land in Holland is reclaimed, it must constantly be drained by canals and pumps—or else the water will rise again!

one een
two twee
three drie
four vier
five vifj
six zes
seven zeven
eight acht
nine negen
ten tien

Graham worked on a series of photographs of water, water in the Netherlands. The sea, the canals, the rivers, the whole country was knit by the presence of water, actual water, and the water which was no longer there by always threatened. The silver, shining, reflective surface. What, he took a picture of Rachel standing in a fountain ecstatic in a great fount of spray, is the nature of vision? Photographing Jess the light caught and recorded a magnificent aureole. Then sunlight on your hair! an extraordinary and beautiful luminescence. The phrase became a joke and a password.

TRANSLATE

The house was built a year ago. We were seen by his brother. The new ship has been sold. When will the letter be written? The boy was bitten by a dog. His name is Richard but he is called Dick. Have the horses and cows been rescued? I love you. The ship is not expected today. The raven was flattered by the fox. The books must be sent to my house. The country has always been governed well by its statesmen. He was trusted by his friends. The wheat has not been mown. I love you. The children were sent home. Were these vases sold? These glasses have not been washed. The bird was caught by a small boy. The girl was called by her father. The church had been built in the middle of the village. The roof of the house is on fire. I love you.

Saskia! No justice and early death. Such a beautiful Flora, the flowers in your hair, the oval face, slightly fat, the fine, bumpy nose and most stunning, endearing, dimple-forming, slight, up-curving smile.

The broad-brimmed hat of the Dresden portrait casts a shadow over Saskia's smiling face, so that her golden complexion, her strawberry-red lips and rosy cheeks lie partly in brightest light, partly in shadow dappled with surface reflections. Borne on a ray of light, this graceful image of a happy wife rises out of a fiery darkness.

As Rembrandt wrestled with the mighty task of the *Night Watch*, Saskia wrestled with death; on June 14, 1642, she died, aged barely thirty.

This might have come as a terrible shock to Rembrandt, for in the light of his art we can guess what Saskia meant to him, kindling and inspiring his imagination in all his work. Then, abruptly, after the abounding joy, the radiant delights of his life with Saskia, came darkness. While she lay dying, her features haunted his fervid imagination and pursued him into the thick of the soldiery peopling the *Night Watch*, conjuring up a world of strange imaginings in which we see her in the guise of a child, in a realm of fantasy where time has ceased to be.

The *Night Watch* and the dead Saskia. The life of Rembrandt. Bad news, bad news. All over Asia and Africa men are doing violence to each other, the Chinese are reported to be carrying out a genocide of the Tibetans, and in the West the grip on order is also precarious.

A letter at American Express, Aunt Kate is dead of cancer.

As though the devolution had its own momentum, they became more and more unhappy. With all the shaking glass, the sound of beams breaking loose, Graham became enormously hungry, a frantic hunger. He would eat huge meals, potatoes, bread, sausage, and then would rise, leave the restaurant, and peer into the window of the first food store they came to. The windows of candy stores and bakeries were stuffed full and bright as Christmas. Biscuits, cakes, cookies, glazed fruits, creams, huge crusty pies. The most splendid pastel candies, fudges, truffles.

Truffles were one of his favorites, the flakey powdered chocolate coat, the lump, and, breaking the faint tension of the surface, the cream which was itself a marvel of transience. It did not rest on the tongue but melted immediately into pure sweetness dripping down the throat.

Bitter Ballen	meat balls with mustard
Blinde Vinken	stuffed veal or beef rissoles with bread, milk, salt, nutmeg, egg, bacon, breadcrumbs, butter, margarine
Boerenkool met Worst	Smoked sausage and cabbage

Ertwensoep	Thick pea soup with smoked sausage, cubes of pork, pigs' feet, leek, celery
Hangop	A kind of gruel with milk
Paling	Smoked eel on toast
Rolpens met Rodekool	Minced beef and tripe topped with apple slices, served with red cabbage
Uitsmijter	Bread with a slice of cold meat topped with fried eggs. This is a popular "quick lunch"

Rachel became obsessed with mirrors; she would stand on a chair in front of the oval glass in their hotel room and stare at herself for long periods. Sometimes she would make faces, talk, but most often she would just sit and look.

With all the food Graham began, for the first time in his life, to grow fat. Layers of new flesh folded themselves around his bones; he slept for hours each day.

ARTIFICIAL RESPIRATION

Artificial respiration is used to make a person whose natural breathing has stopped start breathing again. It must be done deliberately and regularly for at least an hour, if the patient does not recover before then. Resuscitation as a result of artificial respiration may occur many hours after apparent death.

While artificial respiration is being applied, an assistant should loosen clothing at neck and waist of the patient, make sure that there is nothing in the mouth blocking the airway, get clothing or rugs to keep the patient warm, and massage the limbs from below upward. This assistance must not interfere with the application of artificial respiration which is all-important.

One night, slightly drunk on beer, making love. She perceives her body, defined by its contact with his, as construct, architecture and earth. The old truisms sharpen their teeth. Body like a building, like a mountain, huge.

1. Lay the casualty face downward with head turned to one side and arms stretched up beyond the head.
2. Make sure that the mouth and nose are not obstructed.

Haul out the analogies between the body and the landscape, the female earth. You down there, trying to get in, hey you. Help, help, knocking. Shifted to an exercise in communications. Pilot to tower, repeat, pilot to tower, request landing instructions. Instruments, radar. Nerves and switchboards. Shift to an art history lecture, images move through her head like slides projected on a screen, illuminated from behind. *Click.* An old Egyptian drawing, the sky as man, stars on his chest, legs and thighs, arching over the female earth. *Click.* Art Nouveau, the excited line which is its own purpose, vegetable energy and proliferation. *Click.* Persian miniatures, warped space, and pattern warring with form for ascendancy. *Click.* Bosch. *Click, click.* Rothko, Stella, the modern colorists. Colors. Oh. Colors.

3. Kneel to one side of the casualty's hips, facing his head.
4. Place your hands flat in the small of the back, over the lower ribs and just above top of the pelvic bone. Your thumbs should almost touch each other in the middle line, the fingers being over the loins.

Monumental sculpture. Two great pelvis pans pressed against each other. Picasso on the beach; a single eye in the center of the face, the warping of vision at close focus. *Click.* The body as earth, Henry Moore was right.

5. Sit on your heels, no weight being transmitted to the casualty, though your hands are maintained on his back.
6. Swing your body slowly forward from the knees keeping your arms straight and hands in place all the time, so that a steady pressure is transmitted by the weight of your body. Maintain this position for two seconds. This action

presses the casualty's abdomen against the ground, forcing his abdominal contents up against the diaphragm, which is raised and expels some air out of the lungs—expiration.

7. Keeping your hands in position and arms straight, relax the pressure by swinging gently and steadily back on to your heels, counting three seconds before swinging forward again. This allows air to enter the lungs—inspiration.

He looms over the horizon of her chest, drinking, great hills of breast. Lips, wet interior caves toothed and toothless, then the careful game with pace, form and time, equations of falling and acceleration, free fall, float, float, surface down from the air, up from the roiled water depths to the clear bubble of the middle space.

8. These swaying to-and-fro movements must be repeated regularly at a rate of twelve to fifteen a minute, and continue this, if necessary, by relays of helpers, until natural breathing begins. Even then, artificial respiration should be continued for another quarter of an hour. When apparent recovery has taken place, the casualty should be placed on his side in a warm bed, given a hot drink, and encouraged to sleep.

Now, the current off, the touches are neutral again. Peripheral parts, hair, the rim of an ear. Both have survived.

Jan van Eyck
Hieronymus Bosch
Pieter Brueghel the Elder
Frans Hals
Rembrandt van Rijn
Jan Vermeer
Vincent Van Gogh
Piet Mondrian

What is de Betekenis van het zien?

She filled their hotel room with flowers. Finding the aging flowers as beautiful as the fresh, she kept them for weeks, and the air smelled of the animal stink of the decaying blooms as well as the lighter odors of the new bouquets. He recognized some of the smells as cousin to those of their own flesh.

The colors of flowers as they decay grow hotter, pale yellows turn to bright yellows and golds, bright clear blues to redder blues and violets. (The hues in Cézanne's paintings undergoing this same transformation, early to late.)

In the Netherlands in 1963 there were 44,597,000 chickens, 3,645,000 cattle, 2,423,000 pigs, 468,000 sheep, and 149,000 horses.

Bad news from America. Divorce, separation of friends. Death by drugs. Mistakes, wrong decisions, futile journeys, flawed plans.

FLOWER VIEWING

For flower-growing enthusiasts, or for tourists who simply appreciate the beauty of miles of flowers, a visit to the flower-growing areas of the Netherlands is a must. At "tulip time," particularly April through mid-May, a thirty-mile strip of land between Haarlem and The Hague is covered by a dazzling blanket of tulips, daffodils and hyacinths.

The most *massive* display of these floral wonders is found in a sixty-acre flower garden located near the town of Lisse, called Keukenhof, where there are greenhouses containing tens of thousands of tulips, vast areas of open-air gardens, a pavilion with photographic exhibitions of flowers, flower arrangement demonstrations, an information office, and all else a flower enthusiast could possibly desire.

Mirrors are water made abstract. They do not quench, nourish, flow. They simply reflect, reverse, reflect.

You're welcome. (nothing to thank) Neits te danken.
Excuse me. (take me not badly) Neem me niet kwalijk.
So long. ("until see") Tot ziens.
Do you understand what I say? Verstaat u wat ik zeg?

What are the sounds a drowning man makes?

Things were falling apart. One day, coming back to the hotel, he found Jess sitting in front of the mirror cutting at her hair with the sewing scissors. The dark pieces lay all around on the floor, and she had left only a short, curling cap, which made her head look suddenly very small, her neck very long.

Why do you do it? His face hung white and quivering in the mirror above her.
She was sweeping the clumps of hair into the waste paper basket. It was too much trouble, I was tired of it.
But I *loved* your hair. He was shaking.
Graham, it's not important. It's *my* hair. Don't nag at me.
His bowels churned. It was such *lovely* hair.
Oh for God's sake can't you leave me alone? Her voice went shrill. He saw it as the severing of another of their connections. When she went out of the room he bent, shaking, sick, he picked up one of the dark, separate pieces and stuffed it in his pocket to keep.

He was drowning in the multiplicity and lack of order in the world. Order is a lucky, rich, sexy, privileged, sought-after bird. She does not answer invitations to dinner.

Going to see the flowers in Holland had at first been rather a joke, like going to see the Eiffel Tower in Paris, or the Statue of Liberty in New York. But having reached the gardens and finding themselves surrounded by the banks of glowing blossoms, the scent thick in the air, they became high with it, drunk, carried away.
What is it about flowers, he asked her, in bed, they had been

fighting again, what is it about flowers which stuns and fascinates? Scent on a stalk, form on a stalk, color on a stalk. She lay propped up on pillows, her eyes still red and puffed with crying, the street light falling upon her face in spots, like the skin of a fawn. What makes a flower supremely beautiful, he continued, his voice taking on the juicy orotundity of his college debating team, is the fact that they are a paradigm of our own mortality. Their brief perfect lives are an example to us, a preparation for our own deaths. Bud, bloom, decay. These sights became for Graham so full of message, so supremely the case of the sensual wedded to the didactic, that he wondered why the other visitors to the gardens were not caught up in the grip of it along with him. They wandered casually through the massed fields of scent and color, seemingly indifferent to the enormity of the drama being played out there. Whenever he saw flowers now his eyes would sting, he was afraid he might break down and start weeping in the gardens or the parks some day, in front of all those people, in front of Jess.

Fug, fump, fook, fack, fub, fuck, feek.

Lovemaking in that sweet, stinking room. Things are falling apart. Alternations of light and dark, flashes of pattern, street light on the ceiling as they turn and swim through each other. Comes, and she, released, moves upward to her goal, the progress is made in distinct steps, clear quantum jumps of sensation until the strings are finally tightened to their limit, vibration, spilling, breaking, overslowing. Limp, companionable grunts, thank you, OK, yes, I'm OK, great, wow. Off, on. Sense again of body as landscape, connections, movements those of the natural world, ebb and flow. Marks us with the sense of movement toward a goal, life as a journey, life as a cycle, goop, off, great hard rod, lovely loose balls; playing with the doorway, finger in, out, in, the tremoring of a pianist's trill inside, jokes in the ears suspended miles away, finger in the dyke, good Dutch boy.

On that involved bed, the salty sheets and confusion of limbs in the strippled urban dark. In Ann Arbor the summers got so hot I wanted to strip off my skin and join the inanimate world. Jess, lying on her back, gesturing vaguely at the ceiling as she talks. In the partial, sporadic light her movements fall a bit behind her words like a movie out of synch. Showers four times a day, she chants, gallons of ice cream. Completely unbidden, some childhood trigger not yet dismantled, juices squirt, Graham's mouth fills with spit. Chocolate, vanilla, strawberry, peach, butter pecan. Turning over on her stomach. There was a huge sign on the front of a bank, the time on one side and the temperature on the other. The sign would swivel slowly, all through the damned hot day: my mind too pulped with heat to think about anything else I used to fix on that sign. I used to wonder just how many calories the damned thing was adding to the atmosphere. Sweet entropy.

Good day! ghoeden-DACH Goeden dag!
Good morning! ghoeden-MORghen Goeden morgen!
Good evening! ghoeden-AAvent Goeden avond!
How. HOE hoe
goes GHANN gaan
it Ghaa-ĕt gaat het
with you met-UU met u
How are you? hoe-GHAAT-ĕt-met-uu? Hoe gaat het met u?
Well, thank you GHOET DANK-uu Goed, dank u
And (with) you? en-met-UU? En met u?
Quite well HEEL GHOET heel goed.

Graham grew fatter, little pouches of flesh hung in his cheeks and there were rolls of soft, white meat around his waist. He bought food for the hotel room now, on top of the meals; jars of pickles, sausages, chocolate, loaves of bread, just in case we get hungry in the night, he said.

One morning at American Express, the place was always filled with caricatures of their countrymen, a letter arrived from Graham's sister. He put it in his shirt pocket first, then read it as they sat in the café. A thick envelope, there were snapshots, and the letter covered several pieces of that very thin airmail stationery. Jess could see through to the other side while he was reading, could see, backward through the skin of the paper, the loopy ballpoint script, exclamation points, underlinings. His face flickered as he read the letter, shuffled the photographs. Blond nephews and nieces arranged on the front steps of a large house, freckles, missing teeth, and another of the family group spread out on a beach by a very blue sea, the tanned forms dark against the brilliant sand. Dear Linda he wrote to his sister that evening. It was very good hearing from you. The kids look great. I envy, in a way, the solid life you and John seem to have made for yourselves. Amsterdam is very fine, very polished by history, but things are somewhat askew. Jess and I haven't been getting along too well, same old thing. I simply don't seem to be able to hold things together. There are too many things to balance, to keep in repair. (Don't tell Mother any of this, of course, it would just worry her.)

This is probably just the autumn getting to me, please don't you worry either. By the way, do you remember whether there was a secret passage in the big closet in Grandma's upstairs bedroom? I asked Mother, but she keeps forgetting to reply. Rachel is growing big and beautiful. Do you remember the autumn at home when we were kids, the giant molding heap of leaves in the back yard that we used to jump on? I find, curiously enough, that I am homesick, but for nothing that I can return to. It's like being homesick for the past.

DENSITY OF HOLLAND

Holland is the most densely populated country of Europe. With its 11,938,000 inhabitants living in an area of only 13,514 square miles, it has an average density of 884 people per square mile, compared with 783 per square mile in Belgium and 794 per square mile in England and Wales.

Since the population of Holland has more than doubled in the last fifty years it is not surprising that the Dutch authorities are much concerned with the problem of overpopulation. Though fresh areas are constantly being dyked in to provide new land for farms and villages, there is a steady stream of emigrants especially to Canada and Australia.

TRANSLATE
What are you doing? How many fish are there? The blue
house is next to the red house. Please speak louder, I cannot
hear you. Why are you crying? Can you speak Dutch? New
York was once called New Amsterdam. What is the divorce
rate in Holland? About three quarters of the surface of the
earth is covered with water. I cannot hear you. Please speak
louder. What is wrong? Why are you crying? Why are you
crying?

They were fighting again, sitting in a restaurant, almost
yelling in that public place, although he hated such scenes and
she was weary of them. Accusations, disappointments. She was
angry, she was shaking, and she didn't want to hear the replies he
gave because she knew it all, hadn't they been through all this a
hundred times before, they knew their parts. They could have
changed places, changed scripts, and the dialogue would have
been the same.
There was nothing to say but they kept on. In the mirror
across from them, on the wall of the restaurant, they saw
themselves, dark stiffened figures, leaning close together,
gesturing, lifting and cutting chunks of air with the edges of their
hands. Things were falling apart.
Het zonlicht? op je haar. Het zonlicht op je haar.

Springtime, especially April and May, is the most beautiful
period in which the tourist has the opportunity to admire the
Dutch bulb fields in full bloom. But then the large flat
polders from Haarlem to Leyden and in the neighborhood of
Alkmaar are a unique carpet of color from the roadside to the
distant dunes, with mile after mile of waving tulips,
hyacinths and daffodils.

At the house of some friends for dinner Rachel, climbing on a
chair to reach a large, three-paneled mirror, fell, cut herself, and
knocked over a bowl of four goldfish which lay, gasping, on the
floor.

They were sitting on the bus which ran from their hotel to
the museum, half-dizzy from fucking through breakfast, no food,
no coffee, too many cigarettes. On to the bus climbed a large,
square Dutch mother with the number one pattern Dutch face:
small straight nose, large, rounded eyes, round head, half-wide,
even mouth. She had with her three children, of size increasing
by regular intervals, and with faces exact copies of her own. So
precise in fact was the rendering that it was as though no one else
could have taken part in their making, no large Dutch husband
full of beer braved those great pink thighs, she had seeded herself
and given birth to these replicas.

Saskia, inflation, despair. Americans on a moral peninsula.

On January 15th, 1637, a bunch of tulips was worth 120
guilders, only a few weeks later 385 guilders, and on
February 1st 400 guilders. For very rare examples as much
as 10,000 guilders were offered, which in those days was
equal to the value of 12 oxen, 24 pigs, 36 sheep, 6 bottles of
wine, 12 barrels of beer, 6 casks of butter, 3,000 pounds of
cheese, 3 silver beakers, 3 boats, and 20 tons of wheat.

Suddenly she saw that he had begun to save the bits and
pieces they had accumulated on their journeys; pamphlets,
guidebooks to places where he had lagged behind because his feet
ached, matchbooks. Just to keep tabs, he said, stuffing the ticket
stubs and the used Rittenkaart into a large manila envelope he
had labeled with date and location. He dropped an ash tray he
had been attempting to steal from a restaurant on the canal.
      Why?
The waiter came with a broom.
Don't why me.
Why?
The new flesh beneath his chin quivered.
Don't you see it had a little map? It said just where we are.
His eyes had moistened. He pointed at the glass, the waiter's
back, the broken glass under the checkered table cloths. Right
here.

MADURODAM—NOT TO BE MISSED

Not to be missed is the miniature city of Madurodam, between Scheveningen and The Hague (street car 29, bus 22). A visit to Madurodam is both instructive and amusing for it contains a typical Dutch town in miniature—4% of the normal size—with all the buildings, streets and squares as they are in reality.

Rachel, cranky and out of sorts, tried to kick in the sides of one of the buildings of the tiny town, Jess was too tired to care, and Graham disliked it because, he said, it gave him an unwelcome glimpse into eternity.

There was an old friend, Richard, a friend of Jess's, living in Amsterdam. An academic, he had just got back from some months in Germany. They had been to college together, had known each other, had, at one time, almost been lovers, but the occasion had passed, other things intervened, and a miss was as good as a mile in those things, in these times, with these people. They had, in a casual way, kept track of each other, through some friends in common, through a few long letters full of talk. They had always loved talking to one another, it had been their big connection, endless conversations of an indeterminate architecture.

Come and see us, he wrote Jess, I'm married to a Dutch girl and we're going to have a baby, she, that is, come to dinner.

They brought flowers with them, red tulips. The apartment was large, greenly lit with the reflected light from a canal. Richard greeted them, effusive, louder and more jocose than she remembered, hawk Jewish profile growing blurred. He was an historian with the university, was going to live here forever, relished the city, loved the people. His wife, Anna? Anneke, very quiet, blonde, small nose, breasts and belly swollen but not yet fully extended, sixth, seventh month. They talked, had cocktails, talked. Civilization, sweet sauce, a precarious prize. A fragile, delicious, delicate thing, a product of thousands of hands, always ready to tumble, fall, headlong, splashing, finally, without a trace, into the sea.

The sky outside turned from gray to blue to a bruised black, and Anneke lit a cluster of fat candles on the small table, the tulips in a bowl in the center, and began serving dinner. With the light coming only from the one source, all the gestures magnified into shadows around the room. The little area of warmth in the candles' pool of light was the energy center, the drama of plates and cups and moving hands and cold, bearded beer was carried on in this nucleus, and from that hot center everything graded off, fell away into the blue, deep corners of the room. Well, Richard was saying, it's as though Americans still believed (more ham) in the perfectibility of humanity, and Europeans (please pass the bread; tomorrow we're going to visit Anne Frank's house) know that it's not possible. That's what gives Americans this optimism and this terrible energy. They're just now learning (they?) that the story doesn't necessarily have a happy ending. Cinderella murders her sisters and sets fire to department stores, and the bears really do rape Goldilocks. The bubbles in the beer rose and burst themselves upon the surface of the air. Smells of cabbage and potato and hot sausage; a real Dutch meal. Richard stretched his mouth and puffed out the place where his belly would be in a few years. He patted Anneke's round bottom in a show of jocularity. The perfect burgher, this Jewish boy from Brooklyn and Harvard.

Jess was talking, her mouth full, her face glazed in the wavering glow. Light in some paintings is the equivalent, at least the analogue, of love. God's gaze on the world. Graham's face muscles began to ache with the effort of maintaining the creased smile. Richard and Jess were still at it, talking and talking, society, civilization, the arts, war and revolution. Graham let himself sink into the silence from which Anneke watched the show. Her hair was very blonde, lighter in tone even than her skin, her ears slightly protruding, her face shiny. The mild Dutch face. She seemed several years younger than Richard and the rest of them. The talking and eating continued. The pregnant girl moved back and forth from the table to the kitchen, in and out of the light, blooming, unconcerned for the categories and fine distinctions being established. She moved slowly, weightily, pushing her full front before her. Watching her carrying the heavy, steaming dishes Graham, a little drunk, found himself flooded with a clear and sodden, irrelevant desire. He felt he could almost hear, through their common thick silence, the beating of the baby's heart, as though the instant love had created a stethoscope of spirit between him and the blind small creature in its waters.

Their mouths filled over and over with the eating and drinking. The level of their glasses and plates rose and fell until it seemed a function of nature, and flushed with food and beer and his new love Graham followed Anneke into the kitchen. He stood in the doorway watching her wash plates, cut bread with her deep, slow, underwater movements. Her cheeks red, her short nose red and shining, she filled the platters again. He moved toward her and bent to kiss her. Later, reviewing this, he was amazed at his gaucheness. The potatoes and beer and the stiff, quick pair waiting for them at the table, he would not have blamed her, this fat, fair love, if she had screamed and pushed him away amidst pieces of broken crockery. But her reaction was, wonderfully, not that. Simply, she accepted his embrace and stood, holding his head to her full breast, he standing stooped, pressed against the plate of cabbage which she still held in her other hand. The fragrant gray steam rose, enveloping them both.

Returning to the table Graham felt the tightness of the other two, trespass rank in the air, hell to pay. The reckoning would come later. For the moment, insulated from them, he was fed and full and they were only shadows on his eye. Fantasies in that pure, drunken moment in the kitchen, it had for Graham the taste of the annunciation paintings with the dove, Mary, and the seed sliding down the ray of light from God to Mary's *ear* (zap), that baby in the womb *his*, a miraculous infant.

Holland is not quite as big as Vermont but the dykes if placed in a straight line would reach from New York to beyond Chicago.

(De) dingen Vielen uiteen. Things were falling apart.

They would walk and walk through the city, gray skies,

reflections, in the water everything was doubled. The city regarded itself, whole and multiplied, shimmering, in every piece of water, every shining surface.

Built entirely on huge piles driven through the marshy surface soil and intersected by countless canals, Amsterdam has inevitably been described as "the Venice of the North" though its canals differ from the Venetian in being almost invariably linked with quays.

They were it seemed to Jess like very early humans, prehistoric, cave-dwellers, fumbling around with the beginnings of speech, clumsily attempting the shaping of tools, a small stirring in their muddled broths of brains. Hairy, cold, wet, scared, they groped their way through the peaty darkness, trying to reach each other, trying to read the marks scratched on the walls of the caves, but it was no use. There were not enough words, they were not fine enough, the ice age was coming and it was cold, there wasn't enough food, there wasn't enough fire, it was dark, they were lost.

In the next room the child cried.

The Zürich Doctor Konrad Gesner was the first to discover the tulip in the garden of the Fuggers in Augsburg in about 1555. The true home of the tulip, however, is not Augsburg, but much further east, in Armenia, the Crimea. In about 1560 the Austrian Ambassador at the court of Ibrahim Pascha brought a few tulips with him to Vienna and presented them to the botanist Carolus Clausius or Charles L'Ecluse. When the latter was appointed to the University of Lieden, his tulips came with him to the Netherlands to be ever afterward associated with the name of that country.

bread broad
doof deaf
vies dirty
waar true
geel yellow
dun thin

It was his birthday, Thursday, and he must have a treat. he wanted to go to the Hilton Hotel for a celebration dinner. Come on, she said. You must be kidding, she said.

No, I really mean it. I want to go. His face was puffy and white. I want hamburgers and a milk shake and french fries and the whole deal. Just like home, he begged, just for a joke.

So they sat in the Drug Store Restaurant, the three of them, eating the American meal. Rachel was overexcited, her face bloody with ketchup. Graham had eaten three hamburger specials with all the trimmings, and Jess grew sick at the sight of the plates stacking into squat towers on the table.

He called the waitress over again. "It's my birthday," he said. "Do you have a cake?"

"Jesus, Graham," Jessica hissed.

The waitress brought a large cake, ornately iced, pink frosting roses on top and candles in plastic holders.

Jess stood up, "I'm going home," she said. "I've had enough."

"Wait, wait just a minute." He was pleading. His forehead was wet, and there was grease on his mouth. "Have some cake, please. It's my *birthday*." He bent to blow out the candles. "Look, Ray," he said. "I'm making a wish. I'm blowing out the candles."

Jess began putting on the child's coat. "No more," she said. "You can come back with us, or you can stay. We're going back to the hotel."

"Not yet," he said. "Just have one piece. It looks like very good cake." Rachel, bewildered, began to cry. "Cake," she screamed, growing more excited, "I want cake." People were staring at their table. Jess picked up the weeping child, and Graham grabbed her arm. "Please," he said. "Please." She tried to pull away. Rachel, suddenly, began to gag. She vomited, shuddering, covering Jess and the table.

In the ladies' room, cleaning up, Jess and the child cried and cried.

He grew fatter. None of his clothes fit any more. Gluttony is not a modern sin. His stomach distended, his face was wreathed with fat, he panted now, going up the stairs. They fought, were quiet, fought again. He brought her flowers, armfuls of flowers, they filled the vases, bowls, all the surfaces, and rotted sweetly in the room.

Remission and relapse. A cowboy movie was on in the center of town and they decided to go, on whim and something deeper, some obscure, pervasive homesickness that led them to a frantic consumption of American totem objects when they found them. Jess had bought some peanut butter and marshmallows in a shop and brought them home, they fell upon them, finished them all, and were sick through the night. Laughing, rueful, the ache persisted.

The cinema musty with generations of cigarettes and once gorgeous hangings of gilt and plum velvet (van Eyck), they sit in the front row. Rachel, sitting between them, is rapt; her hands stuffed with melting chocolate which she forgets, in her abandon, to eat. Half-full, an audience of devotees and the aimless on this Tuesday afternoon.

The newsreel is full of death. A bull in Spain, a group of anonymous, blurred soldiers in Vietnam, a black woman in a riot in Milwaukee. In that film, through some oddity of camera, her fall from the second-story window to the street seemed endless. She falls and falls, the only movement on the screen, everyone else in the chiaroscuro scene frozen with inertia or surprise. Finally she lands, a small heap, strangely jointed, and the other figures, released, begin to move again, gesture, cry out. Fire, flood, war, disease. Bad news, bad news.

A man somewhere behind them coughs and spits, a boy, about ten, runs down the aisle and back. Then a fresh turning toward the great screen, a rustling, a hush, and the giant American West is spread out before them, the mammoth pan of grass and the immense blue sky. Beyond the grass, in the weird hills glowing pink and purple in the coming sunset, the band of Indians wait. Big-nosed, feathered, striped with paint, they grunt to their spotted ponies, they wait to set upon the band of pioneers. A puff of smoke rises from a mesa toward the cloudless sky. The attack is about to begin.

The subtitles give an odd extra dimension to this drama. Warhoop, smack, bang, thud, the attack. Only the horses are surprised. The air fills with bullets, with arrows and the sound of arrows. Indians, pioneers, horses are hit, quiver, fall to the grassy ground.

Blood and dust mingle, and the colors swim in Jess's eyes, the gum turns salt in her mouth. She cries for the pioneers adrift on the huge prairie, their wagons burning, their children screaming loudly in the flames; for the Indians who, victorious in this battle, she knows to be doomed; she cries for Graham and herself, and for the little band of believers huddled in the movie house, and for America, torn and awkward, rich and bewildered now, fumbling through history, the fat boy hated by his classmates.

The film ends and they stumble out into the streets of the foreign city, their pupils clench, their vision blurs. The lights and shops and herring stands, Wyoming is more real.

TRANSLATE

Who can sing this song? Who knows the answer to this question? Who has lived in this house? From whom did you hear the story? What have you painted your house with? What shall I talk about? Which man is your neighbor? What kind of cigarettes do you smoke?

The fighting went on and on, and it was about no reason in particular, it was about all the reasons, simply all the facts about them and the world, their lives, their birthdays, politics, the colors of hair, toothpaste, painters; it was that the islands and the dykes, and the sanity and the civilizations were too hard to build, they could not build it, they had run out of stones and sand, there was not enough daylight, not enough words, they weren't strong enough, there was too much water.

They were so tired, they allowed each other no rest, and they couldn't leave each other alone, not even for a little while, just for a week or two, just for a break. But their unhappiness had paralyzed them into a kind of puppet show, an absolute routine of sleep and anger, and she couldn't break it, couldn't get away.

He followed her through the streets one day, and kept asking her the questions they both knew, she wanted to be alone, just for a few minutes, but he followed her, into the café, down the street, through the park. They were standing on one of the small bridges over the canals. He pulled at her arm, her shoulder, and she tried to get away, and he kept holding on to her. Then she grabbed the camera from his other hand and while he yelled at her she threw it, threw it up and over the side and into the canal; it splashed in the dark green water, sank, circles spreading outward, and he hit her, twice, over the ear and the side of the face. She tasted blood. She cried leave me alone, and ran down the street. He didn't follow her.

Hours later he found her, sitting in the American Express office, tears sliding down her face with no sound coming from her mouth, staring at all the Americans, fat and thin, who came and went in the rooms. He took her back to the hotel.

That night, Jess asleep in the hotel, he screwed one of the prostitutes who sat in the windows looking out at the streets. She was young, with long legs and gray eyes which, whenever he looked, were open. Afterward he remembered mostly the calendar on her wall, a picture of a windmill standing against a very blue sky.

"Could it be," he said to Jess one night, "that where the water has been it still holds power? That this whole trip has been through water, under water, in that way?"

They got a wire telling them to phone Graham's sister in Oregon. The two-languaged operators' voices and the strange mechanical syllables of sound seemed to Graham the tickings of a huge brain; such a black space extended from the receiver in his hand, pressed to his ear. The key hole at the other end of the space illuminated, his sister was on the line.

Her voice sounded very small and only just familiar.

"Graham," she said. "Graham, hello, I have some bad news." There was some interference on the line, a crackling like the sound for forest fires on a radio program.

"What, what?" he was shouting into the phone. "Linda, I can't hear you. *Linda.*" The operator's voice appeared, floating above the static, and then the line cleared.

"It's *Mother*," he heard Linda's tiny yell from the other end of the cord, six thousand miles away. "Mother. There's been a plane crash and Mother's dead."

Graham could hear that she was crying now, a strange grating noise that seemed to be some more of the machine's own mechanical conversation.

"She was on her way to visit Gary in Ohio—some kind of freak storm over the Rockies." The line fizzed again, then healed itself. "Everyone on the plane was killed."

When his sister hung up Graham held on a minute, listening to the links and synapses click themselves out. He hung up, and the silence roared in. The bottom dropped out of his bowels, and he barely made it to the toilet. In the great light of the men's room, in the spotty mirror, he looked like an old man.

There are sixty canals in Amsterdam.

When it came, it came quickly. Afterward, looking back over the way they had traveled, they could see the signs which pointed and announced that *this* was coming, this and nothing else, but at the time it had not been so clear. The condition itself obscured their vision of it and left them unprepared, if one can ever be prepared for such a thing, all set, bags packed as it were, like getting ready to go to the hospital to have a baby, the new pink bed jacket, the Kotex and the toothbrush.

All the bills came due at once, this in the sense of all the personal debts incurred, the most intimate transactions, the banks failed, the chickens came home to roost (this in the flat voice of the midwestern grandmother), the dykes, the dykes finally broke and the water came in and over, filling everything, covering everything.

Graham, surrounded by water, lay flat and quiet in that bed, in that room. People moved in the corner of his vision, forward and back, blurred white shapes, he could hear sounds come bubbling from them at him, but there was no sense to the sounds. Later they learned to wall off the sea by building dykes—first out of earth, centuries later out of stone, and today out of concrete and steel. The Dutch are presently building their gigantic "Delta

Works"—a series of five new dykes that will seal off further large estuaries of the North Sea. And remember, too, that even after land in Holland is reclaimed, it must constantly be drained by canals and pumps—or else the water will rise again!

Creatures joined him in the fluid life, ugly fish with shining scales. With unclosing bulbous jeweled eyes and long transparent tails they swim around him, bumping into his flesh, chewing at his fingers and the bottoms of his feet. He could feel the snails creeping up his arms, leaving behind the trails of slime that are their histories. Other creatures, those convoluted in shells, and those made of clear, brilliant jellies, nestled in his crevices, his ears, beneath the sheets, between his legs. New Orleans was burning. Denver was burning. San Francisco was burning. Vietnam is bigger than Rhode Island but smaller than Texas. Van Eyck, the Chinese, salt water, the secret passage, the starving millions in India.

As Rembrandt wrestled with the mighty task of the *Night Watch* Saskia wrestled with death; on 14 June 1642, she died, aged barely thirty. While she lay dying her features haunted his fervid imagination and pursued him into the thick of the soldiery peopling in *Night Watch,* conjuring up a world of strange imaginings in which we see her in the guise of a child, a realm of fantasy where time has ceased to be. Saskia! Saskia!

Holland is the paradigm of civilization, of the attempt to make civilization; the island, bailing to keep above the sea, planted with flowers.

They walked among the massed flowers. The sky was blue. De bloemen waren rood, gell, wit, roze, blauw, violet, and other colors, mixtures of colors. The scent, that compound scent, was indescribable. Het warme continent, de rode daken. To attempt to describe it would be foolish; it was like the smell of hair, of wet ground, het plekje tussen de borsten van een vrouw. Fish do not close their eyes. Little is known about the life of Vermeer. Translate: Do you expect your uncle today? De hond blafte en maakte de kinderen wakker. Waar is het toilet? What is the nature of vision? Het zonlicht op je haar. Food is good and plentiful in Holland, and need not be expensive. Saskia! De dijken, de bloemen, het water. De Koninklije Familie gaat per fiets. Spreekt u Engels? Spreekt u Italiaans? Spreekt u Duits?

Another shape bent over him, the waves leaping up. He could remember that this was Jessica, and she was talking to him, but he was too tired. Make sure that the nose and mouth are not obstructed. Kneel to one side of the casualty's hips, facing his head. Artificial respiration is used to make a person whose natural breathing has stopped start breathing again. Saskia! These swaying to-and-fro movements must be repeated regularly at a rate of twelve to fifteen a minute (what are the sounds a drowning man makes?) and continue this until natural breathing begins. *Drowning* is caused by complete immersion of the *nose and mouth* in *water* for a length of time which varies with the individual circumstances. At "tulip time," particularly April through mid-May, a thirty-mile strip of land between Haarlem and The Hague is covered by a dazzling blanket of tulips, daffodils and hyacinths. When *apparent recovery* has taken place, the *casualty* should be placed on his side in a warm bed, given a hot drink, and encouraged to sleep. Saskia!

The waves died down, and the water began, very slowly, to recede. Graham could feel its level with his fingers over the edge of the bed. He was asleep.

It was a long way back. Streets, and where they led, were impossible for a while. The fragile dominion he exercised over the bed was gradually extended to the boundaries of the room. In the faded blue pajamas he would rise at noon and sit silent for moments on the edge of the bed, trying to extricate himself from the drugs. Then, later in the day, the slant light yellow in the air, he would walk, carefully, holding his breakable self, on short journeys around the room. From the bed to the desk, she had put red and yellow flowers in a pot on the desk, from the desk to the chair, a cup of coffee. Then he would move to the window, now the shade was left up for part of the day, but the street and even the look of the street still threatened, and he would move back to the bed, in a rush except at such a slow pace, and fall back, his eyes shut, his face closed and drawn.

Work not so hard as delicate, this gathering up and putting together of parts. As the waters receded, they could inspect the damage done, the carpets ruined, veneers curling, paint rotted away. The holes in solid things. Jess had thoughts of the acrobats in circuses who built, with apparently ordinary apparatus, extravagant structures. The careful, precise piling up of tables, chairs, bicycles, bottles, into a trembling tower, and the final triumphant perching of the sequined, sweating performer on the top.

Slowly he began, with Jess and the child, to take short walks again, out to the shops to buy milk, a newspaper. The first ventures seemed possible only when they had a goal, to go out and bring something back. It was as though without that he might be distracted, detoured, lost.

He had become, through this thing, very thin; the flesh he had put on so quickly fell away as though it had been a costume, layers of cloth, Now he was very thin and strangely hunched over. The doctor described this bent state as common in cases of severe depression, and predicted that with the return of health he would straighten. It was true. Jess watched him unfold, slowly, like a calcium flower into the precarious, upright, human state; head erect again on the fine bone stalk of spine.

Sometimes he wondered whether the answer lay in that lost six hours between New York and Amsterdam. CITY ON THE WATER. Amsterdam has been called the "Venice of the North." It is built on huge piles driven through the marshy surface soil and intersected by countless *canals*.

The breakdown, they referred to it by name, his breakdown, "my" breakdown, proprietorially, like old ladies talking of operations; became a node to date by. Things had happened before or after the breakdown. Going there and coming back. As he grew better, things took on some of their old shape, the outward forms of eating, sleeping, seeing friends began to be possible again without the conscious effort of holding things together. But it was in the invisible area that permanent change had taken place, the mind's dark library. Some of the things he had known or thought he knew, were gone, swept away with the floods or rotted away with water and mildew afterward, and some new things were there. He understood now that the world, and his purchase on the world, were less protected and more vulnerable than he had thought. He knew of the way in which we build our islands out of the empty sea, how we fail, and how, with temporary dykes erected and windmills pumping out the brine, we inhabit our failures. He had discovered what we know and do not believe, that he was breakable, and that the dykes made only an uneasy peace with the water and that, in the end, the water is bigger and can wait longer for victory.

Jess was going back. Jess and the child, and he was to stay. They would see each other again, no final decision had been made, he would return sometime before too long or she would recross the water. But though these reassurances were made and given, he no longer had any sense of a sure future containing himself. It might happen, they might survive and meet and come together again, but he knew now the odds against any plan, against anything built staying built and he could admire the architecture but not invest.

TRANSLATE

How big those apples are! How we laughed! What nice apples these are! What a strange story! There is still some food in the kitchen. There are some old trees in the garden. Whose picture is this? Whose are these flowers? How beautiful!

They said goodbye at the airport and he had, the whole time, the sense of a reel winding backward. A last beer in the restaurant. Rachel was excited, wanted to see the airplanes, and they held her up to the window, her face against the glass. That morning, making love, Jess's face had tasted of salt. Now they were just polite, there seemed little to say, and she was extinguished, tired. The multi-language voices purled in their ears. He had the quick thought to take her, kiss, slap her, reach her again, but they talked, quietly, until it was time for her to go.

On the coach back from the airport, worn out, he fell asleep almost at once and dreamed a strange dream of the burning of New York; he dreamed that, over the ocean, Jess had leapt out, the child and the blue pig in her arms, and floated down; he dreamed of Holland and of moving through Holland, *the flowers, the water*.

Instructions for Exiting this Building in Case of Fire

First and primarily the reader is asked to radically visualize a particular child. Employing extreme breathing, sensory looping and the usual bio-psyche techniques, please call up into vivid present a real boy or girl, one whom you know well, and preferably one with whom you enjoy a largely positive relationship.

(If given the partitioning of modern life you do not know any children, you will have to borrow one from literature or painting, or perhaps from the movies. One candidate, an archivist, recently utilized the younger Shirley Temple, and another fastened on the tiny blonde Infanta Margarita looking warily out from the Spanish court, at Velasquez the painter and past him into the middle distance.)

We have found it useful to provide some framework devices to assist visualization. Initially, call up the brute dimensions of the child: mass, weight, reach, height. You will find that you can revive, through whole-body recall, the received pressure from those occasions when the child's body has rested against your own. The next array includes the color and fragrance continuum. Fill in hair color, eye hue, the pigmentation of the skin and particularly the shades of mouth, cheeks, the palms of the hands and the soles of the feet, and the skin beneath the fingernails. Please be as exact as possible. Numbered swatches and color chips are enclosed. Try next to specify the smells relating to mouth, hair, skin and gaseous emissions. What textures do you associate with this child's skin and hair? Characterize the teeth.

We have found that the reconstruction of auditory sensa are especially difficult for some. It facilitates to summon up the image of the child in action, bending, turning, pausing to speak—insert here a typical utterance, coming from lips of such and such a shape, with the head tilted how many degrees from the perpendicular, and the brow set with just these curves and arcs, the nose at such and such an angle, the gesture, the gaze, the tone of voice.

Now quickly, at a grosser matrix, fill out the time-space context around the individual: specifying surroundings, time of day, presence of others, color inventory, humidity and pressure, noises, smells, emotional tonus. There is your child now, squarely placed in an amply detailed continuum (I am reminded of the exercises in "particularization" in the Creative Writing Syllabus at Chicago Tertiary College), and there we leave her (my resolutions for gender-neutral language break down—when *I* tell this story, I see a little girl).

She is sitting athwart her young brother whom she has tickled into hysterical submission, they are wrestling in our back garden, sending up gusts of yellow aspen leaves which litter the ground like coins of fairy money. She is wearing hand-me-down denim overalls and a red sweater on which the motif ducks and rabbits have gathered for a pre-Easter meeting though it is only October. And one's sense of her person is of a highly variegated surface so covered is she with her usual rents, tears, bruises, paint marks and other smudges and her fine brown hair escaping every which way from the double security of braids and barrettes. Her earnest and passionate researches into the nature of things leave her decorated with testamentary marks of contact, stones and worms in her pockets, twigs in her hair, blue and green daubs across her cheeks and chin. She has the aspect of a tribal citizen, very powerful and intact, with an extraordinarily direct and unabashed intelligence. In the broad sunlight it is warm, though there is an autumn chill in the plum-colored shadows. Her eyebrows are drawn with a two-hair Chinese brush, her eyes are blue. Now her brother is bawling over some rough justice, and to soothe him she delivers a new rhyme, a choosing device which she has learned, she is shouting out, "My Mother and your

Mother were hanging out the clothes/My Mother gave your Mother a punch on the nose/What color was the blood? Shut your eyes and think/Green! G-R-E-E-N spells green and out you go/With a jolly good clout upon your big nose!" Successful solace, and they are both laughing uproariously and will not stop.

*   *   *

And now, patient reader, without at this point questioning the mechanism, let the Goddess Hariti act as *dea ex machina*. She who began as a child-devourer but was converted by the Buddha into a cosmic nurse-maid will whisk that altogether palapable child to Moscow, to Gorky Park. It is spring and the ice is continually melting and freezing, and what is this child, my child, my luminous girl doing in Moscow, on a park bench, wrapped in foreign winter gear and licking a chocolate ice cream?

It was as the Middle East rended itself mortally, the crazed wolf in a trap biting his own flesh. And it was as the pendulous Siamese twins of Africa and South America, now separated, seemed still continuous in their joint misery and suffering and accelerating frenzy. There were so many wonderful and urgent reasons for dissent, and only the one overwhelming reason for accord which was both absurd and too vast, so that most of the *homo sapiens* population, up on our hind feet, sundered from biology, found it invisible. The little wars flickered and acted as beacons to the larger interests; the global theater was filled with acute excitement. The situation became daily more extreme. It was when the minute hand on the Domesday clock fluttered and hiccoughed in those rare seconds before midnight that we finally acted on this set of premises, to change history.

Angleinlet, Minnesota

Anyone viewing the video of Dakota Saltz and Michael Benjamin, the newly-sunburned Saltz-Benjamins, making the beast with two backs in the 60s Nostalgia Room of the Hotel Sands Susie on election night would have concluded that her attention was only partly taken up with the bumpy union of their bodies. The camera, though expected, was tactfully secreted in an expensive lighting fixture which mimicked live candles. The décor featured hanging strands of beads and bells, souvenirs of Vietnam, political posters in four languages and voluminous folds of Paisley cloth. Spot-lit and bolted to the floor was a display case in which a bit of moonrock set in a lucite block was on show, and the theme was picked up by a "one small step for man" photo mural.

"My mother was a hippy," Dakota snorted, on top, lazing back and forth, she sneezed at a drift of smoke from the automatic, everlasting, self-igniting joss sticks. "She believed that a creative and spiritually evolving life-style would save the planet."

The television blatted out the terrible and expected results, the bright and dark forms of the victorious flickered across the lovers' substantial flesh, bad news, bad news. From all over the globe the media shepherds and shepherdesses rounded up and brought forward their unnatural flock, the members of the world's various governments, to react and reflect upon the American elections. Mesomorph, ectomorph or endomorph, bald or hirsute, rhetorical or confiding, pompous or humble, religious or secular, dressed in emblematic duds, they all bared their teeth at one another and uttered patriotic formulae and threats.

Moaning, Dakota willed herself to focus on transactions between her body and her husband's. She called on some partially understood tantric discipline to transmute the corporeal into the spirit, to map the personal body onto the cosmic body, she meditated on a terrible form of the Goddess Kali seated in intercourse on the male Corpse-Siva, resting upon severed heads. The fanged and bloody goddess is the same as the beautiful Mother and Lover. The images flickered and incremented, Michael's red mouth shaped an O, the pulses of orgasm married the opposites for a moment. Panting, grinning, tasting the sweet oxygen, the newsflash immobilized them as though it had been a jolt of ball lightning zapping through the room:

The young son of a top Russian General and the four-

year-old daughter of a US Senate leader had both been kid-napped from their homes within the past twelve hours.
BEGIN!

* * *

Dakota found herself standing in the middle of the room, holding some socks and underwear, starting to pack, standing still, tears flooding her vision. Michael side-stroked into view, looking preoccupied.

"*Kismet Hardy, or Kiss me, Hardy, pie in the face,*" she babbled. "*Here we go!*"

The news bulletin is repeated on the screen. The relatives of the kidnapped girl are being interviewed, they seem hardly to be able to construe the reporters' questions, so deeply absorbed are they by the enormous event which has overtaken them. The father's brows leap and punctuate independent of his sentences. Dakota's mouth is a hot cave from crying.

"Crossing the Rubicon, I can't remember the Latin for the die is cast," and she wept and roared for a few moments, into the labeled hotel pillows, and then she was calm again. They had their instructions with them, a micro-dot mole on her right shoulder-blade. *Eat this note.*

The shaman reconstruction ritual was an eclectic and corrupt piecing together. About fifty women were bussed from St. Paul, through the vast acres of sleeping suburbs, through the farmland, into the northern woods, and then deeper and deeper until they stopped at a place that looked to the untutored eye as leafy and indefinite as all the surrounding landscape. Dakota wondered afterward whether the hot drinks passed around in polystyrene cups had been drugged. Certainly the colors in the nimbus around the fire began to vibrate brilliantly in distinct bands. They took off their clothes, undressing in the bus, joking and talking in the instant equity of bare flesh. Outside their breaths formed steamy clouds but the big fire heated them at least one side at a time. Silhouetted against the tall flames the organizers read out bits of potted prophecy from Hopi and Kiowa texts, from the

Bible and the Koran, and also from Nostradamus and other dubious sources. Then all were encouraged to run around the fire circle springing and roaring, leaping, barking like a dog, sniffing, lowing like an ox, bellowing, crying, bleating like a lamb, grunting like a pig, whinnying, cooing, imitating the songs of birds, and so on. It is said that the descent of the spirits often takes place in this fashion.

And so, the preconditions having been satisfied she was now an "activated agent." Outside the snow had begun again. Carrying messages too secret to entrust to technology, Dakota was on her way to Florida.

* * *

No one invented this, everyone did, all at once, like a miracle. No one is the leader, we all are, and it just happened that way. That's right. And if that all seems odd, unlikely, too much the paradigm of what used to be called new age organization, then you will have to find out for yourself, if there's time, if it seems important. The stories we tell ourselves are whatever is necessary for going on. Personally, I've never really thought of myself as a group player.

In the crisis room in Kansas the red crisis lights are on, and the sirens blast at frequent but random intervals rendering all thought impossible for that period and leaving an auditory after-image suspended in time for a little like the ghost flash bulb that hung over the head of the importunate school photographer. I am explaining this to you just as I find I am explaining it to myself, over and over, since I made the initial, irreversible commitment; since we began.

The very notion of approaching a family situation, and invading that family and violently removing a young child from that family and taking that child away so fast and so far and promoting so many changes that any future connection between child and family is uncertain; even the *idea* of that action is disgusting and abhorrent.

And so I come to you with unclean hands. And also, in the midst of so much distress and tragedy, I speak with authority of my own, of our family's tragedy.

* * *

It was during the early months of the exercises, I had returned from Florida, we were aping normality and even the pretense was precious. Judith, our middle child, second daughter, first-grader, our blue-eyed indomitable, always joking darling, is late home from school. It's Halloween and we're going to carve the pumpkins and then go out trick-or-treating, so she wouldn't be late. The costumed figures of the smaller children stumble from doorstep to doorstep, the bigger children are readying themselves, and yelps and calls escape from the upper windows. *Where is she?*

Checking the bus stop, which is on our side of the street, a two-minute walk. Pacing up and down the street, making the phone calls to friends' houses to see if she has, please God, broken the rules and gone over to play without permission; walking around the empty school, the deserted playground, the town park full of children but not that one special bright face, green jacket, fast runner, good climber. Talking to her teacher, to the bus driver, the school head, to the police, the FBI, and for those few hours, until it grew dark, sustaining a hope that some reasonable logic was still operating and that she would be home for supper, our radiant girl! But the dusk gathered and the clouds grew bright, never have I dreaded more the sunset's gorgeous rose and cadmium sacrifice, so quick.

We had known, of course, that in order to remain covert, and also to maintain a basic justice, the members of the organization would have to be part of the big computer's horrid lottery, along with everyone else. And now I think of Judith always, every hour, every time I look up at a peripheral flicker which isn't here. My dilettante's essays into non-attachment have been worthless, of no value whatsoever.

What could justify this offense to Person, Family and Natural Law? Only this. The extreme and growing likelihood that we are finally about to do it, blow ourselves to kingdom come, extinguish our species along with the multitudes of others that journey along with us, and perhaps the planet itself as a life-sustaining venue. That, coupled with the dreadful, finally unavoidable conclusion that sane, liberal, powerful, even very evolved persuasion cannot any longer save the day—simply because we've run out of time!

At the ultimatum meeting in the buried solar motel at the Kansas headquarters a fat Polish woman stuttered through the pandemonium to the heart of things.

"Suppose yourself in a burning building, full of confused adults and children, a trickle of blue smoke, the intoxicating scent of roasting hydrocarbons, soon it will turn into an inferno but the inhabitants seem not to notice. The only way, *the only way* to set off the alarm which will alert the crowd is to lower a child, yours or another's, out of a window and drop it to the ground to its probable destruction. *Would you do it?* 'Yes.'"

Key West, Florida

The "living diorama" Seminole village, which was said to be on the site of the *actual* Seminole village, was made up of two rows of structures that looked like giant, stripped-down four-poster beds minus the organdie. These Seminole dwellings were open on the sides and covered on top, some with a kind of rough thatch, others were roofed with sheets of galvanized metal. On the platform, families in antique dress were assembled, playing Canasta, cooking fry bread, singing to babies who were slung in hammock-like devices fixed to the corner uprights. In short, going about all their domestic business before the eyes of the delighted tourists. These Indians were, on close inspection, a savvy blend of warm humans and androids, the mix favored by the most successful modern theme parks.

Pearled, striped and blotched with sweat, Dakota followed behind a group of heavily swathed Jordanians, and was herself followed by a cadre of handsomely equipped Japanese. She limped along on her sore ankle, viewing this odd, highly artificial and decadent interface between cultures, of which there are no others. Peering along with the others into the faces of the native Americans, first to make the rough division between humans and subs, then to enter behind the opaque gazes of even the living

Indians. "How can I find my 'contact' if no one will look back at me?" Just a trill of panic, had she spoken aloud? Their eyes were obsidian. And so, not paying attention to what lay immediately underfoot, and limping on her left, the ankle was swollen and still swelling, progressively, a chronic sprain, *damn!* and so she was next a victim of the instantiated national characteristics of the tour packs who surrounded her. The Jordanians, intrigued and amused by the quaintness of the exotic infidel, dallied. They hung back to point and discuss, they stopped to open picnic baskets and napkin sacks. They planted themselves just so to clean the face of one of their spotless children, they retraced their steps to catch another look at some special sight; they gossiped, they lingered. The Japanese, hung about with all manner of mid-tech recording devices, pressed forward with determined enthusiasm. They photographed, videoed, filmed, taped, they pushed. And so Dakota is caught up between the aggressive Orientals and the dilatory Arabs, the light dazzles her eyes and her leg is hurting and she is getting too much sun and how would she ever connect with her contact.

Thump! she is knocked flat into the pink dust, coughing; a large pyramidal shape looming above her resolves itself into a heavily draped Arab woman. Bending over the topsy turvy "agent," she lifts gauzy purdah and speaks directly into Dakota's large-lobed left ear *"Follow the squaw who overcomes the dragon-reptile."* She then shows the sign which marks her as indubitably part of the exercises, the sisterhood, the Mothers of Invention dubbed by some old lady who did or did not remember the 1960s. Spitting out dust, Dakota picks herself up and moves forward. "Not a particularly glamorous bit of espionage." Had she spoken aloud?

And there at the end of the street which is formed by the two rows of houses, a dusty widening, trampled clay pricked out with weeds, a primitive gas station with one pump, closed, and a café-type highway restaurant which had fallen away from its chipper franchise crispness and exhibited curl all along its perimeters. The multi-cultural crowd thronged and surged, according to their deep natures, toward a deep, flat-bottomed pit fortified by adobe walls. Dakota was bundled along with the crowd, pushed forward on a wave; she could see at the bottom of the pit, crouched on the fissured red mud, the green, segmented, long-jawed, quizzical alligator, ticking its tail in display to impress the young Indian woman who crouched opposite. The woman looks both tough and oddly casual. Her blue-black hair is cut very short, her face, in concentration, contains but does not reveal. A fat Indian man in a Hawaiian shirt printed with orchids and parrots gives the signal for the 'gator wrestling to begin.

The woman enters within the attack range of the animal and then must immediately, avoiding both the switching tail and snapping jaws, move to hold the jaws shut with one hand. Then with a sudden twist she flips the animal onto its back and maneuvers to sit astride the beast, and then, most amazingly, she proceeds to rub its belly in a clockwise fashion. And thus did the reptile fall into a hypnotic sleep which continued until the young Seminole woman cease in the stroking of its stomach's pale, shining skin. And then its eyes unbuckled and its body kinked and jerked and its tail began to pendulum again and the woman leaped off and out of reach and scrambled up from the pit to much applause and electronic whirr. It was only at the last that Dakota remembered she was to follow this woman, and she dodged through the crowd after her, into the café.

Having attracted the attention of her quarry by pouring Bourbon on the rocks into her lap, the lap that is of Laverne BitterWing who, as a radical feminist 'gator-wrestling Seminole had seen more politicking than Dakota had had hot dinners, Dakota apologized and bumbled out the password, which was "authenticity," and felt herself blushing head to toe as Laverne looked on with a kind of irritated tolerance. Drinking the replacements, seated in a red naugahide booth, Dakota gave Laverne the message, whispering about an exercise that involved Manila and Peru with Florida as the third critical point. She hissed the names of the children who had "won" the lottery; she outlined the network for each child's retrieval. Laverne's perfume rose up into her nose, she was thirsty from the dust and heat and the whispering, "another Scotch, or rather Bourbon, that's what we're drinking." And Laverne tells Dakota the scarey stories about the "hot" submarines nosing in close to the Florida coast, playing games of chicken. Recently military chemistry has covered the beaches with stinking, phosphorescent fish. Obsidian.

*   *   *

Sometimes it seems to us that there are signs that the exercises are beginning to take effect. In the boardrooms, the factories, the bedrooms, in the chambers where governments grind out their extraordinary decisions, everywhere human creatures act and move, there is now this enormous consideration. With the kidnapping and the "specified" resettlement of all these many little children, increasingly, the *we* and the *they* have become irrevocably, irretrievably confused, all mixed. This mixing, this sense of shared consequences, is not of our making. The exchange of the innocents simply points out what is in fact already the case, that finally, at this extraordinary juncture of history we are members one of another, not in some abstract rhetorical sense but at the most practical level of survival. "The bottom line." Who spoke?

We remind ourselves that some small initial success is not sufficient for us to do what we all long to do, to stop this terrible work. The danger of absolute conflagration is immense. We must not weaken. We must be resolute.

Yes of course there are casualties. The child who fails to respond adequately to surgery, the anaesthetised child who aspirates vomits and suffocates, the families ruined beyond repair, the child who goes mad. Please refer here to your own illustrated file on the after-effects of nuclear war.

Lubec, Maine

Flying to Lubec, Maine, the Saltz-Benjamins, diminished with Judith missing, no longer fill the five-seat middle bank of the airline's economy class, and Dakota finds herself between four-year-old Max who, naturally exuberant, has been numbed and practically muted since the kidnapping of his sister, and an extremely elderly man. This gnarled and transparent gentleman introduced himself in heavily accented English as the proven and established oldest man in the world, a claim he substantiated by drawing out of his wallet various laminated newspaper clippings which pictured him and explained that, as a political prisoner in the Soviet Union during the 40s and 50s, not a young man even then, he had undergone repeated hunger strikes which had provided just that periodic shock to the genetic material which was required, as science has since demonstrated, to extend the human life span dramatically. The old man chattered on about his history, stories of doves and hawks and the species' ultimate games. He entertained Dakota with the recitation of a menu from a great diplomatic dinner in Geneva—oysters in truffle sauce, smoked swan, beef Wellington, eight vegetables, world-wide cheeses, six wines, black bread, baked Alaska, pumpkin pie, and a whole living peach tree wheeled in so that the guests, all now deceased save for her interlocutor, could pick the fruits with their own hands, Dakota yawned until her jaws creaked, she was desperately tired and, of course, it should be Judith sitting there.

Jenny, their eldest, turned pale and Max grabbed at his ears as the plane banked and made for Ape Island, the teardrop-shaped artificial bauble of land which had become famous as an exclusive resort and tax refuge, it winked up at them out of the foaming, Guinness-colored Atlantic.

*   *   *

Fragmentation of directions is necessary to confound our pursuers. Dakota walks, with family in tow, through the Theme Park of the Evolution of Culture, *"just pretend to be ordinary,"* on the lookout for a sign. Displays, rides, exhibition halls, museum complex, *son et lumière,* the mother and father point out the items of interest to their children, see the walls, the cities, the gardens, the modes of transport, the sophisticated techniques of warfare, all the works of art and culture which make up the inspiring models of *homo sapiens* achievement. Jenny was paler still at the Rembrandt Arcade, and finally threw up just outside the Lincoln Compound, observed only by a group of robot darkies. *And on this hand is the special activated genuinely scientific demonstration and statistical display*. They walk under an arch lettered in Revival Nouveau vegetable cursive MONKEYS TYPEWRITERS SHAKESPEARE. A "living exhibit" organized according to the premise contained in the "archaic humorous saying" *Put enough monkeys with enough typewriters for enough time and they will produce the complete works of William Shakespeare* (which see).

No doubt the recent cataclysmic events have interrupted the day-to-day running of organizations even so far from the epicenter as this bit of hypostasised pastorale. Notwithstanding the fascinating character of the display, the monkeys and apes disporting in a charming conjunction of nature and culture, there was on every hand the evidence of neglect and order distressed. Citizens goggled at the primates interacting with all manner of typewriters, word processors and computers. They applauded the drama of these hairy cousins reinventing culture in picturesque vignettes, "the taming of fire," "clothing our nakedness," "invention of the fishing hook," "the commencement of poetic diction," and so on. But, as father commented to mother, despite the lavishness of this rhetorical Darwinism, there were, to the observant eye, many signs of "making do." Since the cancellation of Malaysia the severe interruptions in supplies and personnel have resulted in a certain amount of barely adequate habitat and noticeable psychological dislocation among some of the animals.

They come upon a group of gorillas dressed in rough tags of Elizabethan costume, laboring away at the construction of a replica of the Globe Theatre. Max and Jenny press forward in a gang of children up to the barrier to watch the action. They have taken up with a charming, peach-skinned, French-speaking blonde child, smaller than Max, and Jenny struggles to lift her to the top of the barrier so that she can see. The apes move gracefully about the building site, there is a sense of mock decorum about many of their movements. Dakota noticed that they seem to build and unbuild with almost equal assiduousness, and they frequently stopped in the midst of some effort to act out a line or two from one of the plays, or to quote a mangled couplet from a sonnet. Their language was vastly imperfect but it was language. They glimpsed Hamlet and Ophelia in conversation under a willow tree. Ophelia seems upset, and Hamlet grunts and plucks at her, then turns away. And then a massive young silverback male catches Dakota's attention. He is standing on a precarious cantilevered joist which swings, barely pinned, from the top of the north wall. He is mouthing a speech: *"Lie with her!—We say lie on her, when they belie her.—Lie with her! 'Zounds,   that's   fulsome!   Handkerchief—confessions— handkerchief!"*—he gabbled. *"Pish! Noses, ears and lips. Is't possible?—Confess?—Handkerchief!—O devil!"*

"Act IV, Scene 1," says a voice at her side. She jumps sideways, startled; it is the certified most ancient man. "His name is called Otello, in the Italian manner." Dakota watches *as though in slow motion* the gorilla Otello moves down through the construction and over the grass and rocks to the barrier, and, at more frames per second, clambers over the moat and simply bounds to the top of the barrier. Voices cried out "Otello, Otello!" And then, as Dakota realizes that she has known that this would happen, with grotesque but inescapable logic, Otello reaches down and lifts the little blonde from Jenny's arms. *"Daphne!"* An ear-splitting shriek from two throats, French, the armaments magnate and his spouse who are ravening bootlessly at the edge of the crowd. "Daphne!, Otello, Otello!" These two musical names curl out over the scene as the gorgeous Otello mounts the heaped elements of the theater, the wailing baby in his arms. Perched on top we can all see that she is in grave danger as he dandles and dangles her and teases her with the unsecured space. There is nothing anyone can do without spooking the ape and endangering the child further. *"Otello, Otello!"*

What are these words in her mouth? Dakota is calling to Otello, he listens, he replies. This woman who has always disliked and avoided heights is climbing the structure, scaling the walls, she has gained the top, she is facing the gorilla and flailing child. *"I'm terrified of heights."* Had she spoken? *"Otello,"* she said through dry lips, and he made a dignified nod and handed over the little girl who was rigid and purple with continued screaming. Dakota held her tightly and climbed, bit by bit, shakily, carefully down. As she touched the ground she heard the crowd sigh collectively, the parents were coming toward them. But Dakota felt with her hurt foot for the trigger to the trap door in the burned knoll. *How had she known it was there?* and it swung open to let them in, then snapped shut, decisively. The hammering continued against the massive door which fitted seamlessly into the bank, it held steady. Dakota exited, down and out. She injected the wretched child and watched her twitch into unconsciousness. As they transited, Dakota was apologizing to the ashy, crumbled baby in her arms.

Cape Alava, Washington

We delivered Daphne to Cape Alava, Washington. She was to undergo further training, briefing and "conditioning" which is a dump word for surgically and drug-induced consciousness alteration. Drop-off was a veterinary clinic in a shopping mall. Anaesthetic music accompanied their progress through the bland reflective corridors constructed at a giant's scale. Daphne held tightly to the collar of the bumptious Newfoundland puppy, her decoy. He terrorized hamsters and kittens in the waiting room, a distraction, until they went through to the examining room where the agents stood with sad, drawn, severe faces that Dakota recognized from the mirror. Then the child was screaming again, and trying to hold on to her, and the huge puppy was barking and leaping, and people were falling on the slippery blue linoleum, and Max yells out in a rusty voice, *"Daphne, Judith! Daphne!"*

* * *

Now, gentle reader, please call up into your mind's eye your selected child as already visualized. Go through the reification processing and mass out significant traits as indicated earlier. (Refer to instructions.) Remember, having filled in the broad descriptive categories, it is often the subtle level of detail which strongly evokes an individual child's presence.

What is this child like in silhouette? The typical thrust of shoulders, the gait. What kind of temper does the child display? Describe the child's appetite, singing voice, mood spectrum. It is of utmost importance that you carry out this program of recollection with maximum thoroughness, as recent evidence indicates that the psychic numbing of which we have heard so much cannot withstand this kind of focused attention to vital, loving detail.

How does the child look when asleep? What is the sound of your child crying? And now, place the child here, right here at this place in the text. PLACE CHILD HERE. It is *your* chosen child being viewed, stalked, snatched, taken.

As I write there are sounds of hideous wailing coming from the isolation ward above. And it is your child, your little Nan or Ted or Mary, your Miguel, Saleem, Makmuda, Ku, your Jonathan, Joseph, Mario, Zephyr, Chen, Boris, your Alice, your Sam who will be "adjusted" to the fabric of another nation and culture.

And please let Judith play along with it, like a game, and not turn magnificently stubborn, our radiant girl!

And please let the big computer remember so that when we may find her, we can.

Some of the operatives have killed themselves.

Osborne County, Kansas

Good times, bad times. And now here we are, autumn on the Great Plains and the wind howls down through the high grasses, juddering and wailing over Canada, all the way from the North Pole. In the grounds of the Best Western Motel which we have taken over as headquarters the gardens are being organized as a didactic and formal mechanism. To walk through its lanes and avenues, and to look upon its sculptures, ruins, topiaries and fountains is to move through the powerful arguments, logical, aesthetic, political and metaphysical embodied in the artifacts made by angry, grieving, grimly optimistic women.

Was Clio, the Muse of History, a mother? Did she grieve while the necessities of process destroyed her young? Now so many children have been shuffled and transported: Israeli children have been taken into all the Arab countries, and there are defiant Jordanians, Syrians, Iranians, Libyans and so forth now living in Israel and in the West. As for the super-powers, Russian, American and Chinese children have been scattered all over the planet like grains of rice; in Northern Ireland such is the nature of the horrid conflict that Catholic and Protestant babies have been exchanged and re-worked so that they are often living down the street from the biological parents. And so throughout the world, every barrier of nation, race, class and religion has been crossed and recrossed with our tender future citizens. And all over the globe, along with the massive grieving and anger, there is a kind of stirring consciousness, a kind of glimpsed recognition of this pattern, the strategy and its point. Can humans, we sapient ones, come to take care of our offspring with the same concern and good sense shown by the other beasts? If a nuclear missile aimed at my "enemy" is now, also, by definition, aimed at my children, will it stay my hand?

* * *

We strolled through the white garden, the red garden, the scented garden, the garden of physicks. We picnicked quietly by a vast turf maze. Max seems calmer, here in the open. He and Jenny are braiding weedy flowers together into a chain which they put around my neck. A bent figure bundled against the blustery wind approaches us, and as he unwraps several layers we recognize the "oldest man." We offer to share our lunch with him, and he sets to with gusto, launching with a full mouth into one of his rambling stories about past days and the adventures of his prime, about the cold wars and the biological wars. . . . As he talks we finish our meal and decide to wander together through the maze. The path winds round the reproductions of the Sphinx and Camel Rock, then through the water garden. Max is tired and I pick him up. Carrying one heavy, silent baby, longing for the lost one, we push on until we come to a life-size statue of Avalokitesvara, the Bodhisattva Mahasativa of compassion, eleven-headed, and there our ancient companion regales us with a tragi-comic tale of another elaborate conference on disarmament which had once again finished in histrionics. He told of a subsequent feast of fools in the Embassy and ended, "*I was at that feast and drank beer and wine, it ran down my moustache but did not go into my mouth."*

Michael laughs *haha* at the ironic and habitual Russian ending to fairy tales and fables. Max is snoring softly. And here we are at the center of the maze, a niche, a minor cave carved into the side of a hill, an invented hill in the flatness of Kansas. And in the cave there is a grotto, lined with seashells and fossils, and inside the grotto is a robot facing a blank of TVs which are showing the 24-hour news from all around the world, burning buildings and etc. Jenny says amazed, "the robot is weeping."

Mothers, forgive us.

Mothers, join us!

Sheep

Prologue

The Cowboy's yellow silk shirt is fringed, and the yellow wings of the clothes moth are fringed, and dressed in her woolen nightdress which is full of moth holes the Sleepwalker, her eyes open but unseeing, her arms outstretched before her in the classic manner, walks barefoot across the moonlit wooden floor of the bedroom, opens the door, across the landing, down the stairs, and stumbles into the arms of the waiting Cowboy. The sheep from which the wool had been shorn to make the nightdress huddles with the rest of the flock just outside the door, standing on the green lawn which has the look of blue enamel in the moonlight. She is wired up to a monitoring device which measures and records her brain waves, eye movement, the tension and relaxation of her throat muscles, and her heart beat as she sleeps.

Numerous recent electroencephalographic studies have revealed the cyclical alternation of two distinct types of sleep (Dement and Kleitman 1957a), which have been termed "fore-brain" and "hind-brain" sleep by Jouvet (1962), (or "orthodox sleep" and "paradoxical sleep"). The former is accompanied by slow waves and spindles in the electroencephalogram (EEG) and the latter by a low-voltage, fairly fast EEG pattern; spasmodic, conjugate rapid eye movements (REMs); relaxation of neck and throat muscles in cat

(Jouvet, 1962) and human (Berger, 1961); and recall of dreams following awakening (Dement and Kleitman, 1957b).

The bald moon casts the sheep and her fellows in stone and soap.

The group of mammals known as ruminants—cows, sheep, goats and others—go on "ruminating," or cud-chewing, throughout the night. They go on doing this while asleep, even though their eyes remain open. They become unresponsive to things going on around them and have the EEG of sleep. The peculiar arrangement of their upper digestive tract relies upon gravity for its proper function. In consequence the head and neck have to remain erect even during sleep. What will happen if their muscles become paralyzed during paradoxical sleep so that they cannot keep up their heads? Will their food "go the wrong way"?

They get round this problem by eschewing paradoxical sleep. The lamb before weaning spends much of the night in paradoxical sleep. As she grows older and begins to ruminate, paradoxical sleep is almost lost. Only rarely does it briefly appear, and at these times rumination ceases. This is very interesting: it implies that her brain processes have matured in such a fashion that they need scarcely any of the particular restitutive virtues which one must assume normally stem from paradoxical sleep.

The fringed Cowboy, and the Sleepwalker who is still asleep, walk arm and arm out the front door and into the moonlight. They begin a slow dance, revolving about the garden, a fox trot, in which they are joined by the sheep, and the sheep dog.

THE FIRST LOOKED to be about 14 months old, she had not reached her full growth, a standard commercial cross-breed, well-fleeced, not yet with young. She was not sufficiently mature to be the bellwether, and so it was evident that she had strayed away from the main body of the flock, come in advance. She put her head down and touched her lips to a few spikes of the bright green early spring grass, her warm breath ruffled the grass, she lifted her head again. In the birch tree by the stile 5 blackbirds improvised, the wind eddied inconstantly, blowing up sweet-smelling dust. She ambled over to the fence (it was, at this point, 3½ feet of galvanized twisted wire set with red cedar posts), then backed off a few steps and leaped easily over the barrier. Number 1.

At the left-hand side of the picture the stream and the bridge, the meadows rise up in the middleground, and then in the background, rinsed blue with the distance, the woods, the hills, a suggestion of mountains.

The second was clearly another stray, being of about the same age and size as the first. It was now possible to recognize both of these animals as members of the breed known as "Oxford Downs," a blend of the Hampshire and Cotswold breeds. These sheep combine the meat-producing properties of the Hampshire with the wool-yielding qualities of the Cotswold. This individual lifted her dark face to peer shortsightedly over the fence and follow the progress of her companion who could be seen, halfway up a gentle rise, cropping the grass which was green and lush, having not been grazed over for some time. The *coulisse* stage right is empty of predators. This peaceful scene seemed to fire the second sheep's decision, for she made a short run and jumped the fence; it was a jump higher than it needed to be, higher, perhaps, for sheer pleasure as her heavy woolen body described a pure, curved, Norman arc in the air. Number 2.

And here the bed lies between me and my fall toward the center of the earth. And the substance of the bed is protean between rock and swamp, and I feel the heart, like an engine of uncertain warranty, counting in the chest.

And the Sleeper's list of omissions and commissions grows, and with each entry a shift, a turn, a quarter turn, each joint flexing for relief, in vain. There is a moth in the room, it visits each light, the lamp on the bookcase, the bathroom's mirror bulb, and now it comes to batter itself against the light by the bed. The Sleeper turns and mumbles, grinds her teeth, turns over in the bed whose four feet, carved into lion's paws, perch on the spinning earth. A Suffolk ewe and her lamp approach the fence, scan, jump the fence. Number 3, Number 4.

And then, coming from the North, from the woods which cast such long morning shadows, came the sound of whistling; not bird-song but song which had been schooled in that primary mode, up three notes, down two, up a long note, held. And after an interval, perhaps twenty beats of silence, an answering whistle from the East, off-screen, from beyond the bright rim of a bright hill. And then five sheep come out of the woods, six, eight, and then the figure of the Shepherdess, more sheep, a black-and-white spotted dog. The young woman gives a hand-signal to the dog whose milky blue eye constantly studies her hands, her face. The dog melts back among the trees, the sheep issue out, they forge up the hill, and when they stop to graze the dog nudges them on. The woman strides up the hill in the lead. She moves easily among the elements, her skin is bright and tweaked about the eyes from being so much out-of-doors. They gain the crest of the hill and stand waiting, looking to the East whose blush is shifting to blue, and then they can see far off, approaching, some sheep, a dog, the figure of a man. Phoebe stands with folded arms and an air of anticipation, the creatures churning about her legs, the wind mixing with her hair. At the edge of the page some tardy sheep hurry to join the flock, they jump the fence, Number 5, Number 6, Number 7, Number 8, Number 9.

The Sleeper rises and goes to open the window, but the air outside is as still as the stale air cubed inside the room. The alarm clock ticks loudly.

Butter

To dream of eating fresh, golden butter, is a sign of good health and plans well carried out; it will bring unto you possessions, wealth and knowledge.

To eat rancid butter, denotes a competency acquired through struggles of manual labor.

To sell butter, denotes small gain.

Elbows

To see elbows in a dream, signifies that arduous labors will devolve upon you, and for which you will receive small reimbursements.

For a young woman, this is a prognostic of favorable opportunities to make a reasonably wealthy marriage. If the elbows are soiled, she will lose a good chance of securing a home by marriage.

Fleas

To dream of fleas, indicates that you will be provoked to anger and retaliation by the evil machinations of those close to you.

For a woman to dream that fleas bite her, foretells that she will be slandered by pretended friends. To see fleas on her lover, denotes inconstancy.

Lawyer

For a young woman to dream that she is connected in any way with a lawyer, foretells that she will unwittingly commit indiscretions, which will subject her to unfavorable and mortifying criticism.

Lice

A dream of lice contains much waking worry and distress. It often implies offensive ailments.

Lice on stock, foretells famine and loss.

To have lice on your body, denotes that you will conduct yourself unpleasantly with your acquaintances.∙

To dream of catching lice, foretells sickness, and that you will cultivate morbidity.

The grizzled ewe, Breakmouth, one of the grandmothers of the flock, was severely afflicted with lice, *Linognathus ovillus,* one of the sucking, as distinct from the biting lice. As she approached the fence she was rubbing and gnawing at her skin, her back was patched and raw. She jumped the fence, ticking her left hind leg on the top wire, it hummed the length of the valley. Number 10.

The great stone outcropping at the end of the valley was fantastically shaped and colored, rosy red, purple, pink, salmon, brick, it served as a referent for names and visions for the inhabitants for the region. When ranchers and ranchers' wives, the wealthier ones, began to make the Grand Tour to Europe it became common to call it "The Castles," with special mention of that Chateau, Pallazzo, Rheinish heap, that had won the heart at B_____. Before that, when memories of the great sea-crossing still featured, dimly, so far inland, it had been most often "The Ship" or "Shiprock." What the proud and secret people who lived here before the anglos came nominated the sacred mass that defined their horizon is not recorded.

Visible now picking their way around the bulk of the rock are several horses and riders; they wear the hat and the silhouette of ranchers and cowboys; when they hit the flat they let out their horses and rush in a gallop and a cloud of pink dust into the foreground. The tallest one, called "Blackie," was tough, bronzed, quick, slate-eyed; he was the Range Boss, and had the "hero" configuration, nose, posture, dominance. He controlled the operation, and the motley group of men. They came from all corners of the globe, but they all knew the rules of the range, and they lived by them, or died by them. The fat cowboy with the red complexion, called "Tex," could draw and shoot faster than any other man in the territory. The young lad, scarcely more than a boy, was "Johnny," the Cookie was a half-breed, "Injun Joe"; and there were others, "Roger," "Harry," "DW," "Tom," "Swede," "Slim," "Danny," "Mungo," some as dry and spare as the land they rode. And now the herd of white-faced cows filled the mouth of the valley, bellowing and lifting dust, the cowboys riding loose in their saddles, shouting now and then to each other, or their horses, or the cattle.

A little fussed by the disturbance down the valley, a group of sheep stopped grazing and trotted back and forth a few times. They then made purposefully for the fence, and began jumping over. Number 11, Number 12, Number 13, Number 14, Number 15, Number 16, Number 17.

First Bion's dog, a yellow hound, gained the hill and greeted the black and white collie. They approached each other stiff-legged, sniffed and presented hindquarters, then their tails started wagging and they bounded off together, old friends, side by side, patrolling their flocks. Then Phoebe and Bion came together, their glad cries, the kisses, the words and looks of lovers in the spring of the year. All the birds, the insects, the creatures, even the vegetable life joined in this politics of the pastoral landscape, the dream of mankind's happy state *(sic)*. The Shepherd and the Shepherdess, with their fingers interlaced, swinging their arms; their dogs, their glances braided together, their flocks straying together, move out of camera, exit stage right. A Hampshire ram, fresh from love, leaps the fence. Number 18.

The Flock moved with a single psychology through the morning, up the green hill, chewing, their mouths full. The lambs were resting now, asleep in the pools of shadow cast by their dams. The old, spotted ewe, Blotchface, who was the leader of the Flock, startled first; it was the smallest breath of scent, one part per million on the fresh breeze. She threw up her head, the Flock froze, they stopped chewing. They had caught the scent of the Wolf who was patrolling the margins. The smell was distant, it was a trace, but the Flock was on its guard, grouped closer. A few young ones, frightened and playing at being frightened, broke away from the Flock, ran snorting with flying heels, leaped the fence. Number 19, Number 20, Number 21, Number 22, Number 23.

Crumbs in the bed. A hot drink, shake out the pillows, turn the page. Somewhere in the maze, a few streets away, an ambulance howls. Turn over.

Touch collar,
Never swallow,
Never get the fever,
Touch your nose,
Touch your toes,
Never go in one of those.

The gas roils in my belly.

Amputation

To dream of amputation of limbs, denotes small offices lost. The loss of entire legs and arms, unusual depression in trade. To seamen, storm and loss of property. Afflicted persons should be warned to watchfulness after this dream.

On the desk the little plaster bust of Dr. Freud, reviewing this insomniac display of ego, id, and super ego, staring blank-eyed and unflinching on civilization's bad bargain. I toast you, Doctor, tonight, in warm milk.

If you see an ambulance hold your collar and don't swallow till you see a dog. If you don't do this the person in the ambulance will die.

If you see an ambulance you must touch wood or you will have bad luck. When the ambulance is out of sight you must keep your fingers crossed until you see a four-legged animal and if there is more than one of you, you must have it the one who saw it first can uncross their fingers, and the others not until they see other animals.

And the lungs balloon and deflate, and the heart goes on da-daà, da-daà, da-daà, da-daà.

Ba ba ba goes the lamb to his mother, ba ba baa goes the ewe, they come to the fence, the ewe jumps over, Number 24. The lamb tries to jump, he does not clear the fence the first time, he falls back. His mother calls to him, he tries again, he jumps over, Number 25.

Over the second hill, all growing with daffodils and dandelions and wild garlic, the office building and the crow's nest that make up the Border Control. The fence is higher here. Road, crossroad, flag, gate, guardhouse, telephone kiosk, eight or nine government cars and jeeps, and a similar constellation on the other side of the fence. From time to time a vehicle approaches from one side or the other, stops, someone in uniform comes out of the guardhouse, talks with the people in the car, examines documents, sometimes the people are required to get out and enter the three-story office building which looks as though it has been uprooted from its neighborhood shopping center. But more often the gates open and they drive on through. It is a very minor bureaucratic node on the line of red tape stretched between two countries ideologically at war.

A little way off a camouflage-painted jeep rushes into the landscape. The camouflage has been designed to blend with a desert environment of brilliant sunshine and deep shadow, which renders it highly visible here in all the thousand greens of temperate spring-time. It stops, a woman and two men leap out and begin to dig. The woman is cinematically beautiful, a Red Head who, a good telescope would permit inspection to conclude, has one glass eye. She speaks in highly accented English. One of the men is very tall, bald, dressed in a tuxedo, the other is small, hairy, dressed in camouflage, he gesticulates hugely as he talks. In the upturned earth, earthworms wriggle in the sudden light.

From studying their faces and their movements, a trained behavioral psychologist might conclude that the three spies are both exhausted and bored, and are filled with the malaise which attends their profession in these latter days. The psychologist might further speculate that it is only constant pressure of danger which serves, any longer, to tug at the causal strings and compel them to action. There was, indeed, a religious, left-wing androgynous psychologist, wavy haired, who was training a number of monitoring devices on the spies at that very moment. She had drawn these tentative conclusions, and further remarked to herself that the anomie which they were exhibiting was a much wider *fin de* millennial phenomenon, and not confined to such citizens of the netherworld. She sneezed, and beaded the lens.

The trio is in a hurry to finish the job and get back home. The Romantic fallacy has ceased operation, and there is now no connection between their mood and the constructs of the landscape, the weather, the wind, the light and shadow, the hierarchies of flora and fauna. There is no reflection and no answering vibration, they are post-modern and altogether sundered from their bucolic and bureaucratic surrounds.

The sheep are frightened at first, then curious.

Another blip appears on the view-field of the scope; the red limousine speeds down the road, then leaps the curb and starts off cross-country toward the jeep. Inside are the Russian, the Canadian and the Arab. The chase is on. A movement from A to B. Some older merino lambs, agitated by the activity, jump the fence. Number 26, Number 27, Number 28, Number 29, Number 30, Number 31, Number 32, Number 33.

The old gray Wolf pads along through the brush, keeping a set distance between himself and the Flock, keeping downwind of them, not in a hurry. He sees three more silly sheep leap over the fence, Number 34, Number 35, Number 36.

Fortified against predators, the range crew had just set up their new camp—Slim, Danny and Mungo were posted as out-riders, working their way around the edges of the herd, pushing along the stragglers, looking out for coyotes and wolves. There was a bunch of new calves in the herd, and more due over the next few days, they needed a quiet place with good grass and sweet water.

The cowboys sat in a circle around the cookfire, eating a mess of beans and eggs, hunkered down on the heels of their boots. Blackie chewed tobacco and rubbed his nose, a sign that he was ruminating over some deep matter. Some of the other punchers were playing poker-knife, and little shining stacks of silver dollars rose and fell in front of first one, then another. The Swede was the only one winning with regularity, his lap was full of silver. The fire painted their faces, the air smelt acrid and fragrant at once, burning wood, sage and dust, the sweet breaths of herbivores.

In the distance, a puff of dust announced a horseman, riding at top speed in their direction. They accorded it the interest that any event in the landscape promoted. News, trouble, blessing, all arrived heralded and crowned and robed with dust in those parts. The dust resolved itself into a cowboy on a palomino, a big horse, a stud.

Reaching the camp the rider leaped off, he looked small and young close to, belying the authority which which he handled the big horse. He addressed Blackie, The sheepherders have come down from the mountain pastures, they're bringing their flocks onto the range! The cowpokes mutter at the news.

The boy pulls off his cowboy hat and foam-pale hair, released, tumbles and flows down his back, her back, for it becomes clear that this is a girl, a woman. Exclamations from the crowd.

Blackie says, That waterhole is low, ain't enough water here for our cattle and those damn sheep.

As if to mark his words, in the lower corner of the page three sheep jump the fence, Number 37, Number 38, Number 39.

And Phoebe and Bion/ those two/
who resembled each other in height/
in swiftness and stature/
And to Phoebe and Bion/ those two/
known to each other as children/
from the locality and the same—

Pan to Phoebe and Bion swimming in their favorite pool, the pool ringed with weeping willows, where they had splashed and dunked and learned to swim as children. The willows, sighing, trail their leaves, and those two dive in and out the self-made hills of water, like porpoises relishing their material selves and their joint society. Then she stands, half-revealed in the shallows, and the boy lies out on his back, stretched out on his aqueous couch. As the water quiets, the standing girl is doubled downward from the waist, a monstrous and enchanting repayment for the cancellation of her lower parts by the silver substance of the pond.

And then tall Moschus comes with his flock to the watering place, looks with interest upon the scene, reads other meanings into their water play, he who comes from a town in another district, he too is quickened by the sight of Phoebe, he has an appetite for her, he loves her too, though Bion is most generally the favorite. And while their various sheep drink with dark lips from the water, Moschus joins the shepherds and they splash and puff together. Throwing themselves finally upon the leafy bank, and gaining land, a certain modesty comes on them again, they throw on their shifts and fall to talking.

Phoebe, who is not yet so much a lady, grins and knuckles her grin, suggests a versifying contest.

BION: I will poetize upon our life here, its qualities, how sweet the climate is, and how mild.

PHOEBE: And how our rams and ewes are so loving with one another, that our flocks prosper and grow fat.

MOSCHUS: And our wool is of the finest, tightly curled.

BION: So that the folk from cities bid hotly for it.

PHOEBE: In the orchards, the trees are heavy loaded

MOSCHUS: And bees do their work from flower to flower

BION: And we have such sweet wine that when we drink it transports us from common sense to ecstasy.

PHOEBE: And when we play the wanton games of love, we lose our heads and take on such fond madness

MOSCHUS: That every other mode becomes as dust

BION: For, as with our fruits, our cheeses, and our wines, you must bend to use them when they come, by stages, to perfection.

PHOEBE: Wait too long and you will have but rotten viands and vinegar, our mortal selves give us but short space to employ this corporeal bliss

MOSCHUS: And that at the best of times, when we grow hale and old. There are many, alas, cut down before such ripening

PHOEBE: So come and kiss, my boys, and let us prove, this day, at least, well mannered by our love.

All through that summer's afternoon, as long as the afternoons of childhood, they called forth the glories of their life in that local place, with poetry and kisses, removed from the city's gross machines, without an appetite for riches, or much curiosity about the workings of the world beyond their valley.

And of that sour bargain for civilization, they paid only part, for, in truth, they lived a life half-civil and half-wild.

And while they sported, so their dogs played also, and some sheep escaped their usual vigilance, and wandered reckless and hopeful as is the nature of their breed, and leaped the fence,

Number 40, Number 41, Number 42, Number 43, Number 44, Number 45, Number 46, Number 47, Number 48.

The chase had ended in confusion, the limousine losing a wheel and plowing into an oak tree, the Russian had somehow, in the excitement, managed to shoot the Arab in the left foot, the bald man and the hairy man had gone to earth and disguised themselves as peasants of the area, the lovely monocular Red Head had aged herself with makeup and now appeared as an old hag selling apples in the empty square fronting the Border Control office building.

She had sold three apples to a Customs Officer, and one to a munitions expert, when along came the customer for whom she had been waiting. He was a slight, sandy man, strangely bundled up in the heat of the summer day. He approached her, and said in a conversational tone, "When the sheep call Wolf Wolf, the Shepherdess gives heed" and the apple woman replied, "The Wolf's great teeth can make the sheep to bleed." He continued, "So good folk guard your cattle and your brood." "The Wolf prays in a Church of bones and blood" she concluded. "Amen to that, come with me Comrad, Buddy, Amigo, this way." She led him down the street and off up a track through the scrub and rock where a few stray sheep were grazing. The Red Head, whose name was Vanessa, knocked sharply on the face of a great slab of purple rock, and a large door swung open on a soundless track, revealing steps leading downward. They followed them down, one hundred and eleven steps, the door swinging shut behind them.

It was hot underground, they had entered a kind of library, lined with books and files. On a table food and drink were laid out, and they were eating pasta and drinking South American wine. "Where is the message?" the Sandy Man asked of Vanessa, who was regaining her youth in stages as she wiped the grease paint from her lovely face. Vanessa, her mouth full of noodles, grunted, "Freckles, back." "What?" "Freckles," she repeated, swallowing, "Look" and in a swift and graceful movement, like the rapid peeling of a fruit, she had pulled her dress over her head and left the Sandy Man staring at her creamy torso, her rosy budded breasts, a shy man even through the years of international intrigue, he blushed. She turned her splendid back to him, and sure enough, the delicate pelt was splashed with three handfuls of freckles, like the tiny Swedish ore coin that kids used to buy sweets in the Sandy Man's boyhood, like spices liberally sprinkled on the Christmas eggnog, like stars, like tiny amber beads scattered from a broken string, like red lentils sprinkled round the mouth of the bin. Vanessa directed him to a particular freckle, just *there* on the point of her poignantly articulated shoulder-blade, he touched it, he scraped at it, it came off in his hand to reveal a microdot. A movement from B to C.

Up at the surface, bewildered and made uneasy by the opening of the stone door, three sheep made tracks to another area, they jumped the fence, Number 49, Number 50, Number 51.

The curtain rises on a drama within the Flock. They have cropped the grass steadily since the first mists of morning tattered and dissolved. Now, the sun had mounted in the flawless sky, hot and high, and most of the members of the Flock had lain down to rest on the carpet of herbs and flowers. Bucklefoot, the wisest ewe, and Big Cock, the great horned ram, were, along with Blotchface, the leaders of the Flock, and there existed beneath them a strict chain of control, as well as a network of psychological communication so sensitive that it was often telepathic. To be part of the Flock was like being plugged into radio contact with every other member. The order: One Eye, Torn Ear, Toothless, Winterborn, Blackbreast, Twinsdam, Shamble Trot, Limper, Broken Mouth, Stinkarse, Baldback, Lambless, Blackcoat, Twisthorn, Big Gut. . . . It was Torn Ear who first scented the odd perfume of Wolf, he fluted his black nostrils, testing the mix, the chemical notice threw an ancient neurological switch, he lifted his heavy head and uttered ba's of warning.

And they they ran, keeping well together, their legs flickering over the grass, with their odd rocking gait, faster than it looked, blowing and snorting.

And when they had covered a certain distance, and the

shadows held no visible wolves, and the air was clean of wolf component, they slowed and stopped. And the dog found them and rounded them into a tighter group, pushing at them with her nose to reprimand them for dashing off. A sub group of young ones thought to jump the nearby fence, to prove their independence of dog, they run, they leap the fence, Number 52, Number 53, Number 54, Number 55, Number 56, Number 57, Number 58, Number 59, Number 60, Number 61, Number 62, Number 63, Number 64, Number 65, Number 66, Number 67, Number 68, Number 69, Number 70, Number 71, Number 72, Number 73, Number 74, Number 75, Number 76, Number 77, Number 78, Number 79, Number 80, Number 81, Number 82, Number 83.

In the fresh pasture they circle, and seek to calm themselves with great jaw-fulls of grass, and then, as they take the census of the flock, Long Tail reports her lamb is missing. Her eyes roll with fear, her child lost and alone, and the Wolf abroad. The Flock mutters, the dog, nose to ground, travels in incremental concentric circles. She finds the lamb, trembling and tired, flattened into the shadow of an overgrown privet hedge, the first time in his life that he had been alone. The dog brings him back; returning to the Flock, he jumps the fence, Number 84, and he greets has dam with glad cries, she bellows her joy, and she noses and smells him all over as he starts, voraciously, to suckle at her teats.

A well-trained sheep dog can be of inestimable help in the care of a flock. There are certain breeds which have been developed over the years with just those talents and abilities to fit them for caring for their charges. A good sheep dog can be trusted to mind a stationary flock, without human support, for several hours at a time. It also serves as an invaluable aid in guiding the movement of the flock from one location to another.

In choosing a sheep dog, the shepherd can acquire a mature dog, already trained, or a puppy. If choosing a puppy, it is important to select one from established working progenitors. Either bitches or dogs serve equally well as sheep dogs. Sheep dogs can be trained to work to whistles, hand-signals, voice command, or a combination. It is an old shepherd's adage that a good sheep dog is worth half the flock.

The rattler gave its characteristic warning and then struck, biting into the tender flesh of Pete's inner thigh, he was dressing after swimming. And then its head had been blown off by shots from two guns, fired almost simultaneously. This was the sequence, the metallic flash of the snake's form echoed by the glint of sunlight on the pistol barrels, then Pete's pale body crumpling suddenly as the venom hit his nervous system, all this took less time to happen than it does to tell.

The bullets had come from Tex's gun and from Amanda's, and there was some dispute over whose bullet had ended the snake's life, and whose had followed along behind. In the course of things, this parley led to a shooting contest being arranged between the vast man and the skinny girl, and the targets and rules were specified. They set up in the natural amphitheater of black rock, while on the other side of the river cowpokes worked to suck the pizen out of Pete's leg, and to cauterize the wound. Bang bang bang bang bang. They each shoot ten rounds, standing, sitting, lying down, at a trot, at a gallop. Bang bang bang bang, each bullet burns a tunnel through the air to the breast, to the eye, to the heart, to the very center of its target, followed by each report splitting the afternoon into before and after. Amanda is the winner. By a trick of literary riddle-making, referring back to the implied guarantee of "Tex could draw and shoot faster than any other man in the territory," indeed he is the fastest *man*, but Amanda, who can beat him five out of six on a regular basis, is a woman. A topical joke, and a weak plot fastener, but strong enough if you account the witches' fatal punning to Macbeth as sound enough to bear the weight of all that Scottish blood.

Shouts across the river, Pete is dead! The vultures circled. Amanda, squinting against the wind, shot out the name "Pete" on the horizontal bar of the wooden cross they put to mark his grave. It was at this moment that Blackie came to love her.

Awakened by the shots, a Rambouillet ram clambered to his feet, shook himself, and went off in search of company. He jumps the fence, Number 85.

In the dream the dreamer was walking down the street in a big city, London, maybe, or New York, it was cold and she was wearing light summer clothes that didn't really keep her warm enough. The clothes were of a silvery material, and they sparkled and glowed, very faintly. She remembered wondering whether the other people noticed them glowing. She was also wearing, though it didn't seem odd at the time, long white gloves on her feet. She noticed a man selling something on a street corner, he had quite a crowd gathered round him. She went closer to see what was going on, and after a bit of pushing and shoving (she was more aggressive in this dream than she would be in waking life) she was able to get close to the huckster and she saw that he was an older man, rather stern. He was delivering a high pressure spiel, talking at a great rate, and at the same time handing out little wooden boxes to those closest to him. He pressed one into her hand, and she took it eagerly. It was finely made, a little larger at one end than the other. It took her several minutes to open it to reveal a human nose inside, set on velvet, like a piece of jewelry. The nose wasn't gory or unpleasant, though it was obviously a real human nose from a real head, it seemed self-contained and neat, like a piece of dried fruit, a peach or an apricot. She looked around, and saw that all of the other boxes that people had opened seemed to contain noses too, she saw that they were of varying shapes and skin tones, each one fitting neatly into its little box. The next bit is unclear, but soon a group of them were lining up to enter a large baroque fountain, the kind with spouting whales and little boys pissing into the wind. When it was her turn to climb up and get into the fountain, the attendant, who was wearing a uniform that looked like a movie house usherette's, said to her, Open your mouth, she did, and the usherette looked disgusted and said, You can't come in, your teeth are too bad. But then she thought to show her the nose in its little box, and the usherette let her by.

Voilà, Dr. Freud, she addresses the white plaster head, What is the proper interpretation of this dream? (She can see the Dr., rubbing his jewish nose, wrinkling his brow and giving other behavioral evidences of thought.) Let's mention some of the oddities, they may contain keys: she likes that business about wearing the white gloves on her feet, though she doesn't really know what it means, maybe it has something to do with acrobatics, or ambivalence, or androgyny, or being a frog. Again, she finds the glister of the flimsy clothes a rather interesting feature, she who doesn't think about clothes at all from one month to another in her waking life. Note both her concern with the opinions of other people, *she remembered wondering whether the other people noticed them glowing,* and her willingness to push and shove to get right up to the salesman, indicating, does it?, that at some level of her character, self-consciousness and casual aggression form an unlovely pair.

Now what about those little caskets, for surely they resemble caskets, and their odd contents, noses, *noses!,* we've all known about the possibilities of noses since Cyrano. And indeed, are these little phalluses all boxed neatly in her dream? A wish to bury (male) sexuality? reproduction? A wish to "have" it, to appropriate it? Or maybe these are noses in their own right, as organs of breath and smell, and the transaction has to do with the encapsulation, or burial, or appropriation, of that which breathes, that which scents.

The salesman is described as a high-pressure huckster, but she gives no evidence of trying to resist the salespatter, indeed, she presses forward to hear the pitch and get her sample. Is it interesting that she remembers only the affect of the sales talk and not the content? And what is this about the nose looking like a piece of dried fruit? What about the huckster himself, eh? *An older man, rather stern,* well of course it's Papa, the central characters in the puppet show don't really change so much from year to year, Papa, whatever are you up to this time?

The whole of the second part (with the fountain), would seem to have to do with a rite of passage, a birth, a rebirth? And the encasketed nose proves to be a ticket, more powerful than the awfulness of her *bad teeth, (disgusting)*. Who is that woman in the usher's uniform anyway?

So how's this? Herself in a pretty course and unboiled state (aggressive, self-conscious), presses her way up to a man who turns out to be (at least in part) her Father. He gives to her (and to many others) a coffin containing a severed nose, that is, sexuality, male sexuality, sense, the sense of smell in particular, the organ of breath. So her Father gives her a gift which later wins her a place in the fountain, (birth, rebirth?) in spite of her dental unworthiness. (This leaves out of reckoning the part about gloves on the feet and shining clothes, of course.) Does it scan? Maybe. Maybe so, maybe not.

And of course, Herr Doktor Jung would go about this somewhat differently. She rather thinks he'd make quite a lot of the shining clothes, and the concern for whether other people perceived them. As a good Swiss, he was always rather conscious of ourselves in relation to the community, and she thinks he might feel that the shining quality had to do with virtue, or maybe aspiration, and note that she was also concerned with whether the other dreamfolk recognized her worthiness. The gloved feet still elude her. Perhaps the salesman, the Jungian "elder," the "Father" the "Teacher" would have a less personal, a more general parsing in a Jungian analysis. But the Jungian theory also urges "amplification," expansion outward from the manifest content. In that case, she wonders what they'd make of the noses and the dried fruit, the dessicated fruit of knowledge?, a laying up of provisions? And the nose set into a casket like *jewelry?* What kind of ornament is this, and where indeed are the noseless who have sacrificed to provide it? The inhabited casket also has some resonances of the occupied womb, is she pregnant?

She thinks that Jung would find the generality of the fountain/birth/rebirth image impossible to resist, drawing from it, perhaps, more communal and uplifting theory than the sour Viennese could muster.

What time is it?

Nose

To see your own nose in a dream indicates force of character, and consciousness of your ability to accomplish whatever enterprise you may choose to undertake. If your nose looks smaller than natural, there will be failure in your affairs. Hair growing on your nose, indicates extraordinary undertakings, and they will be carried through by sheer force of character or will.

A bleeding nose, is prophetic of disaster, whatever the calling of the dreamer may be.

Now I lay me down to sleep,
I pray the Lord my soul to keep,
If I should die before I wake,
I pray the Lord my soul to take.

Too hot. Hungry. When she opened the window, the barking of the neighbor's King Charles spaniel, lusting after the Scotty bitch in heat three houses down, shattered any hopes she had of sleep, and frightened three old ewes into jumping the fence, Number 86, Number 87, Number 88.

A summer storm, the clouds heaping up into mansions, camels, winged machines, and then deconstructing again into gusts of blowing rain. There is movement on both sides of the border fence. The cave to which the Sandy Man had been led by the information on the freckle was cut deep into the purple rock of the north-facing slope, but it was so overgrown with spreading evergreen and ivy that to find it one had either to have very explicit instructions, or to get lucky with the statistics of the pure operation of chance, or benefit from the synchronous universe. He stops just inside the mouth of the cave while his eyes adjust to the gloom. The only illumination is a small finger of light from his pocket flashlight. His nose wrinkles with disgust at a sudden acrid smell, "Pah, fox!" and he half stumbles across a pile of bones, sheep bones, cow bones, peering deeper into the cave he finds more bones and then, grinning up at him, a human skull. He grins back, he is getting closer to what he's looking for.

On the other side of the border fence the limping Arab and the morose Russian have returned to their headquarters after a fruitless day of digging, they are wet and chilled, the Russian speaks: "If we don't find the packet, we will have to agree to deal with them somehow." The Arab hisses through blue lips, "Our instructions are to find the packet, not deal." And the Russian, peppering his vodka, looks at him pityingly, "Our objective is the information, it doesn't matter how we get it." He gestures to the pale child who lies, bound to a chair, in the corner of the room. The child is asleep, but his eyes are still partly open, slits through which his eyeballs can be seen following his dreams. His hands are tied. "That's our insurance, over there." A movement from C to D. A few meters down from the passport control, her steps leaving dints in the wet grass, a fat Cotswold sheep jumps the fence. Number 89.

Phoebe's final "Ah, ah, ah" seemed to set the natural world in motion again, the blackbirds and the robins and the finches, the larks, the cicadas and the bees all recommenced the sounds and movements which had been stilled, for a few breaths, there in the glade, while the lovers labored. The wind picked up its song again, and teased the water, the dogs lifted their heads to gaze upon their charges, who ba-baed again and bent to eat, their constant task. Bion pointed toward the sky, "Look, Love, the sky itself is filled with sheep," she followed his fancy, "Some eat, some sleep, some hurry to make lambs."

There is an odd, loud, grinding from up the valley, the dogs lay their ears back close to their heads. It is a sound that none of them has ever heard before. The dogs growl deep in their throats. "Look, Love," Phoebe points again to the sky, a sudden wind has broken all the cloudy lambs and sheep and sent them scudding away.

As above so below, seven sheep break ranks and jump the fence, Number 90, Number 91, Number 92, Number 93, Number 94, Number 95, Number 96.

Sunlight on the saddle. Sunlight filtered through the purple dust which was everywhere, filling the air, covering each surface.

Midsummer drought, and the cattle are thirsty. The range gang has just pushed the herd on a long, dry trek back to the Shiprock and the only waterhole in the district that had not gone dry. As the skinny beasts hurried forward to slake their thirst, Blackie called a parley of the men, and his face was grim. "Lookit the tracks here" he said, gesturing. "Sheep," his mouth contorted with disgust, the cattleman's hatred of sheep, and of their tenders. "Mountain maggots" Dexter spoke up, and spat into the dust. "There's not enough water and not enough grass for the both of us" Blackie continued, "an this here has bin cattle land since the white man first got here." "You want us to deliver a message to the sheepherders, Boss, tell them they gotta git out?" "We'll do that, Joe," Blackie said, "and if they don't listen, we'll do a little persuading." "Madre mia" said Mex, crossing himself.

And a few miles up the valley, in the sheepherder's camp, there was worry over the sparse grass and dry weather, and some of the sheep were sick. Gathered around the fire were Buffalo, Ricardo, Danny, Otto, Sonny, and Kennedy; others were out with the flock. They all expected some sort of trouble from the cattlemen, it had happened before. To add to their troubles, some of their crazier sheep jumped the fence again, Number 97, Number 98, Number 99, Number 100, Number 101.

Crouched in the cave, breathing in the dust, the Sandy Man opened the leather case and rifled through the contents. There were documents in four languages, and maps, and a few photographs. Not much to the uninitiated eye, but he knew that this handful of papers would shake the governments of several nations, and shift the international balance of power. He permitted himself another rare, rusty grin.

In the information landscape, the camouflaged computers sang like exotic birds. Another machine, a mid-level robot programed to "search and report," comes upon a sheep and, having no code for such a creature, kills it.

The Russian was working over the short-wave radio, he had just received a long message in code. When he had translated it, he looked up in triumph, "We're going to make an exchange," he said. Outside, besieged by the summer flies and looking for new pasture, two sheep jumped the fence, Number 102, Number 103.

Shifting and groaning, the unsleeping Sleeper turns in the bed, farts, turns. In the next fragment of dream the Sleeper and her friend, her lover?, her husband?, had been captured by some powerful enemies, and were being daubed with gouts of a greasy yellow substance which went on like awkward war paint, on their faces and all over their bodies, in a pattern. It looked like mayonnaise, or artificial whipping cream. They were told that this substance was poisonous, and that they had to *go out into the world and rub this stuff off onto other people and animals*, this would kill those people and creatures, but would, apparently, spare her and her companion in the end. Ugh! She was disgusted and disturbed within the dream itself, and into her waking state.

The censor, wearing a fez, speaks in tongues. He has a deck of wild cards; he pantomimes the transvaluation of all values.

woman = man
dark = light
up = down
sun = moon
sweet = sour
positive = negative
yang = yin
chocolate = vanilla
yes = no
black = white
good = bad
left = right

"A breeding record can best be kept by smearing the breast of the ram and the area between his forelegs every day or two with a thick colored paste. Then, as the ram serves the ewe, a mark will be left on her rump."

The heart, da-dà, da-dà, da-dà, da-dà, The Lord is my shepherd, da-dà, da-dà, da-dà

There are a number of methods in use for docking and castrating. Castrating may be done with a knife, a Burdizzo, or an elastrator. When cutting instruments are used, the hands should first be thoroughly washed. . . . The lamb is usually held with his back to the assistant, who grasps the hind and front legs of the same side in each hand. When the operation is performed with a knife, the lower third of the scrotum is removed, exposing the testicles, which are then drawn out. Some sheepmen prefer to draw the testicles with the teeth, thus securing greater speed and keeping the danger of infection to a minimum.

In recent years, the elastrator, which is a bloodless method, has been used in docking and castrating lambs. It consists of placing a small rubber ring around the tail or scrotum when the lambs are only a few days old. The elastrator is the invention of A.O. Hammond, a sheep farmer of Blenheim, New Zealand.

As in castrating, there are a number of methods for docking lambs. The important thing, however, is to use one of them and to use it at the proper time. It may be done with a knife or shears, hot iron (pincers or chisels), emasculator, Burdizzo pincers or elastrator. There is the use of the hot docking rion or chisel. However, the wound heals more slowly than when the operation is done with a knife. For most rapid healing the instruments should not be heated beyond a very dull red color, and the tail should be severed rather quickly, avoiding any more burning than is necessary to prevent blooding. Also, with heated instruments, the lamb's buttock should be protected by placing the tail in a slot in the end of a board or by putting it through a hole in a board.

> Little Bo-peep has lost her sheep,
> And can't tell where to find them;
> Leave them alone, and they'll come home,
> And bring their tails behind them.
>
> Little Bo-peep fell fast asleep,
> And dreamt she heard them bleating;

But when she awoke, she found it a joke,
For they were still all fleeting.

Then up she took her little crook,
Determined for to find them;
She found them indeed, but it made her heart bleed,
For they'd left their tails behind them.

It happened one day, as Bo-peep did stray
Into a meadow hard by,
There she espied their tails side by side,
All hung on a tree to dry.

She heaved a sigh, and wiped her eye,
And over the hillocks went rambling,
And tried what she could, as a shepherdess should,
To tack again each to its lambkin.

The Lord is my shepherd, and two more sheep have jumped over the fence, whose fence posts are of osage orange, Number 104, Number 105.

"The Great God Pan is dead" roared Bion from the top of North Hill, and standing opposite, cupping her hands to her mouth as a trumpet, Phoebe answered, "Yes, He is dead, and we are His children" and from the West, astride a great outcropping of blood-colored rock, Moschus bellowed, "Come, then, heirs and followers of Pan, fill the cup, tip it up, let the revels begin. Give over to ecstasy and the fruits of ecstasy . . . " "We begin!" shouted Bion, in a voice like a wolf, and the three ran headlong down the slopes to the glade where they had stored their wine skin cooling in a stream, it was the time of new wine, it was the season of passion and forgetfulness. "Drink." "Sing." "Dance, hands in a ring." Throwing off for today their common shifts, they had dressed themselves in sheep skins and appeared now half-naked, half-beast.

Resting, they tease each other and frame riddles: Who smiles and smiles no matter what the politics or weather?/The skull has a smile that does not stop. At festival, of all the dances, who dances last?/The little, quick worms always dance the final dance.

Tussling about, wine spilling, the gravitas of passion . . .

Phoebe and Bion had a selection of wooden and clay pipes, and Moschus had an ornate metal flute which he brought from the city, the contest was to fool the birds. They construct false bird song, seduction, play, passion, to call the birds to them. The melodies unfold across the meadow, the sky fills with flapping wings, birds of many types. Phoebe is the winner.

Bion and Phoebe come together, fuck; Moschus, as a joke & release, makes do with a sheep, Winterborn, an open-faced six-year-old with a kindly and subordinate manner.

Another wolf scare in the flock.

At the top of the arc of these drunken revels, they come upon a track in the grass, unlike any track they have ever seen before. The ground shakes, it is something completely new. Ordinary heroics do not serve, and they tremble at the altogether frightening and disorienting sight of a great machine, an engine of destruction. The sheep are also frightened, as much by the spectacle of their guardians' terror as by the thing itself, a Debouillet jumps over the fence, Number 106, a Corriedale jumps over the fence, Number 107, a Karakul jumps over the fence, Number 108, a Targhee jumps over the fence, Number 109, a Panama jumps over the fence, Number 110.

LAMB FORESTIÈRE OR MOCK VENISON

Wipe with damp cloth:
A 5lb. leg of lamb or mutton
Marinate refrigerated 24 hours or more in:
Buttermilk or Yogurt Marinade, 528,
turning occasionally.
Preheat oven to 450°.
Drain, wipe dry and lard meat, 444, with:
Blanched salt pork or bacon
Put roast on a rack in a pain in the oven and bake
for 15 minutes. Add:
1/2 cup hot Vegetable Stock, 524

1 bay leaf
2 small whole peeled onions
Cover. Reduce heat at once to 325° and allow 35 minutes to the
pound. When roast is nearly done, remove cover, degrease, 340,
and add:
1 cup Sauteed Mushrooms, 308
Pour over roast:
1 cup warm cultured sour cream
Cook uncovered 10 minutes. Make:
Pan Gravy, 341
Serve roast surrounded by:
Browned Potatoes, 320, or
Pureed Turnips, 280
Garnish with
Parsley

Structuralist Exercises for the Primary Grades

Sheep/not Sheep
1. Sheep/Goats
2. Sheep/Cows
3. Sheep/Wolves
4. Sheep/Humans

And the Flock could smell the Wolf's scent, which was sharp,
and they could hear the Wolf's voice, which was loud, and they
could see the Wolf's markings, which were fearsome, and they
saw the Wolf's shadow, which was subtle, they became very
afraid. Agitated, they ran this way and that, a group of them
leaped over the fence, Number 111, Number 112, Number 113,
Number 114, Number 115, Number 116, Number 117, Number
118, Number 119, Number 120, Number 121, Number 122.

Autumn. Deposed like the players on a stage within a
procenium of rock, and set against the afternoon sun, the
cattlemen and the sheepherders faced each other. They took up
the postures of ritualized insult and confrontation, threats of
violence. Damn sheep/ our rights/ dirty farmers/ get out/ water,
grass/ you bastards/ damn cattle/ bones, blood/ it's been a long

time/ damn sheep/ government land/ watch out/ free range/ need grass/ damn cattle/ last time/ damn sheep

In the aftermath of the argument. Blackie and Amanda, sighing violently, kissed each other, the two-vase profile brilliant against the smoke, the autumn blossoms, burnt leaves.

A jet draws a chalk-line across the sky which acts as a membrane between that time zone and a restaurant/motel round a bend in the road. The modern Westerners inside wear Navajo jewelry and acrylic outfits, the Dining Area is called Café Internationale. Some of the characters: "Daphne," 5'11", her hair, which is a brilliant orange, is heaped on top of her head, to a height of 6'1". She signals elder dominant female. She is a Christian Scientist. She owns three houses. She wears many pieces of heavy Indian jewelry—beaten and cast silver set with large pieces of turquoise—six rings, four necklaces, four bracelets, several pins and barettes. She visits the Reservation to buy jewelry from the Indians which she then sells retail. Before his retirement, her husband was the Governor of a Women's Prison in New Mexico. "Jim," a young man with a soft, fleshy appearance and a large, back-slapping manner, he is pale, he sells real estate. "Claire," a young woman with eyes obliquely set. She is a mountain climber. "Jack," a man of about 50, of medium height, he is dressed in jeans and work shirt. He is ranch worker, he votes Republican. His face and hands are weathered and deeply indented, he walks at a slant, as though against the wind. He wears a cowboy hat of shallow capacity. "Sidney," sixty-two years old, a huge man who dabbles in the occult, obese to the point of androgyny, he is a successful capitalist, he wears a silk monogrammed shirt and carries a silk, zippered purse. At the imported English Pub Bar they are drinking: Cuba Libre, Grasshopper, Black Mumbo, Rabbit Punch, Pina Colada, Singapore Sling, Virgin Mary, Blind Eye, Warm Fuzzy, Rusty Nail, Gorilla Gorilla, Sloe Gin Fizz, Mother Tongue, Camouflage, Rusty Nail, White Russian, Black Russian.

And meanwhile the chase continued in the hills beyond the checkpoint, the machines looped in and out of the lengthening shadows, the wheels of the Porsche, the Range Rover, the black limo, the Triumphe, the Ford, the dented Mercedes threw up the dry leaves, they spun, they danced in the late slanted light, the drivers cursed the dazzle. Among them they represented 17 national groups, 12 religious persuasions, 9 political philosophies, 5 eye colors, 4 sexes. Deer startle, a fox runs out, the partridge flutters up. Gun shots, a helicopter of advanced design, the camels, a flock of sheep come out of a side road and fill the roadway, and the chase vehicles are bogged down in the mass of wooly creatures, the cars leap the pavement and set off cross-country, in every direction, gone amok.

And at that moment the President was just finishing a supper of lambchops prepared with spinach and minted cherries which he had eaten at his desk, he had come to a decision on the matter of the border exchange, he picked up the green telephone.

A movement from E to F. The limping Arab held a knife to the throat of the naked Turk. The child was wired to a fail-safe device. (Note the activities of the Red Head, the Russian, the mute, the Marine.) And the landscape read as war-scape, mined, ticking, traps, ha-has, the art of camouflage is perfected, is that tree real?, that mountain?, taste the stream!

The bald man, to trap the Jews, puts a lighted match to the yellow grass, the parched ground-cover took up the flame with a passionate advocacy, the landscape burns and burns. The helicopter hovers, ready to land on the burnt-out stubble, A terrified two-year-old Shropshire sheep jumps the fence, Number 123.

And as the seasons shift, the bees store up their honey, and the prudent lay-in provisions for the coming scarcity, and lovers grope closer in the night to share their bodies' heat.

The Wolf's menu, *à la carte*, includes grouse, insects, rabbit, deer, salmon, mice, and mutton.

Bion and Phoebe riddle the time away, they joke about the

oncoming winter, the constant presence of death, they joke about the threat to the pastoral characters and to the pastoral vision.

Moschus comes upon a dead sheep in a meadow, the sheep has been killed by collision with a vehicle, something that Moschus cannot make sense of. It is Winterborn, the sheep with which he had performed the act of love. He lifts her heavy body in his arms and walks, weeping, following the machine tracks, oil, spoor.

Bion and Phoebe watch the fire burning itself out across the landscape; silhouetted against the smoky edge of the canvas they remark a procession of men on horseback, men wearing oddly shaped hats.

In the pastoral strategy the poet, dressed in silks, retreats from the salon and the ballroom to the garden park, and the court follows; they enjoy a garden party, in costume. The sheep are played by servants. And two of these phony sheep, more nimble than the rest, decide to escape the festivities and climb over the fence, Number 124, Number 125.

Little Boy Blue,
Come blow your horn,
The sheep's in the meadow,
The cow's in the corn;
But where is the boy
Who looks after the sheep?
He's under the haycock,
Fast asleep.

Bang bang, bang bang bang. The cowboys and the sheepherders have taken up position across a territory of open riverbottom, most are hidden behind rock and trees, shots follow any break from cover but as yet no cowboys or sheepherders have been hit, three sheep and two cows lie dead in the No Man's Land between the two forces.

The Wolf is hungry. Traveling behind the Flock he has come to know them, their individual scents, their tracks, their habits.

And now the winds are cutting cold, and the casual bounty of summer and early autumn is gone, and it's getting to be time to risk the dogs and the humans and their weapons and go after the sweet, tame meat of the Flock. In the Wolf's mind is a map of his territory in which every tree, bush, stream, ditch, hill, pathway is featured and remembered.

He sought out the ridges and the high slopes where the scents were clearest. Since he had become separated from the rest of the wolf pack, he had been forced to develop his strategy and learn to hunt alone.

He located the Flock again, half a mile downwind of him and moving at a slow pace Northward. He set out to follow them, circling, moving at the tireless trot which he could keep up all day. The ravens, his friends, followed after him waiting for their share in the kill.

the selection of the victim
the eye contact, the contract
the pursuit, separation from the flock
a movement through the landscape, thriller/western/pastoral/bed

The Sleeper cannot sleep, the mind's computer processes the alphabet soup.

Like an anti-shepherd, he looks with great knowledge over the Flock. Like the shepherd selecting a sheep for special care, he turns his great eye on her. He chooses the old balding ewe, Limpfoot, will you dance? His gaze is like a lover's, and she is required to return his gaze. And, like lovers, they exchange a pledge.

He edges her out of the flock, she is solitary, she is on her own, she is running. She is running, alone, the panic of pursuit makes her drunk, it anesthetizes her, she runs and runs.

The sheep runs and the Wolf runs after her, through the area of the Border Control, past the edges of the herd of grazing cattle, upwind from Phoebe's dog, past the unsleeping Sleeper who is dreaming of a drowning mermaid, the sheep tries for one more chance at safety, she jumps the fence, Number 126.

LAMB, HOW TO Roast

1) Season with salt and pepper, if desired.
2) Place fat-side-up on rack in an open roasting pan.
3) Insert meat thermometer.
4) Roast in a preheated oven at 300° F.
5) Do not add water, nor cover, nor baste.
6) Roast until the meat thermometer registers rare, medium, or well-done as desired.

Turn over in the bed, earlier in the evening the spy with the purple punk wig had slipped a mickey-finn into the pitcher of martinis. The Sleeper, drinking wine, had avoided the drugged spirits, but her partner, *the other body in the bed*, had drunk deeply and was now lying, groaning, mumbling, snoring, on the down-slope of the mattress.

Turn over in the bed, the pastoral bargain involves the exaltation of the pleasure principle at the expense of the reality principle. And when she turns and looks at the face of her drugged and sleeping shepherd, her lover, all the things which the earlier shepherdess and shepherd avoided rise up to spoil sleep and to map his face and hers, the money, the work, the children, the illnesses, the politics, the dangers.

Turn over in bed, to ride over the breast of an uncontaminated land, in love with a horse, the endless sunsets, *turn over in the bed*.

Dreams differ from psychoneurotic symptoms in that the opposing wish is always of the same kind—namely, the wish to sleep. A dream is thus the guardian of sleep, and its function is to satisfy the activity of the unconscious mental processes that otherwise would disturb sleep. The fact that sometimes a horrid dream may not only disturb sleep, but may actually wake the sleeper, in no way vitiates this conclusion. In such cases the activity of the endopsychic censorship, which is diminished during sleep, is insufficient to keep from consciousness the dream thoughts, or to compel such distortion of them as to render them unrecognizable, and recourse has to be had to the accession of energy that the censorship is capable of exerting in the waking state; metaphorically expressed, the watchman guarding the sleeping household is overpowered, and has to wake it in calling for help.

Hips

To dream that you admire well-formed hips, denotes that you will be upbraided by your wife.

For a woman to admire her hips, shows she will be disappointed in love matters.

To notice fat hips on animals, foretells ease and pleasure.

For a woman to dream that her hips are too narrow, omens sickness and disappointments. If too fat, she is in danger of losing her reputation.

Hush little baby, don't say a word,
Papa's going to buy you a mocking bird.
And if that mocking bird won't sing,
Papa's going to buy you a golden ring.
And if that golden ring turns brass,
Papa's going to buy you a looking glass.
And if that looking glass gets broke,
Papa's going to buy you a billy goat.
And if that billy goat won't pull,
Papa's going to buy you a cart and bull.
And if that cart and bull fall over,
Papa's going to buy you a dog named Rover.
And if that dog named Rover won't bark,
Papa's going to buy you a horse and cart.
And if that horse and cart fall down,
You still be the sweetest little baby in town.

The Sleeper falls asleep for a few moments and dreams that she is being chased down a long country road by a pack of wolves. On either side of the road the trees are hung with things, what?, necklaces, and snakes, and hoses, they reach down and slap at her as she runs, the wolves are getting closer and she can hear their breathing, her shoes are made of bread and begin to crumble leaving her feet exposed to the stony ground. And then, in front of her, she sees a large dog!, maybe it will help and save her from the wolves, but then, as she gets closer, she can see that it is *a wolf wearing a dog mask!*, caught between the two forces she stops, they gain on her, she can feel their hot breath, their teeth, "help help, help help" she is awake. And chased on and on by the masked wolf, another group of sheep leap over the wall, Number 127, Number 128, Number 129, Number 130, Number 131, Number 132, Number 133, Number 134, Number 135, Number 136, Number 137, Number 137, Number 139, Number 140.

And now it is the hinge of the year, the clouds are rushing to warmer places, the birds, the balding trees . . .

And Limpfoot is running and running, and the Wolf is after her.

Limpfoot is still running with tremendous effort but her flickering feet are not covering much ground, her breath is painful, it does not nourish her, she smells the Wolf, she hears the Wolf, she sees the Wolf, she feels his breath, his teeth on her leg, his teeth on her shoulder, she sighs, she falls. She switches from subject to object. She is switched.

The Wolf ends her life with his bite to her throat, he sets about his supper.

The clerks and accountants and customs officers met for their monthly Photographic Club session, they snapped and clicked at Vanessa, who was posing as "Dawn," an artistic model, and her flaming mane was hidden by a platinum wig. While grinning, and breathing in and out, Vanessa visited her memories of her father playing a headlong mazurka on the spinet piano, while she and her little sister whirled and danced. Afterward model and club, they all went down to the "Streamliner" Bar and drank jug after jug of José's famous margaritas. Salt crusted their lips. They broke into song.

To the tables down at Mory's,
To the place where Louis dwells,
To the dear old Temple Bar we love so well,
Sing the Whiffenpoofs assembled
With their glasses raised on high,
And the magic of their singing casts its spell.
Yes, the magic of their singing
Of the songs we love so well:
"Shall I Wasting" and "Mavourneen" and the rest.
We will serenade our Louis
While life and voice shall last
Then we'll pass and be forgotten with the rest.
We are poor little lambs
Who have lost our way.
Ba, Ba, Ba.
We are little black sheep
Who have gone astray.
Ba, Ba, Ba.
Gentlemen songsters
Off on a spree
Damned from here
To eternity
God have mercy
On such as we.
Ba, Ba, Ba.

Types of sheep: American Merino, Debouillet, Delaine Merino, Rambouillet, Cheviot, Dorset, Hampshire, Montadale, North Country Cheviot, Oxford, Shropshire, Southdown, Suffolk, Tunis, Cotswold, Leicester, Lincoln, Romney, Columbia, Corriedale, Panama, Tailless or No Tail, Targhee, Black-faced Highland, Karakul.

What time is it?

And in the raw panic, scenting the blood, the Flock goes mad and rushes at the fence, and then: four sheep jump over the fence; six sheep get down on their bellies and wriggle under the fence; a frenzied ewe throws herself at the fence again and again, and finally bursts the wood and pushes through, eleven sheep follow her through the gap. Number 141, Number 142, Number 143, Number 144, Number 145, Number 146, Number 147, Number 148, Number 149, Number 150, Number 151, Number 152, Number 153, Number 154, Number 155, Number 156, Number 157, Number 158, Number 159, Number 160, Number 161, Number 162, Number 163.

FENCES FOR SHEEP

Good fences (1) maintain farm boundaries, (2) make livestock operations possible, (3) reduce losses to both animals and crops, (4) increase land values, (5) promote better relationships between neighbors, (6) lessen accidents from animals getting on roads, and (7) add to the attractiveness and distinctiveness of the premises.

The discussion which follows will be limited primarily to wire fencing, although it is recognized that such materials as rails, poles, boards, stone, and hedge have a place and are used under certain circumstances. Also, where there is a heavy concentration of animals, such as in corrals and feed yards, there is need for a more rigid type of fencing material than wire. Moreover, certain fencing materials have more artistic appeal than others; and this is an especially important consideration on the purebred establishment.

1. STYLES OF WOVEN WIRE. The standard styles of woven wire fences are designed by numbers as 1155, 1047, 939, 832, and 726. The first one or two digits represent the number of line (horizontal) wires; the last two the height in inches; i.e., 832 has 8 horizontal wires and is 32 inches in height. Each style can be obtained in either (a) 12-inch spacing of stays (or mesh), or (b) 6-inch spacing of stays.

2. MESH. Generally, a close-spaced fence with stay or vertical wires 6 inches apart (6-in. mesh) will give better service than a wide-spaced (12-in. mesh) fence. However, some fence manufacturers believe that a 12-inch spacing with a No. 9 wire is superior to a 6-inch spacing with No. 11 filler wire (about the same amount of material is involved in each case).

3. WEIGHT OF WIRE. A fence made of heavier-weight wires will usually last longer and prove cheaper than one made of light wires. Heavier or larger-size wire is designated by a smaller gauge number. Thus, No. 9 gauge wire is heavier and larger than No. 11 gauge. Woven wire fencing comes in Nos. 9, 11, 12½ and 14½ gauges—which refers to the gauge of the wires other than the top and bottom line wires. Barbed wire is usually 12½ gauge.

WOOD POSTS. Osage orange, black locust, chestnut, red cedar, black walnut, mulbery, and catalpa—each with an average life of 15 to 30 years without treatment—are the most durable wood posts, but they are not available in all sections. Untreated posts of the other and less durable woods will last 3 to 8 years only, but they are satisfactory if properly butt treated (to 6 to 8 inches above the ground line) with a good wood preservative.

Conjecture for a moment about the modes which the maddened sheep employed to get from one side of the fence to the other, about fencetypes, and about the related question of *style:* The Pathetic, The Humorous, The Heroic, The Decorated, The Romantic, The Sentimental, The Modern, The Post-Modern.

And the Wolf lies in his cave, belly distended, licking his chops, asleep, dreaming already of his next meal.

The camera pans across the smoking landscape, the chase continues. The cloud cover had flattened over the entire sky, and some mists had descended to sit on the very shoulders of the mountains, promising snow.
At the end of the valley the sabotaged oil well sends up three columns of black smoke, and the whole surface of Shiprock is

glowing with chemical fire. The train has jumped the tracks. Trying to speak above the bellow of dying cattle, the Red Head . . . down by the Check-Point a child is crying.

The Sandy Man, as pale as his bandages, had strapped the precious parcel inside his shirt, over his heart. "An old-fashioned gesture" he had thought to himself, as he applied the tape; he had a nature given to reflection but not often to the quixotic. Past the point of no return, no stopping it now, it was with something like relief that he acknowledged the grip of the final causal sequence, and its gathering acceleration. Like Blackie in the template situation, he licked his lips. Blackie, so tanned and sleek, was the photographic positive to the Sandy Man's negative, in his northern paleness. And now it was snowing, and the sun was lit like a blind eye through the cloud cover, "a good setting for the final act," the Sandy Man thought, "my native elements."

In the telephoto excitement of the chase, cars were wrenching themselves from the arms of gravity and hurtling into the air, their heavy bodies describing improbable arcs, ending jammed into barns and mountains, other machines, in unnatural conjunctions. Bif, Bow. The suburbs, the financial center of the city, the bridges, the submarine. The fox lies dead, run over by the jeep, the partridge pecks at the dead grass, the duck-rabbit utters a cry. Moschus, who has the curiosity of a town boy, has followed the tank tracks into the very heart of the Blues' camouflaged encampment. The yerkis, in fatigues and with their heads shaved, captured the confused lad who, amazed by the camp, put up no resistance. They have taken him to Cave L-3, where they are questioning him, employing the modern humane methods. A movement from F to G.

The Border Incident commences, it is, at this stage, a bureaucratic event. The irregular thumps of guns and bombs from the mid-distance keep the Sleeper awake, and drive several sheep over the fence, Number 164, Number 165, Number 166, Number 167, Number 168, Number 169.

Ba ba black sheep
Have you any wool?
Yes sir, yes sir,
Three bags full.
One for my master,
One for my dame,
One for the little boy,
Who lives down the lane.

Western generics turned one more turn of the screw . . .

The landscape gone chiaroscuro in the grip of winter drought, the stubble was littered with the bodies of sheep and cattle. Harry shot Ricardo in the leg. Danny shot Johnny in the side. Albert shot Otto in the head. Johnny shot Dennikin in the back. Amanda shot Sonny in the heart. Lannahan shot Slim in the groin. Burbridge shot Kennedy in the shoulder. Ricardo shot Harry in the chest. The blood ran out of the bodies, and into the earth.

Later, in the saloon, Blackie was challenged in a card game by Buffalo, the head of the sheepherders. They squared off, and the lights came up for the fight scene. A right to the jaw, a left to the bread basket, the body thrown into the mirror, a chair broken, some shots, biting the ear, biting the nose, gouging the eye, shots. The Sandy Man leaned against the bar, drinking whiskey, watching it all. Blackie came up to the bar, took off his hat, "make mine milk."

In the ongoing range war, some of Phoebe's sheep got caught up in Denniken's flock, confused, they trotted back and forth amongst the strange sheep, ba-ing pitifully. They were shot by the cowboys. The ba-ing kept the Sleeper awake again.

Blackie and Amanda have found temporary cover hiding in a barn. Amanda asks Blackie, "Why is it that men are taught to hide and distort their emotions?" Blackie is kissing Amanda and his horse, alternately. She takes down his trousers.

In the distance, in the West, where the burning well and

rock are outlined against the amythyst of the coming sunset, a group of Indians appear on the horizon.

A sheep with a crooked brand, the T-Lazy-7 on her rump, leaps over the fence, Number 170, and is followed by two cows, Number 171, Number 172.

And in the midst of that winter afternoon, with the remains of her flock huddled together for warmth and her dog lying back his fringed ears and slitting his eyes at the wind, Phoebe is looking for Bion. Bion, Bion, she tramps up hill and down dale, the sheep follow grudgingly, the dog pushes them on, *Bion*, she whistles the song which always finds him, up three notes, down two, up a long note, held, but no answer. She goes to their favorite places, the glade, the cave, the swimming pond, where is he, where are you my love, my love?

And then she sees his dog, it wears a strange aspect, it howls at their approach, and then, she sees his sheep, but so few of them, and there are dead ones, dead sheep lie in the grass, their mouths open, their flanks torn, their limbs at odd angles, and then, Oh gods protect us, turn back my eyes, announce that I have not seen what it seemed, oh there, upon the grass and powdered snow, all cast among the bodies of his flock, his own dear body, Bion. The dogs howl. But maybe life remains, and Phoebe rushes pell mell to her Bion, and takes his head into her lap, and croons to him, My honey, Oh my dear, and calls and puts her lips to his lips, but no, he grows cool, My Bion, and his eyes do not open, and his cheeks empty of roses, and the sweet breath does not flow through his chest, Oh Bion, my love, my love.

And Nature cries together, the winds, the skies, the waters, the trees, and the birds and creatures cry altogether, our Bion, Bion's dead, dead in his prime, ahimé. The flower of young manhood has been plucked from us, weep winds, weep fishes, weep poor Phoebe for your lover is gone from you, gone, gone to that land from which, they say, no traveler returns.

And in this country, as Pan and his wild spirits had passed away, so too this generation, with their jokes and their songs.

And even the Wolf, in his den, licking his paws for the last morsels of his mutton meal, hears the message, young Bion is dead, and weeps.

And so the reality principle surmounts the pleasure principle once again, and that fragile early slate is full of entropy, and a sheep, sobbing, leaps the fence, Number 173.

The winter is harsh, and the sheep are in confusion, so many dead, so many dying. Forty killed by the guns of the cowboys, sixty-two murdered by the tanks and bombs of the spies, nine lost and gone to the jaws of the Wolf, fifty dead of poisoned water, alas.

The rimed grass, the frozen hills, (flora, fauna, topography, geology, skies, weather).

And where the Wolf dines well, he will dine again.

The insomniac Sleeper, *in extremis,* is involved in the theory of counting, the manner of numbers, she clutches at her head, the Blues have sent a rigged sheep over the fence, it arcs unnaturally high and then explodes. Number 174. And then the naked numbers themselves are jumping, are leaping over the fence, Number 175, Number 176, Number 177. And the sheep with the crooked T-Lazy-7 branded on her rump (remarked upon before), is jumping back, is jumping back the other way!, Number 178.

And falling out of bed and down the rabbit hole, the Sleeper is waltzing with the Censor, she sees that he is wearing a "realistic" Wolf mask, and with his black grease pencil he edits and amends the environs as they whirl along, *one* two three, *one* two three, *one* two three and.

Steps in Slaughtering and Dressing Sheep and Lambs

In order to avoid undue excitement and make for ease in handling, gregarious sheep and lambs are usually led to the packers' slaughtering pens by an old goat, commonly referred to as "Judas." A reasonable fast and quiet prior to slaughtering are especially important for sheep.

The endless chain method is used in sheep slaughter. The steps in packing house slaughtering procedure are as follows:

1. *Rendering insensible;* shackling; hoisting. The sheep are rendered insensible (by rendering insensible to pain by a single blow or gunshot or an electrical, chemical, or other means that is rapid and effective, before being shackled, hoisted, thrown, cast, or cut). A shackle is placed around the hind leg just above the foot; and the animals are delivered to an overhead rail by means of a wheel hoist.

2. *Bleeding.* A double-edged knife is inserted into the neck just below the ear so that it severs the large blood vessel in the neck.

3. *Removal of feet.* After bleeding, the front feet are removed. Lambs and most yearlings will break at the "break-joint" or "lamb-joint," a temporary joint characteristic of young sheep which is located immediately above the ankle. In dressing mature sheep, the front feet are removed at the ankle, leaving a round point on the end of the shank bone.

4. *Removal of pelt.* The pelt is next removed. Caution is taken to prevent damage to the fell (the thin, tough membrane covering the carcass immediately under the pelt).

5. *Removal of hind feet and head.* Next the hind feet and head are removed.

6. *Opening of carcass and eviscerating.* The carcass is opened down the median line; the internal organs, windpipe, and gullet are removed and the breast bone is split. The kidneys are left intact.

7. *Shaping.* The forelegs are folded at the knees and are held in place by a skewer. A spread-stick is inserted in the belly to allow for proper chilling and to give shape to the carcass.

8. *Washing.* Finally the carcass is washed, wiped, and promptly sent to the cooler. Some of the better-grade carcasses are wrapped in special coverings for marketing.

The all-female string orchestra sawed away melodiously, among the ferns, playing a variation on a patriotic march. The Sleeper, in satin slippers, steps on his foot, and he gives her a greasy kiss. And then, thirteen at table, they sat down to doused mutton with capers, which is prepared as follows . . .

Sweating tripping, doing the tango, she sprained her ankle. All a-heap on the floor her very freckles blushed. In the hospital, going under ether, she was asked to count backward from 100, 99, 98, 97, 96, 95, 94, 93, 92, 91, she got to 90 before the numbers became recalcitrant and began to swim up stream, began jumping back and forth again, the numbers became impure and took on flesh, goats, zebras, oxen, llamas, wildebeest, dogs, wolves, sheep. Number 179, Number 180, Number 181, Number 182, Number 183, Number 184, Number 185, Number 186, Number 187, Number 188, Number 189, Number 190, Number 191, Number 192, Number 193, Number 194, Number 195, Number 196, Number 197, Number 198, Number 199, Number 200, Number 201, Number 202, Number 203.

She itches, she scratches red patterns on her skin, she turns, she scratches, crumbs in the bed.

Matthew, Mark, Luke, and John,
Bless this bed that I lie on;
Four angels to my bed,
Two to bottom, two to head,
Two to hear me when I pray,
Two to bear my soul away.

The five subjects were studied with the combined methods for a total of thirteen nights during forty-four REMS. All showed sleep EEG patterns with recurrent emergent stage 1, apparently no different from normals.

Four black sheep leaped over the fence, Number 204, Number 205, Number 206, Number 207.

Two special forms of displacement should be separately mentioned because of their frequency. One is the representation of an object or person thought of in the latent content by the device of allowing a part only to appear in the manifest content, the process known as *pars pro toto*, which is one of the forms of synecdoche. The other is representation by means of allusion, a process known linguistically as metonymy; it has just been referred to in connection with superficial association. There are still two other ways in which a latent dream element can be converted into, or replaced by, a manifest element—namely, visual dramatization through regression, which will presently be considered, and symbolism. Symbolism, which Freud calls the most curious chapter of dream theory, forms such a special and important topic that I have considered it at length elsewhere; at this point I will only remark that, for some as yet unknown reason, dream symbolism differs from other symbolism in being almost exclusively sexual.

Above the vultures circled, while below the men with bags over their heads struggled with the bad cowboys. The shoot-out happened offstage.

The blue smoke curled up from the campfire, writing Western mottos in script, dissolving and recombining in the purple sky where the clouds wore the faces of dead heroes.

Jouvet and Delorme (1965) reported that bilateral destruction of the pontile nucleus locus coeruleus eliminates the tonic aspect of EEG desynchronization and EMG suppression of REM sleep.

BRAISED SHOULDER OF LAMB
6 Servings

Melt in a heavy pot:
1/4 cup vegetable oil or butter
Sear on all sides in the hot fat:
A rolled shoulder of lamb, remove it from the pot.
Sauté slowly in the fat 10 minutes:
1/2 cup chopped onions

1/4 cup chopped carrots
1/2 cup chopped turnips
1/2 cup chopped celery with leaves
1 sliced clove garlic
Return meat to the pot. Add:
1/2 bay leaf
4 whole peppercorns
1 teaspoon salt
4 cups boiling vegetable stock, or 3 cups stock
and 1 cup tomato pulp.
Cover the pot and simmer meat until tender, about
2 hours. When the meat is done, degrease and thicken stock
slightly with: Kneaded Butter, 340.

Blackie was insomniac, at night, under the stars, counting
the future dead. He could recognize their ventilated bodies,
censored by dust. Blackie mused on the evidence surrounding
the possibilities of continued consciousness after death. Johnny,
snoring beside him, is dreaming a Christmas dream, in it he is a
dumb beast, chewing his cud, one of the animals gathered round
the manger, gazing at the infant Christ, the Lamb of God.

Bion's yellow dog runs across, upstage, they shoot at him and
miss. In the distance is the racketing of a helicopter, a sound
unheard or misunderstood by everyone present in the Range War
Diorama, as they had never heard its like before.

Bang bang. Seven wounded sheep leap and struggle over the
fence, Number 208, Number 209, Number 210, Number 211,
Number 212, Number 213, Number 214.

Put your finger in Foxy's hole,
Foxy's not at home;
Foxy's at the back door,
Picking at a bone.

The Red Head put on a wig and a false nose and stuffed
pillows down the front of her dress. On the radio was the news of
the burning library. The announcer described the scene, a
librarian had run flaming from the building, "a human torch."

The Red Head rubbed her hands with rose water, there was still a faint smell of gasoline. She put on her makeup, rosy cheeks, rosy lips! As she readied herself, she hummed a sentimental tune; domestically speaking, she was soft-hearted.

What time is it?

They had broken the code!, the President had choked on a splinter of lamb bone; Dahlberg, his Secret Service agent, had to slap him on the back. The agents are all taught the Heimlich maneuver as part of their first-aid training, but they are advised to try three or four forceful slaps to the middle back before applying the more complicated, and more "risky," technique. In the President's case, as with approximately 43% of the cases of choking and slapping studied in a recent medical journal, the slaps were sufficient to dislodge the foreign object and restore clear breathing. Dahlberg was later removed to another location. The President was grateful to him, but the President also hated to be touched physically, and found even the memory and its projector unnerving.

"VIRTUES OF WOOL"

It is noteworthy that the antque characterstics and virtues of wool have, through the years, enabled it to hold its position of preminence in competition with other animal fibers, products of plant origin, and the invasion of innumerable synthetic materials. Although certain other fibers may equel or even excel in one or several qualities, none can boast of the total qualities possessed by wool. The virtues of wool are as follows:

1. Wool is porous and will absorb water more readily than any other textile fiber. It can absorb as much as 18 percent of its own weight in moisture without even feeling damp and up to 50 percent of its weight without becoming saturated. This is an important health factor in clothing because body perspiration and water dampness are prevented from clinging to the body in heat or cold, thus removing the chillness from the body.

2. Wool generates heat in itself.

3. W●●l ●s ● s●p●r●●r ●ns●l●t●r, k●●p●ng th● h●●t ●f th● b●d●
fr●m ●sc●p●ng ●nd th● c●ld ●●r fr●m ●nt●r●ng. B●c●●s● ●f th●s
q●●l●t●, w●●l ●s ●s ●ff●ct●v● ●s ● pr●t●ct●●n fr●m tr●p●c●l h●●t ●nd
s●n ●s ●t ●s ●g●●nst th● g●l●-dr●v●n st●rms ●f w●nt●r.

4. W●●l ●s l●ght.

5. W●●l ●s v●ry ●l●st●c; th● ●v●r●g● f●b●r w●ll str●tch 30
p●rc●nt ●f ●ts n●rm●l l●ngth ●nd st●ll spr●ng b●ck ●nt● sh●p●.
B●c●●s● ●f th●s r●s●l●●nc●, w●●l g●rm●nts r●s●st wr●nkl●ng,
str●tch●ng, ●r s●gg●ng d●r●ng w●●r.

6. W●●l tr●nsm●ts th● h●●lth-g●v●ng ●ltr●-v●●l●t r●ys.

7. Dy●st●ffs ●r● l●ss l●k●l● t● f●d● ●nd ●r● f●st●r ●n w●●l.

8. W●●l ●s d●r●bl●.

9. W●●l ●s str●ng. D●●m●t●r f●r d●●m●t●r, ● w●●l f●b●r ●s
str●ng●r th●n st●●l.

10. W●●l ●s ●lm●st n●nfl●mm●bl●. ●t w●ll st●p b●rn●ng ●lm●st
●s s●●n ●s ●t ●s t●k●n ●w●y fr●m ● fl●m●.

11. W●●l c●n b● f●lt●d ●r m●tt●d ●●s●l●.

A crowd of small, yellow clothes-moths, with narrow wings
edged with long fringes, have eaten all the vowels out of the
above text, or fabric. This "editing by insects" is in conformity
with the principles of the *nouvelle cuisine/criticism* advocated by
the French.

The amputée with hair growing from his nose stood close to
the middle of the bridge, the spotlights behind him; he signaled
by waving his flashlight in a slow arc over his head. At that
moment in the synchronous universe his identical brother stood
on a stage in Budapest and pulled a succession of colored silk
scarves from his mouth, or appeared to. At that moment the third
triplet was delivering a 41-year-old black primagravida of a
nine-pound baby boy by caesarian section in a private hospital in
Boston. The Landrover's engine started up.

The cirrus clouds were like generalized sheep, heavenly
sheep.

Blackie, doing heroics in No Man's Land, gets caught up in

the Border Incident, gets a custard pie in his face. A movement from G to H.

At their familiar place, where they had played games with dice, Phoebe throws herself beside the burial mound. At their familiar place, where they had played games with bone dice, where they had kissed—now *his* bones, those lips were so quiet in the frozen earth, she lies beside him. Bion, your bones are so still, you who were never silent with your whistles, and your singing—those rosy lips . . .

Five hungry sheep and two goats squeezed back under the fence. Number 215, Number 216, Number 217, Number 218, Number 219, Number 220, Number 221.

The Wolf's mouth is wet, he is hungry again.

"Yip, yip, yip yip yip," and this queer, crooked creature shambling over the ice is Moschus, Moschus made mad by the brain-washing techniques of another era. He sings, and whines like a dog.

The sheep are in terrible confusion, each sheep has lost brothers, sisters, mothers, fathers, children, husbands. The Flock has suffered terribly, and the Flock is all they know, their base-line, their whole context.

Red sheep, green sheep, amythyst sheep, yellow sheep, silver sheep, black sheep, copper sheep, pink sheep, golden sheep, aquamarine sheep, purple sheep, topaz sheep, violet sheep, brown sheep, sienna sheep, crimson sheep, bread sheep, ivory sheep, ebony sheep, blue sheep, milky sheep, pearl sheep, vegetable sheep, monkey sheep, metal sheep, wooden sheep, blood sheep, bone sheep

What time is it?, the mouse runs up the clock.

I dreamed that the baby was born, he looked about six

months old, he was sitting up, and he had a very radiant, smiling face. He looked blonder than the other two.

In my dream I was playing a slot machine, and after a few tries I won a kind of demi-jackpot, I didn't have anything to put the coins in and they were flowing out uncontrollably, someone offered me a gray cowboy hat, I used it, it filled and overflowed.

The Judas sheep calls to the Flock in a melodious voice:

Oh come, come,
My tender be-lov-ed
Oh follow me
My own wooly tribe
Let me show you
Sweet, greener pastures
Fresh water, warm sunshine,
No wolves.

A movement from H to I.

And the Wolf computes his memories on a bony abacus; that mule deer he ran down near the beaver ponds, the cow elk he had cornered in the red ravine, the ram he teased out from the protection of the Flock, the lamb who fell behind in the melée, he licks his lips.

There has been just one deliberate experimental approach to this question by the researcher who has contributed more than any other to the elucidation of the REM state, William Dement. On the classical model of seeking the function of an organ by determining the effects of its removal, Dement set out to discover what might result from relentlessly depriving persons of REM state by awakening them whenever it began to occur over varying numbers of consecutive nights.

The Mercedes raced along the dirt track, gaining on the Landrover, the Landrover was close on the heels of the Volvo, and inside the Volvo the short, hairy man in camouflage handled the wheel with one hand while with the other he balanced a vial of Super Anthrax toxin. Sweat dripped down and stippled the image of Christ crucified tattooed in the baroque manner across his chest.

The curtain's up, the overture goes thump-a-thump, the stage is set.

Three men and nine dogs are lowered from the helicopter. Types of dog: Collie, Boxer, Wolfhound, Beagle, Bedlington, Doberman, Retriever, Spaniel, Setter.

The skyscraper luridly figured forth the omens and the players, their histories; and silhouetted against the fissionable mix of crimson and orange and gold and pink and baby blue, the stuntmen/stuntwomen play out their antics. The action is dwarfed by the arrested drama of the cliffs and mesas. The scale of the western landscape is always insistently that of geological rather than cultural history.

Getting awkwardly down on her knees, the old Ewe thrust her head under the gap between the bottom rung of the fence and the earth, and attempted to follow with the rest of her body, but the space was not big enough and she could not go forward. Neither, she found, could she go back, for in her struggles her head had become firmly wedged beneath the rail. She struggled, she twisted and thrashed, waving her legs, but to no avail, she was stuck fast.

Old MacDonald had a farm,
ee-ei, ee-ei, oh.
And on this farm he had some sheep,
ee-ei, ee-ei, oh.
With a ba ba here, a ba ba there,
here a ba, there a ba,
everywhere a ba ba

The camouflaged Red Head runs limping across, at the top of the screen, a movement from I to J.

Only black, and black & white birds remain here in the deep winter; the blackbirds, and the magpies, and the rooks. The fox has gone to ground.

God bless Mother, God bless Father, God bless Andrew, God bless Ursula and Anna, God bless Daniel and Sophy,

Jouvet's cats who were deprived of REM state by means of pontine lesions appeared to hallucinate, developed progressive tachycardia, and all eventually died. The frequency of recall of color experience in dreams was found to be much higher than has previously been reported. All subjects recalled dreams in color and two subjects, who claimed to dream in black-and-white at the time of the interview, recalled many colored dreams.

The newly shorn sheep looked white, smaller, stripped of her coat, the air blew cold on her skin. On the floor of the shearing shed, the fleeces heaped up like clouds.

The Sandy Man feels a great weariness and disgust for violence and the dreadful patterns that unroll before him, partly as a result of his own actions and intentions. Justification via the greater good? Ideology vs. the broken bone. The ankle, perhaps.

He turned himself away from the sight of the broken child, the Sandy Man's forehead and upper lip were wet, he spat into the snow.

The Sleeper is awake, her toes finding, probing and enlarging the moth holes in the woolen blanket.

The other body in the bed. The dream of the Sleeper's husband, while she lies wide awake beside him:

I was one of a group of a dozen Jews. We were fleeing with a large horse (?) drawn cart down an unpaved road through an open scrub-covered landscape. It seemed to always be a gloomy twilight; at night things were lit intermittently by bonfires and torches, at day by flashes of sunlight through the densely overcast dark gray sky. All our wealth had been pooled and put inside an enormous leatherbound book with hollowed out compartments within the pages. It was wrapped in sackcloth and strapped on the rear of the cart. Next to it was one of our number also strapped on with rope alongside it to guard it. He was strapped on so that he could fall asleep but would be disturbed if anyone tried to get at the book.

We were refugees, but more—there was a sense of constant panic that we were probably being actively pursued. We were stopped overnight briefly. In the morning I went to wake the guard. I could see blood on his clothes; I called the others; he was dead. The book appeared untouched. We cut it down frantically and pulled off the sackcloth. Someone held it open by the spine and shook it. From its hidden compartments fell stones and dry powdery earth, a little dust, a dessicated mouse. The others were filled with puzzlement that the guard could be killed, the wealth removed and the book repacked without the alarum being raised. It was also so obvious that it was not discussed that one of our own number must have done it.

I however was filled with terrible fear, for I was a gentile and had disguised myself as one of this group. I was being sought by other(s) with great powers and I thought it likely that the inexplicable transformation of the wealth was a sign that my pursuer(s) were on my trail.

I thought that they would insist on a body search as the wealth left behind would be of no advantage. If they found me uncircumcised they would put me to the sword out of their panic without a chance of explanation. However, this did not happen. Instead everyone became withdrawn and suspicious, driven more by the desire to keep moving regardless because of the pursuit than to delay and debate the issue. As we went, all mulled over the manner of both death and theft. One accused another. We stopped. The issue was debated in an intense, quickly reasoned and unemotional manner; it could not be he. We continued down the road rapidly. We came to a small group of simple stone houses in advanced disrepair. We neither knew nor cared if they were inhabited but we saw no signs of life. I had become sure that one of us was the murderer—I accused him—again the rapid cold debate—the alibi found—time to move on. Neither this time nor the previous were there any apologies or recriminations from accuser or accused. It was a communal problem open to reasonable hypothesis and examination, there was not time for anything more. Then, suddenly, the murderer gave himself away, but I can't quite remember how. I think it happened very quickly, that he admitted his guilt and had already been dispatched by the time I got close.

None spoke, but left the body lying and the cart moved on. Dawn broke to reveal the end of the road before us at the edge of a high cliff; behind us flames were rising from the group of stone buildings. I realized I must turn to the side along the cliff to escape this impossible situation, and did so, waking up. I was trapped on a ledge a few inches wide between the edge of the bed and the fiery body of my beloved, pressed into my back.

The poet in the garden extemporizes on the politics of the pastoral. "Removing themselves from the appetites for wealth and fame, and turning aside from the pungent variety of city life—also denying the claims of family, the shepherd and shepherdess give themselves over to the celebration of the beauties of the natural world, and of love. After a space, that world is breached and broken by those energies forbidden to it."

The poet toasts the company with a glass of amber wine, she turns to kiss her curly, baritone sweetheart.

Luminous white angelic cowboys, dusky dark satanic cowboys . . .

Mary had a little lamb, little lamb, little lamb,
Mary had a little lamb, its fleece was white as snow.

The dream mechanics rectified the story, she loved and was loved, she was not insomniac, she had good teeth.

The good cowboys, the bad cowboys, leaping onto their horses' backs from above.

In a recent article Deckert (1964) has reported polygraphically observing pursuit eye movements essentially indistinguishable from those seen in the actual tracking of a swinging pendulum taking place when hypnotized and nonhypnotized individuals were asked to imagine such a device. On the other hand, he was *unable* to obtain comparable results when his hypnotized Ss were instructed to hallucinate or to dream of a swinging pendulum, even after being exposed to an actual one. The EEG segment reproduced here is therefore of some interest as it was obtained from a hypnotized S *spontaneously* dreaming of watching a watch swing at the end of a chain. When instructed on a later occasion to have this dream again, the same kind of record resulted.

The tartan shirt she had borrowed from her new lover set off her allergy to wool, her face and hands became swollen, her skin red and shiny, and the itching was constant and terrible.

Six sheep broke through the fence at a spot where it had been weakened by fire, Number 222, Number 223, Number 224, Number 225, Number 226, Number 227. Four sheep squeezed back through from the other side, Number 228, Number 229, Number 230, Number 231.

The turquoise Volkswagen drew up to the Monument in the Square, the door opened and a troupe of dogs tumbled out—a blond Labrador, a tooth-pick Mexican hairless, a Toy Poodle, a Husky, an Airedale Terrier, a Bloodhound, a grayhound, a Sheltie. Several of the dogs wore tutus and feather boas, others were dressed as miniature cowboys. They pranced on their hind legs, danced, pretended to box, and then, as a finale, staged a doggy wedding.

It was a sheep in wolf's clothing!

Lamb

To dream of lambs frolicking in green pastures, betokens chaste friendships and joys. Bounteous and profitable crops to the farmers, and increase of possessions for others.

To see a dead lamb, signifies sadness and desolation.

Blood showing on the white fleece of a lamb, denotes that innocent ones will suffer from betrayal through the wrongdoing of others.

A lost lamb, denotes that wayward people will be under your influence, and you should be careful of your conduct.

To see lamb skins, denotes comfort and pleasure usurped from others.

To slaughter a lamb for domestic uses, prosperity will be gained through sacrifice of pleasure and contentment.

To eat lambchops, denotes illness, and much anxiety over the welfare of children.

To see lambs taking nourishment from their mothers, denotes happiness through pleasant and intelligent home companions, and many lovable and beautiful children.

To dream that dogs, or wolves, devour lambs, innocent people will suffer at the hands of insinuating villains.

To hear the bleating of lambs, your generosity will be appealed to.

To see them in a winter storm, or rain, denotes disappointment in expected enjoyment and betterment of fortune.

To own lambs in your dreams, signifies that your environment will be pleasant and profitable.

If you carry lambs in your arms, you will be encumbered with happy cares upon which you will lavish a wealth of devotion, and no expense will be regretted in responding to appeals from the objects of your affection.

To shear lambs, shows that you will be cold and mercenary. You will be honest, but inhumane.

For a woman to dream that she is peeling the skin from a lamb, and while doing so, she discovers that it is her child, denotes that she will cause others sorrow which will also rebound to her grief and loss.

Shiprock sailed full speed through the purple twilight.

The baby cries out in her sleep, something about a dog.

The chemicals of panic and pursuit were titrated, drop by drop, into their blood. The Indians said that wolves preferred the flavor of the flesh of animals that had recently run hard.

The Sandy Man gathered the child up in his arms, he was like an unknotted marionette, there was no resistance. Bang bang bang bang.

Displacement: roast meat for the body of Christ, wine for tears, olives for eyes.

Two sheep jumped over the fence and three jumped back again. Number 232, Number 233, Number 234, Number 235, Number 236.

Mr. East gave a feast;
Mr. North laid a cloth;
Mr. West did his best;
Mr. South burnt his mouth
With eating a cold potato.

A movement from J to K.

How many sheep, placed end to end, would it take to reach to the moon?

The sacred Lamb in the Ghent Altarpiece, note the spigot in his chest from which pours the blood.

They panned to the bathtub scene. Amanda in the wooden tub, the surface full of bubbles, she is soaping her back, and the viewer is allowed a hint of breast and nipple. The *character* is lost in the vasty deeps of coyness and pre-fem self-objectification; the *actress* has decided that she still enjoys "flirting" and will allow herself to play that game occasionally. (She's not altogether comfortable with this decision.) She looks up, all webbed with nacre, as Blackie comes in.

Blackie almost swims into the almost substantial fluid of humidity and aromatic bathsalts constituting the inner air of her bathroom, of which she is the exceedingly female-polarized center, "Good afternoon," he says "this is a very heady atmosphere." He breaths in and out, the moisture gathers on the planes of his face and the rim of his hat, and on his dusty, trail-grimed clothes, and makes him amphibious between two worlds. "The fighting's over," he says, "they got some of us, we got some of them, the rest of them have gone back up into the hills." "Until next time," Amanda says, she is rinsing her hair, so blonde that wet it looks like damp fleece; the bubbles on the surface are breaking down and her shrimp-pink body is dimly visible in the dark waters. She holds her face up, at an angle like a Picasso flower-woman, and he bends and kisses her wet face, lightly. She climbs out of the bath and wraps a towel round her, this without coyness, and says to him, "You look tired." "I'm tired" he says.

A sheep turned, bared her teeth, and commenced to begin to savage the dog.

A movement from K to L.

In the documentary movie, displaying scenes of greed, extreme want, irreversible and unnecessary destruction of the natural world, the camera is following the faint valedictory gestures of a three-year-old child dying of hunger, when the projector catches and begins to bubble out loops of unsprocketed film. The image is reduced to a series of luminous stripes of dark, lozenges of light.

Two blind sheep jump over the hedge, Number 237, Number 238.

But what do we really have? A highly sensitive amplifier and recorder at one end. At the other, a sleeping subject with electrodes secured to the skin of her scalp and to her eye muscles, or an animal with electrodes permanently implanted in her brain. The EEG records show only the amplitude and frequency of electrical activity. This is first-order data about sleep. It describes the sleeping states in EEG language. Everything emanating from this is a product of the ingenuity of the sleep researcher. This product may be a deduction, an induction, a correlation, an inference, a coincidence, or pure fiction, depending upon how it was derived.

Mint sauce: the leg, the loin, the rack; shoulder and breast, an inventory of the internal organs, all this. The joke in Peter Pan has to do with eternal youth and the clock in the crocodile.

"How" said the Indians, and "Ugh," their ponies moved, restlessly.

The bottles of pills, the blue tablets, the white tablets, the yellow and orange time-release capsules, the Sleeper lays them out, idly, in the form of a necklace on the bedside table. She is always careful to ingest the right bits of jewelry, the right amounts, in the right order. The moth is back, kamikaze with her hair.

Three hungry sheep jump over the wall, Number 237, Number 238, Number 239, another jumps, it is the wolf in sheep's clothing, Number 240.

I dreamed that the alienist, in his outdoor consulting room formed of wellgrown ewe hedges and topiary details, used the changing cloud shapes as his handy rorschach. I lay on a patch of camomile lawn, the crushed leaves giving up their scents, and parsed the cumulus into emperors, yonis, moose, tankers, continents.

She woke early, lying next to her husband, feeling randy and bemused, she had dreamed that he was having an affair with "Polly," the tall elegant blonde he had loved, briefly but intensely, before their marriage. She asked him whether he had been dreaming along similar lines, he said no, he had been dreaming about architectural innovation.

Another dream involved some kind of surgical process which had to do with "scraping the bones," it seemed to be some kind of medical procedure. Just a fragment . . .

The Leftists, down from the hills, the Rightists, up from the valley, were trying to assimilate the various imported ideologies and correlate them to some substrate of first-order experience. . . . Meanwhile both laid claim to a recent bombing incident, seventeen people of varying ages and unknown political views killed in the blowing-up of a fast-chicken restaurant. The uncooked bodies of humans, and the cooked and uncooked bodies of chickens, were strewn over the lawn and parking lot.

In the puppet show of intellectual history, Freud versus Jung, like Punch and Judy they batter each other over the head and cry out. She takes it as a reminder of mortality, and sentimental Vanessa blubs.

A jet stripes the upper atmosphere, the line unrolling as pink as the ongoing sunset, like a zipper unzipped to reveal pink flesh beneath a blue garment. Over the Red Head's face the warring twins of eros and thanatos played themselves out, tugging at muscle groups, revealing, causing to vibrate. Her eyes blinked, her lips snarled, trembled. She pulls the zipper down on her blue gown, which smells of mothballs.

Wandering around the room, pacing, the Sleeper picks up a book, opens it to a random spot, reads a paragraph or two, puts it down. She pours a glass of milk, drinks half of it, grimaces with her milky moustache in the mirror. She picks up a seashell, listens for the sea. Turning on the radio she listens to a show for truckers, Hey Good Buddy, if you're driving through Montana or Idaho tonight . . . And, "Sioux-City-Sue, Sioux-City-Sue, Your hair is red, your eyes are blue, I'd swap my horse and dog for you, Sioux-City-Sue, Sioux-City-Sue, There ain't no gal as true, as my sweet Sioux-City-Sue."

Displacement: bottle for womb, gift for kiss, sailor for father.

The technicals moved across the bridge, the Volvo and the Ford maneuvered, the barriers opened and closed, the helicopters clamoured above, beaming their spotlights down, all the pieces moved in order like the characters changing the hour in a Renaissance tower clock. The seven ages of humankind are shown, from the puking babe, through grinning youth and lustful and greedy maturity to slothful and frail old age; they are followed by the reaper, who lops off their block-heads, 12 times a day, with the swinging scythe.

The center of the drama, the core, was a small, brightly-lit patch in the middle of the bridge, demarcated by armed soldiers on both sides. The woman walked forward with the satchel, the man stepped forward carrying the child, he was wrapped in a khaki blanket, he appeared to be asleep. The exchanged their burdens, the woman put the satchel on the ground, the man knelt, still holding the boy, and glanced briefly through the contents. Then he stood again and handed the bundled child to the woman, very gently, and she turned to walk back to her side, and he picked up the satchel and turned toward his. Someone, one of the gunmen, perhaps, began to cough in a spasm that continued as the cars backed off and left only the armed men facing each other. They finally turned and walked back to their commands. The bridge was left dark and quiet.

The sheep are tired, they have sun so far, they are hungry, they want to graze.

Displacement, the egg for the ear, the finger for the penis, the tongue for the clitoris.

She tipped back her head and sucked greedily at the wine skin, the red wine ran from the corners of her mouth and down her chin.

Nine sheep leap over the fence, four press through a gap, six crawl back. Number 241, Number 242, Number 243, Number 244, Number 245, Number 246, Number 247, Number 248,

Number 249, Number 250, Number 251, Number 252, Number 253, Number 254, Number 255, Number 256, Number 257, Number 258, Number 259.

Turning away from the bodies, the heaps, the smoking ruins, the dead cattle which are beginning to stink, Amanda jerked up her horse's head, Blackie, Mungo, and Slim followed, they ride off into the sunset. A movement from L to M.

A shoulder of mutton jumped over from France,
Fal lal, lal-de-ro-lee,
A shoulder of mutton jumped over from France,
And the music did play and the people did dance,
With a fal lal, lal-de-ro-lee.

The Sleeper sat up in bed and barked like a dog. Her eyes were closed. Three sheep leap over the fence, Number 260, Number 261, Number 262.

The Lord is my Shepherd,
I shall not want,
He maketh me to lie down in green pastures,
He leadeth me beside the still waters,
He restoreth my soul.
Yea, though I walk through the valley of the shadow,
I shall fear no evil, for Thou art with me,
Thy rod and Thy staff they comfort me,
My cup runneth over.
Surely goodness and mercy shall follow me,
The rest of the days of my life.

The Wolf continues the narrative, mit shadows.

The puny ego clinging to its little length of tape, its flame, the crocodile cries crocodile tears.

A movement from M to N.
A movement from N to O.

Near the river, a group of Navajo sheep, and Indians in war paint.

Yippee ki yi yea
Git along little doggie
it's yer misfortune
and none of my own
Yippee ki yi yea
Git along little doggie
You know that Wyoming
Will be your new home.

And Phoebe was drawn back from her extreme grief, which was so radical that it strained every disposition, it threatened madness. Not her wall-eyed dog, but Bion's yellow one tugged at her hem, insisted, and she woke to herself and went to find the hurt lamb, the weak ewe. She mixed a mash, she found some herbs for them.

Hair/elbows/fleas/lice/butter/freckles/dogs/clouds

Humpty Dumpty sat on a wall,
Humpty Dumpty had a great fall,
All the king's horses,
And all the king's men,
Couldn't put Humpty together again.
Number 263.

The wheel turns and the sheep bend their heads to eat the grass.

The wind shifts, one sheep jumps over the fence, Number 264.

A bookend to the introductory section which featured the Cowboy and the Sleepwalker: the periwinkle blue high-gloss walls of the Green Room reflect the mixed noises of the cast party. Blackie, drunk again, has brought his horse inside, and the poor brute raises his great head at intervals and calls out to be rejoined with his own kind; who's that dancing on the table?

Vanessa ahead, Bion behind, they have joined up to form one of those two-person stage horses, they stand by the bar in conversation with a group of sheepherders. Bion, confined within the costume, complains because he cannot drink. The hot tub is filled with cowboys, at the melancholy stage of drunkenness, harmonizing "Red River Valley" in three parts. Later in the evening, the tenor will swing from the crystal chandelier.

The décor is decco silhouette, the fringed palm trees fringe the green oasis, a mural on "The Sources of Modern Design," massed crysanthemums. It's the Sandy Man cavorting on the table! Winsome fellow, wearing black patent leather tap shoes. His dance can be decoded into messages: statistics as to the numbers and powers of nuclear weapons stored by the U.S. Government, how many in the possession of the Soviet Government, and so on. Poor man, he is obsessed. Even at a party, having fun, he is unable to stop thinking about it.

And Phoebe too, watching the 24-hour news on the television in the corner, swivels back and forth like a spectator at the Center Court, yea and nay, Eros and Thanatos again, as she watches the bad news from all over, and feels as she sees them shoot each other down in the name of religion or ideology the fetus thumping indistinct Morse.

Spin the bottle, pin the tail on the donkey, games of chance, dangerous drugs, necking on the couch. Listen! was that a car backfiring?

Riccardo throws a punch at Jouvet, he grazes the Frenchman's cheek and slams his fist into the bookcase behind his head, Riccardo suffers a broken hand. Tex's nose begins to bleed suddenly, "from the excitement," blotches of bright blood-red blood on the white linen handkerchief.

The company is drawn outside by the noise of the fireworks. On the balcony, the Cowboy's eyes are jade, his fringed moustache contacts electrically with the nape of the Sleepwalker's neck, she shivers with pleasure. The illumination from the fireworks details the giant topiary sheep in the formal garden, leaf by leaf.

The eureka spies have come in strict transformational fancy dress, it is a predilection of their kind. All the men are dressed as women, and vice-versa, some campy, some earnest. The blacks are dressed in white-face, the whites in black-face, and other binaries are switched. They form a human chain and do the "bunny hop" around the room. Amanda passed round a huge silver platter full of delicious little meat balls of ground spiced mutton, served with three sauces, a recipe from the (war-torn) middle east.

The circumscribed, circumcised, camouflaged Russian was eating rapidly from a heaped plate and at the same time arguing with the Stewardess over the old question "what can be said to be more clearly the determinant of the modern Soviet Union, Marxism or the character of Old Russia?"

Striking the set: Atmospherics, a (red) (skin) behind every bush, the burning bush, my lady's bush, our lady of the shepherds, these and other disconnected images phosphoresce in the landscape. And through that landscape, on their own errands viewed with the attendant notion of free will, and also, or perhaps instead, following out their causal chains; the characters, who are not so much constructs as collections of dispositions, wander—having adventures, meeting, parting, messing and tidying, doing *verbs,* making entrances and exits. And the earth aches with its burden of weaponry, and the sea and the air too are mined with the extraordinary engines of destruction. And personal lives and motives are seen to have an odd bright line around them, of the sort observable in television when saturated blue overlay is employed to snatch figures from their contexts and lay them in against another, more brilliant scene; and in this way the unique importance of the personal dims somewhat the kiss in the burning house.

The Sleepwalker, whose education had convinced her that the accumulated articulation of thought represents the antidote to human stupidity and destruction, observes the landscape and is not sanguine about the odds. How much of this assessment is the pessimism of any epoch, and how much justified by the genuine terror of the period?

A cowboy, very drunk, is propositioning a caryatid on the terrace. Vanessa, still half a horse, sings "You Are My Sunshine" to the grips. The party is winding down. At the kitchen entrance, a line of bare-footed children has formed, waiting for the hand-out of table scraps. The Sleepwalker and the Cowboy are watching the finish of the glorious fireworks display. Boom. Poof. The night, and she and he are wonderfully spangled. And so, in spite of themselves, the golden showers and pink explosions of the atmospheric flowerings remind them of the grimmer possibilities stored in the sky, and these images remain later when they undress, leaf by leaf, and make absentminded love. They lie afterward on damp grass with stars buzzing overhead, and he snores and his eyelashes fringe his silver cheek and she counts sheep.

Busy About the Tree of Life

Five, six, seven, eight, bonny Gabriel! He builds a tower with his wooden blocks, the red cube on the blue, then a green one, he sees all these in tones of gray, then a larger cube dented on one corner made of natural wood, careful, balance the stack again, he pauses to move around the room, a stroll. He tries out a large strainer as a hat, a cocky appearance, like a drunken fencer whose protective gear has gone askew. We hear some music from another room, a few notes of Mozart, it's that rascal Don calling to the maid from beneath her window with an argument irresistible in its sweetness if not its sense. The little boy turns around, dip, wobble, and around in pure, primitive dance. He stumbles on a granite pebble brought home from a visit to the seaside, he puts it in his mouth and tastes the salt, Not in your mouth, Gabriel, says his caretaker. Gabriel returns to his handsome tower and adds a ninth block, yellow, and a tenth, which is green with an elephant on it, carved in shallow relief. Then he reaches out his pink hand and knocks the tower over, boom. Boom, he says.

Gabriel will mature with the millenium. The exhaustion, or ripening, of this thousand-year stretch of accelerating history is the boy's mess of pottage. All calendars and clocks are banned from the residential quarters, although the observation room lined with one-way glass and the adjacent three-story laboratory are full of counting devices. Some of these, in the old-fashioned style, are made of paper, wood, metal, plastics and glass; and many are burned into crystals, chips of memory where the data is reduced to *off, on*. And so the equipment banks go on monitoring the vitals of the beautiful child, and the relentless work of counting the absolute unfolding of the universe continuing, continues.

Swimming across to meet her own reflection, the Caretaker moves through the room toward the large mirrored north wall, she is tidying the blocks into the basket, placing the knitted rabbit, or mouse, with the rest of the soft bestiary, speculating (left brain) *(sic)* on the contents of Gabriel's dreams. At the edge of something vast, she knits her brow and her head starts to ache, tears pool at the back of her nose, she drags the dappled rocking horse back to its place, and sits down to rest her feet and watch the sleeping baby.

Gabriel chews at his spotted dog's black and white ear, and the dog endures. The hound, called Smiler, is nervous and wholly devoted to the little boy. Smiler has well-sprung ribs and neat paws, his slightly pop eyes indicate a high metabolism rate. Whenever they play violin or flute music through the loudspeakers, the dog quivers and leans against the boy, suffering the high notes. He is drafted into all sorts of games with the child, who has no human playfellows. Smiler has learned tug of war, injured dog, dead dog, wild wolf hunt, survival drill, and endless variations with balls and sticks, all of which he carries out with a keen enthusiasm. As Gabriel's full-time companion, however, the dog shows other, less optimistic qualities. Vibrating with attention he tracks every potentially significant wrinkle of each face that looks into Gabriel's beloved face. Smiler's swimming topaz eyes worry and watch, often he presses up against the child's body, whining and humming under his panting breath.

The sleeping baby lets off a sweet and pungent fragrance into the room, *balsam and rose and toasted bread,* thinks the romantic, kindly nurse. This smell makes Smiler sneeze repeatedly, and he adores it. Sweet Gabe, as you lie swimming through such profound sleep your pretty face pinks and flushes, your gold curls are damp, your fingers attend your wet red mouth, and the whole room is filled with the eddies of your regular breathing and the scent of that breath. Beneath the eyelids which are of such a fine tissue, pale blue, iridescent with lavender, the eyes are moving, REM, the chart recorder chatters more excitedly and eight pens lurch on the graph, a peal amid the foothills, recording the fact of the dreaming but not the story line, what are these dreams?

What dreams? *Where is Mama?* Gabriel's dreams assume a burden for the Jungian collective consciousness committee. Given his unique inheritance and karmic destiny, he *processes,* but does not deliver us from a whole chorus line of infinite disasters. He dreams earthquake, in which the humpty-dumpty planet's great, plated skin grinds and gapes a terrible hot ditch *in your own back yard!* Gabriel sees the fresh cut green lawn shiver, and then odd deep popping sounds which thicken into a quick roar as the grass buckles and splits, and an abyss opens between the climbing frame and the red brick gatepost. Then it is quiet, except for the cries of the individuals who leap like mischievously animated dolls into the crevasse. *Nursey Nursey! Smiler!*

And then at other times Gabriel dreamed of fire, his cast of intimates incandescing, the nursery landscape of toy houses leaping with toy flames. He also dreams—and this is where Kruger and Deacon and Bernikov and the other scientific prognosticators grow worried and irritable and try to throttle back on their blood pressure, pulse and respiration as they listen to the taped baby lisping out accounts of his nightly voyages—he also dreams of having to navigate terrible scenes of war in his laborious sleep stories. He is galloping on his sea-horse/ hobby-horse through situations of destruction which he cannot quite understand, yet the characters who greet him so boisterously are evidently mad and full of grief. These nightly dramas include a million million strivings for the short-term advantage, the heaping up of the final foolishness. Without a myth sufficiently pluralist to save us; all the bodies emptied of their urgent contents, the cities deconstructed into dust, the wickedness, the greediness and apathy; Gabriel dreams.

5.16/15

In the middle of the race, in the middle of America, on Columbus Day 1871, Great Great Grandfather Maximus Adpo glimpsed the idea which was to make him his fortune. The terrible news had just come re bellowing, tall, black-suited Papa. Papa, who had been the earth's pillar to his adoring boy, had traveled by train to the great city of Chicago to make a deal, selling serge and buying serge. Weeping Aunt Hadassah informed him in the parlor, having to raise her voice to be heard above his Mother shrieking like a cat upstairs in her large bed:

Your Papa will not be coming home again she hooted. *He was caught in the great conflagration. Oh my dear.* This last more quietly.

Poleaxed by grief, young Maximus, like a stubborn sleepwalker, had insisted on going on with his plans to enter the 500-yard dash on the Village Green. Spiced air poured out of the trumpets and palpitated the bunting as six collies, two German shepherds, ten terriers of assorted types, fourteen hounds, six spaniels, a mastiff, and forty dogs of mixed parentage hollered around the volunteer fire engine. Maximus stood with great half-wheels of purple beneath his eyes, there at the starting line, shivering at the gun; then running like an animal in absolute terror. A lap ahead at the halfway point, and then his mind, which had been as blank as new paper, suddenly wrote or was written upon, THE INDESTRUCTIBLE PORTRAIT.

He won the race, and by the age of twenty-three he had made his first million dollars (when a million was a million and a dollar was an iron man) from the busts, reliefs and full-scale portrait sculptures in the round, brightly painted, cast from hardest alloys, the incorruptible version of the perishable flesh. Maximus' color-blindness resulted in combinations of tints that were surprising and distinctly *modernisti*. The portraits were a great success, in use as funerary sculpture and in the finest drawing rooms, and it was from cresting this commercial wave that Max had temporarily retreated to the mountains to fish and clear his head of the world which had so easily become his complete oyster. There on a stone, by a brook, in a glade, underneath the cawing of a large black bird, Max came face to face with the bright-cheeked skinny girl who was to change his life.

She was a poet, he said *poetess* and she corrected him energetically. She came from a moneyed family, she was summering in the mountains due to a recurrent weakness of the lungs. She had no manners to speak of, and was the most direct female he had ever met. She talked and talked, evidently she had been a little removed from congenial discourse at this altitude. She was shocked at his conservatism, and required him to review his whole schedule of political and aesthetic opinion. As they talked, he memorized the way she gestured with two hands, to make a point, and the exact junction of the way in which her head, so heavy with orange hair, turned on her long, arched neck. Just so would he make her portrait.

Three weeks later, when he proposed marriage, she would only agree when he promised that they could travel, unlimited travel, which was needful research for her poems. *My verse is not about the inside of rooms,* she laughed, toughly rhetorical. And then, in the pink summer heat of their honeymoon in Switzerland, Max showed Persephone a whole new vista of feelings, appetites and urgencies that took place within the confines of the pretty room overlooking the bright blue lake.

They became a truly married animal, as connected as the poor monster babies born with two heads and one trunk. Life went on.

The expensive doctors warned Persephone that it would be too taxing to her already mortgaged flesh to risk a pregnancy, but when the brew of wax and whale's fat soap was breached by the insistence of their ardors and she conceived a child, she was secretly pleased.

Maximus worried and paced. He had been most dreadfully concerned since this baby had been started, and watching his cherished wife grow more feverish and transparent as her burden increased had given him no peace. The labor was terrible. She cried out again and again as the force of destiny worked through her exhausted muscles. Clenching and loosening the womb expelled its contents and Persephone, the vessel, came within a hair's breadth of becoming simple mulch for the next crop. Max held her, and roused her, and required her attention to be fixed on the fatiguing task of going on, and she obeyed. *That dear voice*. Very weak, hardly there, she welcomed her large pink infant boy, Thomas, ginger-topped. She held him to her quivering breast.

She never became completely strong again, though she wrote some of her best remembered verse in this period. She formed a very powerful attachment to young Tom, they played cowboys and indians.

The accident that took her life left Max completely numb.

Great Great Grandmother Persephone Kahn was killed, along with fifty-nine miners, in an explosion in the Red Canyon Coal Mine, Red Canyon, Wyoming, on March 20th, 1895, her twenty-sixth birthday. She had gone down the mine on an investigative tour, a little panicky because of her sometimes (mild) claustrophobia, but fortified in her sense that a writer must explore and sample the textures of the world around herself.

As a consumptive her education had been sporadic and irregular, she read hugely whilst confined to bed in the alpine sanatorium, she became imperfectly socialized and a poet. When she met Maximus she knew very little of men and was gratified when he made love to her, and having struck what seemed a reasonable bargain, she agreed to marry him.

Beautiful strawberry-haired Tommy became his Mother's chief delight. She adored him utterly, she worried over his broken sleeping patterns. They traveled for her health to the dry air of The South West, and while convalescent in Wyoming she wrote that of her poems which is most usually anthologized:

> Breathing is a kind of burning.
> Panting combustible in two balloons
> the oxygen sizzles past the cell's membrane
> and into History.

> Around the bonfire of summer grasses
> *you cough too much. Your color is too high.*

Here rest, paddle in your bed.
We swim through fuel.
We wake crossing the wake,
and at the wake the rosy citizens
go bottoms up and toast the planet's turning.
Demeter whiffles through the undergrowth;
breathing is a kind of burning.

Coal was at the base of the new industrial order, and coal she would see. She saw how hard the labor was, it was not romantic, and she would not write about it romantically. When her eyes stung with tears to see the tense grimy faces of the 11-year-old boys already working down the mine she disciplined herself to look more carefully and made notes in her book and more in her head. By way of a little respite, she turned and made much of the tell-tale canary who sang into the bleakness at the head of the shaft. And then later, it was simultaneously the canary and Persephone's half-perished lungs which first registered distress as the mixture of gases in the tight space altered, the bird made little choking sounds, and Persephone found herself coughing uncontrollably, spitting blood. And then the small yellow creature squeaked and fell and fluttered and was still, and Persephone was gagging and coughing and the realization of what was happening came to her just before the event itself, as the gases exploded and they were all blown to kingdom come.

And some time later, Maximus was traveling with a special shipment of the Indestructibles, designed and executed for the crowned heads of Europe. On July 4th, 1898, they had just put out from Nova Scotia aboard the French *La Bourgogne*, and the night was heavy with fog and a strange, slick sea. The dense white screen filtered and diffused the sounds of the ship and the sea birds off Sable Island. So muted was the bell of the British *Cromartyshire* by the treacherous drizzle that the sound did not reach them until too late. *Too late, too late,* and as the ships moved irresistibly toward each other, the white fog opened for an instant, and Max and little Tom caught a flicker of the group of people gathered on the deck opposite. Both sets of passengers were quiet in their panic. White-faced, open-mouthed, there passed between them a glance of desperate companionship as they glided forward to annihilate each other. *Slap slap slap* went the waves against the two hulls, *mew* chorused the sea birds; the collision, the impact, blackness. The boy was saved.

At the bottom of the sea there lay the bodies of 560 humans and 237 Indestructables, all with open eyes, surveying the dramas of the coral and jelly fish, counting the bottoms of ships. The portraits lasted longer.

5.14

Little is known about Great Great Grandfather Hunning Wang except that he worked as a merchant banker at various outposts in Asia, and he married Great Great Grandmother Louisa Domenica Plenciz, who was his "mail order bride." They had one son, Hua Wang, in 1886. After making an heroic rescue of thirty-eight people, Hunning perished in the great flood of the Yellow River in Honan, China in 1887 when more than 900,000 died.

5.13

On the 8th of May, 1902, Great Great Grandmother Louisa Domenica Plenciz made loud and bitter protest as the roaring lava compacted her stucco. She thanked God that at least young Hua was away from St. Pierre, attending an ur-est self-improvement course on the other side of Martinique.

Louisa had never lacked courage. As a postal bride she had chosen a man on the basis of three letters and a dim daguerreotype. She knew nothing of his antecedents save that they were Mandarin Chinese, she knew nothing of his prospects except the reference to banking work for Australian First Federated on assignment in the Far East. To join him, she had turned her back on the dry heat and the shimmering blue substanceless pictures which hung in the New Mexican air of her impoverished childhood.

He had been a peculiar man and a difficult husband. She

learned that he needed to give pain and receive pain in order to become sexually aroused. *It is as great a pity to see a woman crying as a goose going without shoes* this was Hunning's favorite saying. There was a family history of mental instability.

Now in the streets there was the sound of shouting, and of things breaking. The *nuee ardente* would finish off the 30,000 population of the city within the hour. Louisa runs down into the courtyard and sets free the parrots and macaws, throwing open the doors of their rococo cages and then persuading them with sunflower seeds out onto her arm and then up into the reddening sky. And she stands shouting up after them, their dazzle pinks and greens creaking initially at the unaccustomed stretch. They hesitate, flapping from the next door banana tree. They cock their heads and look back anxiously at their only known, dear home. They call out *Come to Mama! Pretty bird! Thy kingdom come, squawk, will be done. Goodnight!*

She hurled cups and oranges, stones, crying out, *Go on, fly!* They swirled again, *in Heaven!, squawk!*, describing arabesques against the glowing, upper air, they flew.

5.12

Great Great Grandfather Felix LeFauvre had been obsessed with fossils since boyhood. He climbed the soft cliffs of Southwestern England digging out the ancient life forms that were so oddly fixed between animal and mineral. According to a family tradition, he trained for the Church. He looked the part, he was tall and stooped with an ascetic's boney prominences and hollows, eel-skinned, pale blue eyes.

Felix officiated at the weddings and funerals, he visited the sick and comforted the bereaved, he attempted to sort out the quarrels that arose within the parish, he christened the infants, and, his diligent attention to all these tasks withal, he remained a gaunt and abstracted figure with the aspect of a giraffe looking over and past the habitats of other animals.

He married Maria Kelly of his parish, and they were soon blessed with the birth of a baby girl, baptised Mercy. Maria worshipped her kindly but absentminded husband. She grew used to his strange ways, his spending hours along laying out his stones and books in his study; she often heard him laughing to himself.

Felix was attending the new opera Les Fossils at Le Diable, on the 25th day of May 1887 at the Paris Opera, and during Old Nick's final address to the audience the theater seemed to ignite spontaneously. Sparks festooned the already heavily decorated surface, they whored rapidly with each other and produced, Lord! what offspring, what quick generations of combustion. The flames reached the orchestra, and quickly critiqued the new scores and sent their embarrassed blackened bars up through the brand new holes in the gilt ceiling. When they reached the instruments they caused each one to be played in a special way, expressing the fact of the absolute transfiguration being brought about. The trumpet blew such a note as could only be produced from melting brass. The cello sounded as it imploded, so beautifully!; and a final note was wrought from each of the singers, and even from the members of the audience, including those who were not formerly musical. Felix himself reached a high C. Two hundred people perished. And so the chorus swelled and fell away, and left the opera to the excited ensemble of the monstrously incremented families of fire.

5.11

And when Great Great Grandmother Maria Kelly looked in the mirror, by accident, the day after Felix's death, she saw that her hair had gone completely white. It had happened overnight, though she was no so clear about that as her grip on sequential time had departed as suddenly and completely as the pigment from her tresses, and she no longer knew the demarcations of one day from the next. Maria moved through the day and night as though it were simply the curtains changing color, from white to rose, from rose to black; the blue was ultramarine, then cobalt, then cerulean. She took care of the child. Mercy's favorite food was porridge. Once Maria thought to check to see whether her pubic hair had also changed color abruptly and found her mound still bristling with the dense, curled, fox-hued muff as it was before. *Is this wifely part of me not grieving then?* she wondered, not having entirely lost her humor. *Felix would have appreciated the joke.*

The little girl adjusted to her Mama's lack of polite schedule, she would nap and wake to suit herself or the weather, and she spent some nights playing with the moon's image in the window, reflected in the pool, striping the library, throwing a boomerang of silver light onto the kitchen floor; porridge by moonlight.

Maria noticed change at all only in connection with the child. The baby's clothes were tighter than they had been. Pulling a shirt on over Mercy's head became an effort. For a moment the cloth envelope stalled, bulged out over the child's tense, masked face, the top of her head crowning in the neck of the garment so that her Mother was reminded of the moment of physical birth, and then the last effort and Mercy's head was born. She uncrumpled her features and opened her mouth to breathe, and to cry a yelp of complaint at the indignity.

Before Maria could challenge reality sufficiently to go on a shopping expedition to buy her some new clothes, she was required to come out one evening by her worried guardians. *Leave the baby with her Nurse, Maria, and come out with us, you must begin to see people, you'll go mad.* Perhaps they had no assessed the degree of madness which Maria had already achieved. They took her first to a meal, delicate yet nourishing, of fish eggs and mayonnaise, pheasant flesh, asparagas, strawberries and tapioca with champagne. She was made to eat hugely. Then they escorted her, perhaps it was a little tactless, to the theater. It was the 4th of September, 1887, and all of fashionable Exeter turned out.

Maria was made sick by all the unaccustomed food and had to hurry to the ladies' room to vomit into the marble loo. She stood for awhile afterward, looking into the depths of the mirror beyond her white hair and white face, and regaining the vertigo potential of ticking time, of the privileged state of the future and the diminishment of the past which was where Felix swam. It became unbearable. She put the tip of her cigarette to the orange velvet curtain which masked the window of the ladies' lavatory from prying eyes, 400 fellow-members of the audience saw their destiny coming toward them as a wall of yellow flame, and she died hoping someone would remember to buy some clothes to fit baby Mercy. *Her pretty nose will flatten in those tight, wee things,* was her last thought, before she reached out for Felix.

5.10/9

As an infant of three weeks Great Great Grandfather Capability Bidwell had been placed on the doorstep of a foundling home in Aberdeen, wrapped in a piece of dirty tartan. Attached to this bundle was a note in an uneducated hand which read, *Take care of the bairn, for the love of God. His parents were decent folk.*

Such a beautiful child! His great, dark, fringed eyes were full of expression, his mop of yellow curls invited the hand, and his brow was high and well-shaped. He was adopted into a well-to-do English family, and he delighted his parents with his air of prodigious knowledge and unnatural accomplishment which marked him out as one of Nature's superiors.

It was one of the little fables of late capitalism which brought him to turn his considerable talents to business, he operated upon whole economies of South America to the profit of many but the good of no one. It was another scene in the book *Strange Tales But True,* which raised the curtain on the soiree in Lima at which Capability was treated to a tableau vivante employing sixteen adults and eight children and signifying Fertile Farming and the Nitrogen Cycle, with the sephiroth of the kabbala as an under text. He fell under the spell of the vivid buxom Goddess who symbolized evaporation. He demanded to be introduced and found himself shaking hands with Olga Janovitch who was visiting from San Francisco. She had little in the way of small talk. *I paint pictures,* she told him.

She treated his courtship with a carelessness for which nothing had prepared him. When working on a painting, his messages went unread and unanswered. He would call and find her smudged with brilliant color, exhausted and stimulated from lack of sleeping, talking to him rapid and staccato about the painting or the union movement and the price of wheat, falling off suddenly halfway through a sentence to stare blank-eyed into the middle distance where the visual field had taken on the texture of Belgian linen. She would pace up and down for awhile, rubbing her hair, daubing him with the bright marks too as she touched his arm to make a point, pink, and hugged him briefly and absentmindedly, endowing him with blue, burnt sienna, lamp-black about the neck. She sent him, decorated, blinking, into the outside world again while she smoked black paste in her clay pipe, poured out fresh linseed oil and turpentine, and went on working. She liked his big nose. She was double jointed, which permitted some amusing sexual postures.

She gave birth to their son, Samuel, in spite of her own wishes.

Capability returned from a trip to Santa Barbara to find that San Francisco had swallowed up his wife and spat out his baby son.

Great Great Grandmother Olga Janovitch drew like an angel. She painted brilliant, radical paintings, unpacking the space in a painted room from the center of the picture outward like a Persian miniature, deep yet flat, several years before Matisse made the art world aware of that strategy as a fresh pictorial possibility. However, in one of the tragedies of the unjust world, Olga was not permitted to enter into the reciprocal *conversation* which is part both of the investigatory and the validation mechanisms of high culture. It is a story too familiar to need telling; as a woman she was consistently overlooked, and she slipped through the meshes. She was bitter.

When she found she was pregnant she made herself so ill with a herbal abortifacient that she nearly died, and lay in bed half-delirious for several weeks. When she began to come to herself again she realized with fury that the little passenger, as she referred to it, was still aboard. It was too late to try again. She gave birth, painfully, to the infant Samuel. It seemed to her he always regarded her with reproach, as though he understood what she had tried to do. She hired a wet nurse, and went back to painting.

When on April 18, 1906, the city began to shake, Olga's studio building folded up around her. Nurse and baby were out for their daily walk, and survived. Olga was trapped for six hours before she succumbed to her injuries and died. She howled over those of her paintings which remained unpainted.

With her death, Capability lost his taste for making money. He planned instead to set up a radical museum of women's art. Having spent some time in Europe preparing this project, he and nervous, finger-nail biting Sam were returning to America to supervise the start of construction. Capability was pleased to book passage on the grand new ship Titanic, pride of the fleet.

The Titanic reproduced in small the layers of the Society which had produced it. At the top the maxi-kapitaliski chew at their great joints of meat and generally enjoy a plentiful variety of sensed pleasures including the large airy spaces of the Louis XVI restaurant, the Parisian Boulevard Cafe, the Jacobean Reception room, the Turkish Bath.

These graceful beings of the upper decks also make much display of willfullness, and they exercise a good deal of care and cunning to keep hold their disproportionate share of the means of organizing things, or power. At the bottom there are many people violently crowded together, supping bad and scanty food, and these folk have a miserable little to say about what happens, or doesn't.

And so this whole unsinkable spectacular craft, lit up like a city, 900 feet long, took to the sea on her maiden voyage, Southampton-New York. Capability and jumpy young Sam were among the meat eaters at the top. They enjoyed four days of parties, games and fine meals. And then, on a night of still sea with no moon, there loomed up out of the darkness one of the rare, dreaded and improbable *black icebergs*, that is, an iceberg so recently upended that its exposed underpart has not yet turned white.

And still the model held true, and when the water filled the unfillable compartments, and the statutory number of lifeboats wasn't enough, the gruel eaters, many of them, were kept back at gun point and locked into their sections, while the meat eaters, most of them, worked their will on the recalcitrant circumstances and survived. The band played *Nearer My God To Thee* as they sank beneath the water, as every school girl knows. Capability handed the blubbering Sam into the arms of the woman to whom he gave his place in the lifeboat, *a sacred trust*. And then with a certain curiosity, looking neither to the right nor to the left, he entered the spangled, tartan waves.

5.8/7

Words won't feed cats. Great Great Grandfather Tonado Gombo learned to put bombs together backward because he was left-handed. Monkey-faced Tonado knew who the enemies were. They were the rich and powerful, and it was Tonado's task, as he understood it, to act upon Society to redistribute both. He gesticulated as he explained anarcho-socialism to Freya, carving the air, and she noticed that he had on his right hand a vestigial sixth digit. He moved crowds to anger and then bullied them into organization.

He was full of wine, his usual authority comical. He mocked himself with her, *the high-born lady with her pet baboon*. And when she drew away from his aroused nakedness he held her and drew her back, protesting, onto the bed. *Women, asses and nuts require strong hands*, he said quoting his Grandfather. *Full bottles and glasses make swearers and asses*, she replied, quoting her grandmother. She pushed him away, she was as strong as he. She pulled on her clothes and pinned up her gray hair around her young face. The next night, as the ivy and yellow roses curled over the wallpaper, cold sober, they consummated their peculiar union.

Freya insisted on playing games of canasta for the first part of the labor. Then, when the pains became more intense, she reluctantly put down the cards, and the baby was born feet first and hollering just a little while later, while Freya's spaniels swarmed around the foot of the bed and howled. When she had finished with suckling the child, and the little lass could eat up her pablum and drink from a cup, Freya packed up her things and took the chattering poppet to live with her father. Great Grandmother Von R went traveling again.

When the train she was aboard on June 14, 1891, collided with another train near Basel, Switzerland, she tried to resist the illusion that the annihilation of consciousness was the main business of this transaction.

And so Tonado looked after the child, Hippolyte, who was a dear little minx, until the year 1898, when he performed his final act of principled destruction, which in the hurly-burly of causality and freewill finished him also. And this took place on February the 15th, when his beautifully detailed sabotage of the Battleship *Maine* caused it to explode (prematurely) into the balmy atmosphere just off Havana. Fragments of persons of all types and political persuasions were raised in a column of bright water high into the humid air, and 260 souls were reported killed, add one more for the surprised Tonado.

5.6/5

When Big John Velasquex heard Great Great Grandmother Patricia Herophilus sing *Vissi d'arte, vissi d'amore* (I lived for art, I lived for love) he came immediately, and permanently, under her spell. She shone like a beacon from the stage. She needed no wig to play Tosca, her black hair was heaped up above her high forehead, and her eyes were huge and bright. This magnificent silver creature filled the entire space of the Opera House with her cascading soprano, and John applauded until his hands were hot and red.

She was raised as a foundling in a large, impoverished family who farmed a small holding on a stony hillside in Greece. Patricia was always bigger and brighter and bolder than her contemporaries, the cuckoo in the nest. She sang so well as a little girl that it moved and stirred all who heard her, and so somehow money was raised and she was trained in the city, and she had risen, with remarkable speed, to international standard.

John Velasquez, rancher, connived a meeting with the diva.

He worked up an acquaintance. He displayed all his lands and his wealth shamelessly, like a prince establishing a bride-price, with great tact he investigated her private library, her passions and turns of mind so that he could strive to meet her there, and converse. He laid a siege.

The beautiful giantess observed his courting dance coolly at first, but as he persisted she found herself amused, and then she became fond of him. He introduced her to more generous physical love, her great shout in orgasm broke mirrors. And then, when she became pregnant, John's insistence that they should marry seemed vaguely reasonable.

When the infant Rachel Velasquez burst into the world much of her Mother's blood immediately followed, and Patricia remained weak and ill for months after the birth. She, who was accustomed to perfect health, had to move carefully and hoard her energy for the brief play sessions with her cherished daughter. The baby flourished, sweet dark-eyed Rachel, and the tatters of the thrilling soprano voice spelt out lullabyes. Finally Patricia was well, though changed, no longer the silver maiden. Having lived the life of a grand rancher's wife for a year or two, she wanted to perform again.

Her first appearance was to be with the San Francisco Opera Company who were presenting Tosca on February 15, 1909, at the Flores theater in Acapulco. Patricia was singing *Chi si duole in terra piu* (Where now have pain and sorrow fled) when the heavy velvet drapes were seen to be smoldering. The crowd began to panic, Patricia too, as she glimpsed and rejected the opportunity for heroic, self-sacrificing action. She wanted to see her baby again, she *would* see her. Patricia felt herself to be stepping on bodies, *Oh Rachel, wait for me*. Only the things that were already burning were visible now, everything else seemed in a preliminary condition. Two hundred fifty-two died that night, and Patricia was clambering to escape when a blazing section of the gilded ceiling came away, falling, the lions and putti glistering and squeaking, and it all roared down upon her beautiful head.

When Big John Velasquez was told of her death he fainted and did not awaken for two days. He clung to the child like a shipwreck.

On August 5, 1915, John had taken his daughter on a birthday picnic, when an enormous wind suddenly blew up. The breeze chased its tail, and in its playfulness it picked up little Rachel, the cake, the dog and the carriage and sent them off on a powerful spiral. It threw Big John to the earth, *smack*. He shouted out to Rachel, but the wind went *kiss kiss* and sucked the sound from his lips. He managed half a prayer before the carriage hurtled back down through the rushing air again, and crashed full on top of him. The child, the cake and the dog continued onward, pell mell, above the bowed masts of the remaining trees.

5.4

Hong Kong was best for tattoos. After the blue and green snake had wound three times around the Oak tree which issued forth with pink cabbage roses, it reared back its head and spat out an elongated mauve heart shape, heavily inscribed. It was at this point that the image, to maintain its vegetable energy, was required to divide again, and Great Great Grandfather Guglielmo Lippershey was deciding between Cerberus in black and red, and more elaborate than the panther on the left knee, or a shift into map form with a diagram of the major confluences of the River Nile.

This was the ship's company's first extended leave since Italy. Now that had been a hell of a time, what he could recall of it. On a major drunk Guggi always lost the middle of the week. For the first two days and nights of a shore leave it was as though he were functioning as part of a mechanism, some kind of complex automation, which was being wound up at the same time that it was being played so that the human figures—leaning, drinking, talking—speeded up, got progressively faster; while simultaneously there seemed to commence a formal extension, a kind of swelling of the volumes of bodies, note the billowing curtains. It was extreme chiaroscuro, and the shadows read as a sign for abrupt laundry chute passages into another zone entirely. The siblings of the heated, tooth bumping intimacy of a few turns of the handle past were now at the other end of the opera glasses and the sound of those tilted, waving mannikins came in whoops and fades. The tilt continued past zero degrees and down through the horizon line as the sailor clutched at the nearest nob, hand, stein or female breast and entered upon the persuasive whirling of the bar room *engloutèe*. At this moment the mechanism is completely torqued, the winding stops and Guglielmo falls out of memory.

It was thus, waking on the next Sunday afternoon that Guglielmo Lippershey had no way to remember the meeting, dancing, and wooing of the foreign nurse. He could not recall her delight at his violently decorated corpus, nor that she had laughed immoderately, nor that the exquisite illustration on his most private parts—which he had achieved at the cost of so much pain—had repaid him by her reading of the lines. *Ach, too much pleasure!* he cried out. He could not contain it. He had no mental polaroid of the knife-sharp profile rearing up against a window, *whinnying*, the auroras sparking around the perimeter of her silhouette. So, *a fortiori*, he had no knowledge at all of the act by which he had fathered a son.

But who knows the workings of the mind? As he lay under the needle, wincing at the exact location of the source of the Nile, some bit of that memory became accessible (this was shortly before the end): that nurse, those hours in the warm white room with the fan droning and ruffling the mosquito netting; and the sensation of her redrawing all his pictures. Her fingers tracked the purple gorilla opening the walls of his chest to reveal a scrolled heart *Mother, forever! Liberty, forever!* She made a special fuss of the border country between the birthmark and the tattoo. The nurse's sharp-nosed, great-eyed face dipping and gliding, he lumbered after her; she speculated with the budding of the great calyx of his most rare orchid, blooming!

The wall calendar read September 19, 1906. The needle doctor had only just completed the lower Kingdom and begun on the egg starting to crack in the Dodo's nest, when quite suddenly the storm knocked first and entered into all the buildings and public areas, and Hong Kong's entire Port ceased to have the ordinary relationship of shore boundary to water's edge. People perished, many in terror and agony, as the earth's stew was violently salted. The two elements were entirely mixed. *I shall certainly make my escape* was Guggi's final thought, as he reached out in the familiar way for the knob; and then he was whirling through the room, reversed. And the violet gorilla, quite unable to draw the blinds, is tête-à-tête with a monk fish, they are embracing sincerely.

5.3

Sharp-featured blonde Great Great Grandmother Rosabelle Atkinson-Smith was raised as the supposed daughter of fundamentalist missionaries living in Rwanda. They insisted on much prayer and despised as fallen not only their own human bodies but even animal bodies, for they forced a young gorilla, whom they kept as a kind of *pet,* to wear a long, loose dress of flowered green calico when at table.

As Rosy reached puberty, her parents grew more and more concerned about the issue of her purity. They dressed her as though she were a much younger child, and kept her well out of the way of any boys or men. They drilled her as to the sinfulness of her own nature, and the great care she would have to take to avoid damnation. They mortified her flesh with fasting and cold. When Rosabelle's father began to whip her each afternoon, with a kind of exultation in his face, she made her decision. She put sleeping powders in their tisane one evening, and sneaked out of the house and off the island. She sold some of the household items she had taken with her, and bought passage to Milan. She arrived on the doorstep of a wealthy and very surprised cousin who took her in.

She trains as a nurse. She is encouraged by the prevailing rational attitude and a very affectionate throat specialist to look at her own body unclothed for the first time. She sees a shucked gorilla in the mirror. One night at a celebration she meets a very drunk and radiantly beautiful young sailor, he is covered with exquisite tattoos. *Show me the rest of your pictures.* Hearing the screams of her mother and her father ringing in her ears, Rosy tumbles and rolls all one night with the lovely illustrated boy.

When she found she was pregnant by the tattooed sailor she was delighted. She traveled to a small town in the South of Italy where she lived quietly until the baby's birth. She had invented a recent widowhood to satisfy the curiosity of her neighbors. She was in correspondence by this time with Maria Montessori, and she planned out a whole radical curriculum. Rosabelle had a clear enough sense of the pathology of the prevailing social order to decide in favor of maximum disjunction with respect to the education of her child, her love child, the baby that she secretly imagined would be born tattooed.

She had her baby scientifically and with effort. *What a glorious child*. She kept him always by her. He had his father's birthmark, the ruby star just below the navel. She would lean over him while he slept in her arms and drink in the exhalation of his milky breath. She wrote to Maria, *1908 is the beginning of a new era full of light, and my beautiful little Papago is its first citizen*. And Papago gazed back at her with complete attention. He modeled her flesh and drank from her abundance. He was later than most in sorting out his boundaries from his Mama's. *I love you Papago*.

When he was nineteen months old, pushing his new 4-wheel Christmas camel along the grassy path in their grand garden, his Mother looking on, smiling at his marching steps, suddenly there were three percussive bangs and the whole earth shook and everything that was standing fell down. All over Southern Italy and Sicily a terrible sorting went on, a shaking and settling of the landscape and inhabitants that left 75,000 of the people dead and much of the physical stuff also cast down to its point of lowest kinetic energy. Papago was left unscratched, hiccoughing, bewildered in the sun and dust. Rosabelle was compressed beneath a heap of neo-Palladian alabaster. No regrets.

5.2/1

Great Great Grandfather Mordecai Isaacs could sell refrigerators to the Eskimaux. In fact, he was engaged on just such a mission when he traveled to Alaska in 1887 and convinced the elders of the *Lugluk* tribe. He demonstrated that the Acme Grand Reflexerating Chiller, an early mechanical refrigerator of his own invention, would keep their salmon fresh in the summer months during the heavy harvest, and give them time to smoke it, dry it or salt it. The early negotiating sessions went well. The *Lugluk* were impressed by the size of the machine, and by the loud humming noise that it made. Members of the tribe stroked and admired the heavily embossed pictorial nickle-plated surface of the great box. The situation thereon depicted was that of recently manumitted slaves, dancing, with geese and bears, under a baroquely conceived (in terms of the gathering in and release of space) display of the *aurora borealis*. The Eskimaux did not recognize an immediate fraternity with the dancing Negroes, but could definitely identify the northern lights, which they appreciated and took as a compliment to themselves. They poked with appreciation at the frozen chunks of fish which stared back at them with infinite patience from the white enamel caverns of the Chiller's interior.

And then having made his sale, in the wait between ships, Mordecai became fascinated by the extreme human solution exemplified by the Eskimaux manner of living. He was greedy for the detail of their anthropology. He feasted with them on fish and whale flesh and seal meat, he smacked his lips, *with a sauce like this a man might eat his own father*, and he belched with a powerful nostalgia. He learned the culture's left-hand/right-hand metaphysics: that the uncle of every *angik-nuk* woman must refrain from eating for three days and three nights and go alone to the sacred place by the cone of blue ice; that certain parts of the slaughtered animal must be set aside; that a particular type of prayer, practiced with a sharp intake of breath, should mark the beginning of every shift of direction. *This is how things began. This is the breast of Mother Earth. In this way do we know that these things are proper, or hdnn-ha, and that these things are forbidden, quok-luk*. He took instruction in the regulations of the ancestor-duties. He learned the thirty words for snow.

Mordecai was thick-bodied, shortish, with a curling beard that sprang with energy from his chin and cheeks, and a loud charming, bullying manner. He viewed with curiosity the separate "woman's culture" within the tribe, which was ancient and full of craft. He sensed that from this perspective, the men were seen as powerful clowns.

He was wanting a woman. His eyes followed the strong, giggling maidens as they worked about the camp, and he began to look out for the one who was a little taller than the others and who smiled more directly into his eyes, her name he discovered was Judith Oss. He knew enough of their customs to risk asking for an introduction, and she soon gave him the clear invitation to "night visit" for which he had been hoping.

She borrowed her Aunty's cabin. The heat of the fire and the strength of the *douk* (a 120-proof clear schnapps) rendered the scene very vivid and also patchy, in the sense of intermittent. Mordecai found himself staring into the girl's clear black eyes for moments at a time; they signaled surface/depth, surface/depth alternately, and suggested a world so detailed and complete that he had only suspected its existence heretofore. He felt himself to be both sinking and swimming in the hot, vivid space, and Judith babbled to him and the undecoded words soothed him. Next he would wake with a jerk to discover that he had been asleep, sitting up, for an instant or an hour he had no way of knowing as she continued on her round of activities, between the steaming kettle and the log pile and the fire and the sleeping dogs. Finally, as the room began to spin again, she came to lie down beside him. She took his hand and admired his vestigial sixth finger. He groped amongst the layers of furs, they seemed to roll for hours on the blanket by the fire, until he found, with a shock of sudden delight, human skin!

Because she had been adopted into this community she was more watchful. She was not quite a part of the village's many headed intelligence, and she noticed how the *rathacuk*, coming in from the South in powerful boats, and seeming at first to bring promise of many marvelous things, left the people disturbed. A line was drawn then between the people and their ancestors. Judith was one of the first to feel the ice begin to creak.

When Mordecai came to the village he was looking to make a deal, like the others, but Judith could feel his eyes on her in a different way, in a way that indicated desire. She was quite amused by his loud voice and his long nose and the sense he had of having come from the far parts of the big world, and as there was no prohibition against the simple satisfaction of simple desires, she took him into her Aunty's (but not her real Aunty's) cabin, and there she welcomed him in the light of the oil stove. He toasted her, *The grace of never having set teeth in Eve's apple.*

The smell of paraffin hit their noses. How sweet, how entire, an ancient seamlessness. . . . And so quite contrary to his plans and better judgment, Mordecai fell to adoring her. He would serve up the world if she would be served. This was not her real Aunty, she would come. And so Judith Oss accompanied Mordecai Isaacs out into the large world, and they were married by the ship's long-faced disapproving Captain. And with each port they visited on the long journey back the newlyweds investigated the architecture, the language, the food and the commerce. Judith began to take the measure of the world she had opted for. She found it fascinating but confusing, *where were the rules for decorum?* Some nights, after her husband had rolled off of her and was snoring, she would get up and sort through her small satchel of possessions from the village, little animals carved from horn and bone, pouches made of seal skin, dice. Weeping was *quok-luk.*

By the time they reached London she was bellying out with her pregnancy, and Mordecai was newly spurred on in his practical inventions for baby tending. She was an outsider and expected to be treated as such. *What she could not understand was how these people related to one another, for it seemed cold and empty and full of show.*

She made up her mind to travel back to the tribe with their baby daughter Venus, for a visit. Mordecai would remain behind to advance the business. She hired passage on the good ship Utopia, she and Mordecai agreed that it was a happy name for a ship, promising as it did a vision of a rectified world. *They would help build it!* The ship foundered, just off Gibraltar, wrecked and was sunk within the sight of a crowd of Barbary apes who massed on the shore, gibbering and shouting at the spectacle. The drowning citizens called out, screamed and shouted, in this case vainly, for help. And then, as that hope dropped away, they called for their mothers and their deities. And so Judith died on March 17, 1891, along with 574 other souls. Baby Venus was rescued from the waves.

Venus was a handsome child, earnest and graceful with deep black hair and brows, and strongly marked features. Mordecai found her to be a reserved little girl, opaque and slightly exotic, like her mother. He died whilst road running a sales campaign for bottled water in Johnstown, Pennsylvania (where the standard joke went *Run for your life the dam's going;* this was always greeted with appreciative guffaws). And on May 31, 1889, the dam broke. A sheer force of water forty feet high hurled itself down the valley with pent up fury, carrying with it a randomized inventory of solid items, trees and houses, etc. Mordecai was drinking bourbon with a prospective client at tea time when the disaster struck. Still holding his heavily diluted cocktail at the end, he toasted fate and circumstance. Venus was sent to London to live with relatives.

4.8/7

Red-headed, color-blind Great Grandfather Thomas Adpo was developing his Oedipus Complex just prior to the period when Freud was organizing his theory of same. He would stand puzzled at the doorway of the great bedroom of the Montana Ranchero and listen to the hoots and cries emitted from the heaving bedclothes. He would pad silently across the lunar floorboards to observe the great, rocking couple. He coughed a false cough and they became aware of him and pulled away from each other. Father loomed plum-colored and angry, glaring at young Tom out of his enormous face, and beautiful Mama was pulling at her shift, her thin shoulders were shaking, hacking, coughing a real cough.

During his second term of psychoanalysis Thomas excavated this primal scene and began to investigate the notion that his other identity, Buck Jones the Hollywood Cowboy, who was increasingly "in the driver's seat," was the fruit of some neurotic connection with the mythic West of his early childhood. As Thomas lost the opportunity to resolve the neurosis, due to the untimely death of both his Mother and Father, he remained stuck. His sexual attraction to his (introjected) Mama generated sexual fears and avoidances, fear of castration, rivalry with his (introjected) Father. These fears were mediated by unconscious fantasies. All this he learned while supine on a succession of analysts' couches, but though he began to understand the mechanism, he still failed to thrust a finger (or some other member) into the works and stop it ticking.

After his Father's death Thomas was raised by an intellectual Jewish family in Vienna and later in New York. He was gifted in mathematics and science, and he took a degree in atomic physics and was recruited by the United States Government to work at the laboratory in Los Alamos. To his surprise this removal to the West provided him with an ongoing parade of madelaines—the dust, the perfume of the sage brush, the particular orange and pink of the sun's daily death, and Thomas took extended leave from his obsessive colleagues who were "tampering with the Universe's essential building blocks." Thomas, or "Buck," learned to play a Spanish guitar in Santa Fe, and he began to sing the local cowboy songs, sometimes with an undertext. He constructed a singing cowboy's gestalt in which the loved and vanished landscape became one with the adored and relinquished body of the primary female.

At about this time he met and married Mercy LeFaure and they had one child, Joseph. Not much is known about their life together.

Great Grandmother Mercy LeFaure was a great beauty, though her nose was perhaps a shade too retrouse. She suffered terribly from tooth trouble. Her marriage to Buck Jones, the Hollywood Cowboy, had lifted her out of penury, and even now she was returning from her tour of the Continent to spend some time with Buck and their young son, Joseph, and to visit her American dentist Dr. Weiss. May 6, 1937, the voyage on the airship Hindenburg had been uneventful, and Mercy, with one greatly swollen cheek, was looking forward to her arrival and relief via Dr. Weiss's capable scrubbed pink fingers. As the ship hovered over the landing field at Lakehurst, New Jersey, Mercy thought she could make out her husband in his stage stetson, holding the child and waving. *How little Joe had grown!* She waved, enthusiastically. It was her last act.

Buck had never worked the Cocoanut Grove before, and had been pleased to be booked into what had become one of Boston's most glittering night spots. It was Saturday, the 28th of November 1942, and the crowd was unusually lively, made up of service personnel, football fans and locals. The floorshow in the upstairs restaurant was stimulating to many of its drunken observers, featuring the chorus line of sixteen hand-picked shapely local beauties known as the Codfish. Downstairs in the Melody Lounge the audience were thoroughly transported by the exotic silk draperies and papier-mâché palm trees, and by Buck's superb delivery of *The Red Man's Lament*.

With the guitar's sweet plink a plink, much amplified, the evening surged along. They toasted all their friends and were coming round to honoring their rivals. War time, and this crush of bodies and their compounded heat were in the service of Dionysus, and perhaps also his darker cousin Ares. *You have to drink hard to really enjoy a war*, Buck whispered to his special friend Andrea. She answered with her eyelashes and bent to sup greedily from her cocktail. She made a rude, erotic gesture toward the flock of suspended flamingos, *Ooh la la!*

Then there was a spurt of pink flame from a nearby palm tree, the whole gaudy world was tinder, and in seconds there was fire everywhere. Lacquer, paper and silk ignited simultaneously and filled the Melody Lounge with asphixiating smoke. The club's gangster owner Barney Welansky had blocked off all emergency exits in constructing his tropical fantasy, and the revelers were immersed in the black, choking clouds. Alas, poor humanity desperately flailing to get out, stampeded. Buck found himself packed skin to skin with anonymous others on all sides. He felt the repeated crashing of shattered crockery and the desperate screams of his fellows pluck like premature harpists along the discs of his spine. He choked. A tongue of heat seared along the side of his head, and he was choking, with the tears leaping from his eyes. One eye stayed closed. The door was blocked. The worst had happened, each person was quite mad to exit, and ignored the fact of the other persons. Four hundred and thirty-three people were in the act of dying.

Buck was making no forward progress. *Mama, Mama* he cried, as the ceiling strut fell and performed that operation he most feared. He was released. *Oh my darling Mama* he sobbed, he crooned, as the flames flickered over him with their unappeasable appetite, and he nourished them.

4.6/5

The double shock of the baby Samuel's extraordinary rescue from the San Francisco conflagration, and the boy Samuel's miraculous escape from the wreck of the Titanic left him, pubescent, gravely etched. Those who were in charge of him noticed that he offered an intimacy to animals that he withheld from people. When he reached 15 they arranged for him to have a job in the local zoo slopping out the small mammals.

Bib-nosed quadroon Great Grandfather Samuel Bidwell, swart and melancholy of face, came to understand the primates, and more particularly the Orangutans, better than any other living human. Looking into their brown eyes he saw an intelligent sadness and a gentleness that moved him greatly. It seemed to him that, contrasted with the human bombast, cupidity, greed and anxiety which he observed on every hand, these old men *(sic)* of the forest were full of grace. His success in dealing with these animals, whom many keepers and scientists found eccentric and difficult, was noticed. He soon became Chief Keeper, and he traveled and worked with a number of zoos, coming to know many of the primates; forming profound and sad friendships with the individual Orangs, he visited them as though calling on old friends who were confined to hospice or penitentiary.

He joined the Masons. He wore one trouser leg slightly rolled and gave the special hand-shake. He married the musician Hippolyte Gombo, and she was now expecting their first child.

Great Grandmother Hippolyte Gombo was a sassy and difficult woman. Raised in her early years by her radical Daddy, she was brought up in a series of middle class homes whose cozy aesthetics would not mix with the Kisimites impassioned evolutionary socialism. She played the Irish harp, with reverse fingerings.

She was recruited to membership in a group of Anarchist Irish Nationalist Occultizers, who were working to establish a new, total and undefiled body of the mystical Irish nation by a variety of practical means, both violent and magical. When after a concert Samuel Bidwell was introduced to her in the Green Room of a theater in Damascus, she was already a stunning and accomplished young woman, with a stripe of bright silver in her black hair.

They were married. Samuel was still in Borneo and Hippolyte, 7 months pregnant, was resting with AINO comrades in Cleveland, Ohio, when they received news that an entire chapter of the Bolshevik co-utopianists had been purged in Novosibirsk. This terrible news, and its implications, caused Hippolyte to go into premature labor, and she was taken to the hospital. There she spent the next thirty-two hours in the labor ward. She was terrified and in agony, the baby's descent was blocked, and the pain of each contraction was very terrible. So she bucked and screamed upon the bed *The Red Flag, the Wearin' of the Green, and Red Men of the Forest, Aiyiiiiii!* Until finally the doctors despaired of any natural outcome and etherized her, strapped her down, sliced her open and delivered her of a tiny, weak but living female infant, Alice.

The babe was wrapped and bundled off to the nursery, and beautiful Hippolyte was stitched up and left to waken from the anesthetic, which she never did, as just at this moment poisonous fumes were rising from a chemical fire in the hospital basement which in the end destroyed the building and dispatched 125 souls. There was some talk of terrorist and counter-terrorist sabotage. The baby was evacuated in time, and on Samuel's return he placed the box with the charred fragments of his wife's body in a hole, privately dug, in a woods.

On October 4, 1930, Samuel boarded the great new airship the R101, the Socialist Airship as it was known. The vessel had been rushed to be ready for the flight to Ismailia, and on to India, where that damned little Ghandi was fomenting trouble, there was even talk of revolution. The R101 was to be a demonstration of imperial solidarity.

Although some protested that the ship was not yet technically ready, Minister for Air, Lord Thomson, insisted the flight was
to go ahead on schedule. The passengers arrived loaded with
baggage, some with twenty cases for an individual, as in the
gracious days of world travel. It was a beautiful ship, and Samuel
walked along its promenade of potted palms and inspected its
fire-proof smoking lounge and its gold and white staterooms with
approval. He might as well try to enjoy himself. He was going to
bring back three adult Orangs from his trip, and the prospect
excited him. His heart beat like a lover's. Ever since Hippolyte's
death only the Orangs had existed for him; he could not summon
up much interest in baby Alice, so much less able than a primate
of similar age.

When the great ship foundered in the air early the next
morning over Northern France, and then fell blazing into a
beetroot field, only a French poacher saw the superstructure
buckle and yaw, and heard the screams of the desperate passengers like whistles at first coming from so high up, but soon, much
too soon, the cries were much nearer, and the birds only just had
time to answer. Samuel had a vision of apes of flame moving in to
release him, not just Orangs, but chimpanzees and gorillas, lifting
him up and into the sky.

4.4/3

And so the petted and adored little Rachel Velasquez was
swooped up in her polka dot organdy dress and carried for a great
distance, and almost killed a thousand times, and spared by fate
or physics, Stripped naked, she lost her silver spoon, she landed
in the coleslaw at the Okeechobee Firemen's Picnic, *num num,
who is this naked, crying baby?*

And playing picnic with her family of dolls on the screen
porch of the house of her poor Irish Catholic foster parents, Great
Grandmother Rachel Velasquez served up dishes of dandelion
petals and mud. She sang parts of imperfectly remembered
lullabyes. Housekeeping on the tilted porch attached to the leaky
house, nibbling bits from her dolls' meals, the quick, dark, pretty
child ingested a certain quantity of lead in the peeling paint, and,

over a time, the edge of her mental acuity blunted, she had little spells of fretfulness, the bright eyes hooded.

Now that Rachel had got to be such a big girl, she was having trouble choosing between going to Hollywood to become a star, or becoming a nun. She talked earnestly about joining a closed order with Sisters Charity and Mustard Seed. She spent long days on the beach staring out at the sea, arranging her shells for sale to the tourists. And along comes handsome Mr. Wang in his blue suit. *Let me tell you about Hollywood, maybe I can get you a job*. She blushed, so pretty, and he teased her. *She sells sea shells sitting by the sea shore*, kissing the lisping lips which tangled with the tongue twister, and then their tongues tangled together. Her wet mouth was guileless and she was shuddering with an excitement she did not understand.

Great Grandpa Hua Wang sold insurance. He was good at his job, being particularly sensitive to the soft spots in the sales resistance of his prospective customers, a nod toward the house or factory which his words could paint with flames, a gesture to indicate the extreme vulnerability of the little family group. Hua would shepherd his terrified customers through these visions of possible disasters, and somehow manage to convey to them the sense that the purchase of a policy would insure them, not so as to pay them if these tragedies occurred, but magically, so as to prevent them ever from happening. He had internalized the tables of statistics as to fires, burglaries, floods, accident, acts of God, and he brought them forth not as dry numbers, but as grotesque items of future suffering.

He was quite a ladies man, and how the ladies did like his heavy, blue black hair and quick hands, his cleft chin and smooth body, his style of knowing more about them than they knew themselves, his air of worldly wisdom.

Hua Wang always declared himself to be a man who lived his life according to the dictates and principles of Nature. And when the sky darkened to purple and the wind came up it was natural for him and Rachel to repair to the lifeguard's hut, and it was natural, as there was only the cot to sit on, for them to sit upon it. And this continued with Hua stroking the pretty child who came to nudge hungrily for more kisses, and surely the stripping off of his clothes and hers could be accounted a great advance for Nature. As for the final act, the moisture, the piercing, the penetration, the blood, the rhythms, the stroking, the moving, the breathing, the sighing, the groaning (while the storm continued to voice with wind and water outside their window), the groaning and the quickening, the pulsing, the arching, the pressing, the calling out; surely here was the very motive part and central seed of Nature, and who would say it nay?

The storm passed. Hua awoke from his deep, sweet, sweaty dream to find the beautiful, disheveled child pressed up against his chest on the army cot. He woke her and told her to dress, turning away from her attempts to caress him. He bundled her outside and across the quay and back to the town. *Goodbye, goodbye* he muttered to Rachel, who was not so bright but very good hearted, and he put a dollar in her hand, which puzzled her. Something had gone wrong with his practical philosophy, and he felt momentarily disturbed, but unbeknownst to him, the most natural consequence of events for the entire species had been well advanced.

Hua Wang died on September 13, 1922, in a gigantic fire in Smyrna, Asia Minor, in which the city was almost completely destroyed, hundreds died, and there was $100 million damage. Much heaped up particularity was destroyed. So many children wandered through the ruins miserable and amazed, they could not find their homes. Every address had become one address. It was a taxing time for the insurance companies. He died never knowing that he was a father.

Rachel was loudly condemned by most of her community when she swelled out and gave birth to a little baby girl. The nuns helped her. She played with baby Sonia, and cared for her, and dreamed about Hollywood and handsome, black-haired men.

On the 7th of September, 1928, Rachel was walking with her little Sonia along the banks of a roiling, troubled Lake Okeechobee. It had been storming dogs and cats and rats for two days, and they were taking advantage of the break in the weather to rush out and buy some lime sherbet, when a great gust came along and rolled that lake right out of its bed and down along the pier, and Rachel was grabbed up and washed out into the water, like a flower, with her red petals outspread, calling *help, help, dear Jesus, dear Virgin Mary.* Along with Rachel, 3 people ceased to exist *in this mode.* And then she entered another formation, and floated above her own drowning body, and fell through a tunnel, on and on, with everybody hugely buzzing, and then the white light, and the radiant sky of near attainment. *Mama! Papa!*

As a testimony to the irregular efficacy of prayer, though Rachel was lost, little Sonia was saved.

4.2

When the earthquake that had taken his worshipped mother from him finally subsided, and the ground had become still again, and the few remaining trees had stopped their swaying and their creaking, little Papago Lippershey, Great Grandfather Papago, was wandering grieving and stunned through the ruined wilderness. And then, by one of those odd coils of fate, he came upon a descendant of the noble wolf who mothered Romulus and Remus so many generations ago. This wolf had lost her cubs in the quake, and her tits were heavy and aching with milk. Papago was desperately hungry, and skilled at nursing, and while the wolf bitch was sizing up this odd human fragment and deciding whether to eat him up or pass him by, Papago stroked her, like the pet dog, and touched her, and somehow, strangely, with what mythic stories coursing through them both, he began to suck, and the wolf let down her fevered, aching breasts, and Papago swallowed quantity on quantity of the hot milk.

He had a few memories of his human mother, in one of these internal lantern slides he was a baby lying naked and at ease on a blanket spread on the grass, the warm sun washing over them, and his mother was rubbing his limbs with sweet-smelling oil. In another she was bathing him, the water was warm and she held him tightly so that he would not slip, soap got in his eyes. He could remember his wolf mother more clearly. She helped him to survive, but there was much roughness and pain in that life. Papago learned to hunt, clumsily, and sometimes he would succeed in running an old rabbit or gopher to ground, catching at it with his hands (his one advantage) and sinking his teeth deep into the hot salty flesh. He learned, also, to read scents, and to sing with the other wolves in a moon-tipsy circle. But he was never a very accomplished wolf, and the others in the pack teased and abused him somewhat. He was at the very bottom of the social order. And then he could remember being hungry, pursued by the hunters and the farmers, baited, trapped, mocked and whipped. He remembered the terrible net, and being taken to the doctors where the medicine odors cut his nostrils.

And then years of dreary rooms, being handled and examined by smelly strangers. Sometimes he would snap out, when he was particularly bored and tired, but usually he would just turn away.

And now they put him on show in the vast exhibition hall of the Crystal Palace, glass within glass, here he was in an odd transparent cage lavishly fitted out like a fancy parlor, Maple's best suite. He didn't so much mind the staring faces; it was not as bad as the scientific people always handling him, and prodding him, and trying to get him to utter.

And so he came face to face with Great Grandmother Venus Isaacs, a well-brought up young lady, darkly beautiful, who was visiting the great exhibition hall this bright winter afternoon, November 30th, 1936, walking through with two girl friends, examining the modern and antique furniture, semi-precious stones, demonstrations of the processing of rubber; surgical tools, African instruments, methods of irrigation, cookery demonstrations, cubism, new world monkeys. Everything was interesting and casual, when suddenly she was stopped short by the intensity of gaze and aspect of the Wolf Man on show. The notice on his cage announced that he had been raised by wolves in Southern Italy and had never been known to speak a word of human language. She saw that he was enclosed in a cage which was fitted out in every detail like a luxurious sitting room, and he moved about restlessly, sitting on the William Morris' flowered-print

Chesterfield, getting up, moving over to the Bluthner boudoir grand piano where he pawed at the keys playing a little in a minor signature, then he climbed up on top of the instrument, scratched himself, and leaped again onto the sideboard. He clambered down and lapped clumsily at a glass of water then pushed some purple grapes into his mouth. There was a little annex at the back where his toilet was just hidden from view, but his every other action was open to the inspection of the crowds. Venus watched, fascinated, her face up against the glass, long after her friends had moved on to another spectacle. Some sense of the wilderness, bequeathed by her maternal line, directed her. The whole energized and uncivil aspect of this man engaged her complete attention, and she felt propriety drop away as she watched his quick, graceful moves and glances.

Later that night, in her suburban home, she pretended to go to bed early, then crept out down the back stairs and made her way to the great glass hall. Pink-cheeked from the chilled night air, she walked the perimeter of the vast building until she found a workman's door unlocked. She worked through the maze of moonlit exhibitions, and located the Wolf Man's cage. Papago, who had been dozing, was instantly awake.

It was evident from the beginning that all the rules were different; none of the citizen's moves and ploys. Venus unlatched the door of Papago's transparent sitting room and walked in. He sprang to meet her, his head slightly to one side, his nostrils dilating, his eyes fixed on her face. She took one step toward him and then he leaped, he was in front of her, already past social distance and as close as they could be without touching, so that they could feel one another's breathing and the heat from the other's body and the odors of the body, and when he moved a fly's foot forward she could feel the sharp prickles of the barbs from the rim of his beard.

And then his hands were running through her hair and rubbing her head and ears, he mouthed her hands, finding the curious vestigial digit, he panted. And she was touching him and feeling what seemed like an electric charge that surrounded his body. What was this, what was happening? She sensed, almost swooning, that this was a moment of impact between the billiard balls in the Humean model of causality, *knock!* and that her instinct to throw over all that she had been taught would issue in profound effects that would move things far beyond herself, the spheres hitting and clicking over the green baize.

They hugged and buffeted each other, they wrestled each other to the floor and there tugged off the intervening garments until they lay, naked and splendid, white as the marble and dark as the granite in the moon's great bath. The clear, unblemished platinum light fell at vast speeds through the thousand lenses of the Crystal Palace, and ricocheted from surface to surface. As Venus arched her back and opened her legs, Papago knocked and pressed at her lower lips with his large, flushed cock, stroking and stroking at the doorway, again and again and then, *ah, ah,* she opens, he enters. She bites him and tastes his blood, she returns it to him as he presses a deep kiss, his lips on hers. The glass is shining and when Venus opens her eyes she sees a hundred moons simultaneously. They are panting. Venus is on top of Papago, moving over him very fast, back and forth, moaning as he moans, his face is very absolute in the cold light. And so they turn and shift, groaning, sobbing, and all their blood and effort is turned to light, glass, crystal, light, light. And when he crests and comes and shoots his million seeds, and she is clamorous, it is the moon fracturing into a thousand moons, his mouth open, howling, a thousand thousand moons, lights, shouts. He howls purely, as he was taught. She laughed aloud with her mouth open and her teeth bouncing back the moonlight. From down the hall, the monkeys were jubbering replies.

He cries out *Mother!*

After the act of love, they enjoyed a Turkish cigarette. There were no ash trays.

Venus, departing, had left the door of the cage ajar, and when Papago roused from his deep sleep and he smelt the air laced with smoke, and he saw the glancing flames admiring their reflections, growing, increasing, he left the cage and began searching for an exit.

Women fell on their knees in the streets to pray on the night the Crystal Palace burned. *Flame Seen Over 9 Counties.* The flames were seen staining the sky all over Southern England. Showers of sparks fell near houses at Beckenham, two miles away. A newspaper could be read in a garden at Norbury, three miles off. Flocks of exotic birds from the aviary were saved in the nick of time by releasing them from their cages. The fish in the aquarium were not so fortunate.

The flames reached the stockroom where the fireworks were kept, and what a display! Like a greedy child who wants all the treats at once, the sky filled with Katharine wheels and pink dervishes, rockets, sprays and bursts, cannon shot, fountains, Pavlovas, two-stage fountains, two-stage rockets, two-stage rocket-fountains, whizzers, giant firecrackers, and the illuminated alphabet. The good folk of London wept and applauded.

The flames were multiplied in those thousand thousand lenses, what a dazzle of matter to energy! So much loss, so beautifully, it constituted a beacon still remembered by the post-imperial Brits. The monkeys screamed what might have been curses or prayers. Were they noted down? The blaze could have been seen by an observer on Mars.

There was no exit, and the molten glass was falling down, and the smoke and flames were thickening. He died like a wolf.

4.1
Venus was sent away from home as soon as her condition was discovered. Prostitutes helped her to bury the two dead babies, and to look after the remaining triplet, Claudius. She was traveling to her wedding with a Polish diplomat on Christmas Day, 1933, when her train crashed near Vishinev, Rumania, like a toy unwrapped that morning and spilled out, upside down in the snow, smashing all the pretty things, and she was killed.

3.4/3
Seven-year-old carrot-topped, color-blind Grandfather Joseph N. Adpo was sent to live with his Aunt Harriet who was a wonderful cook, and Uncle Simon, a wealthy furrier. Simon was also deep into politics, and when he realized the child's abilities, he set up a very special course of training for him. By his 20th

birthday, Joe was a double fish, a master of counter-intelligence, a wild card. He had traveled to the Middle East, where he was doing some preliminary organization of cells, when he met Grandmother Alice Adpo, 19 years old and prematurely gray. She had entered politics early and from a different chute, having been raised in the anarchic woods of far Northern California by the Diggers Revenant, who lived parallel to the law and didn't send their children to school. They became allies. Their work took them to some of the earth's desperate corners, and Alice learned to connect with the violent humor at the bottom of the food chain. She worked to turn the thoughts and efforts of the rebels toward Utopia, Utopia now, by whatever means necessary. No violence that they could mount seemed to her a speck against the violence that went on, systematically, each day to keep these people starving and powerless.

When their baby was born, Alice was working in Agadir, Morocco, and she kept the infant Boris with a native family. She had to dress as a man to carry out her assignment there, and her large nose made her more convincing. She found, though, that she had to bind her breasts tightly to look the part, and the pressure inverted her nipples and made it difficult for the baby to suck.

On the night of the 2nd of March, 1960, a bright moon hung over Agadir and seemed to bless the warm evening. Joseph had traveled to Fez, and Alice, who was exhausted by her recent, heroic and successful efforts to organize a cell of the Utopians in Agadir was tending her blubbering child, stirring her cup of raspberry leaf tea with her left hand, the old women said that it would increase her milk supply. The skinny child mouthed and chewed at her reluctant breasts and would not be comforted.

Alice was singing an off-key fragmented lullabye, *Sleep, sleep, little dinkum, the night is calm, and you are safe with your Mama, sleep,* at which point in the text the earth heaved and broke apart and in Peru formed a large fresh water lake, and at the bottom of the Atlantic Ocean a new 28,000 foot mountain was created and, tit for tat, in the city of Agadir, the quake simply voided whatever humanity had done. Then the earth, having shifted, was still, leaving chaos, screaming, fires, and dust settling over the broken landscape. Not a family was left untouched. Alice was among the many buried alive, and she lived for awhile longer underneath the rubble, thinking long thoughts. Then she died. The infant, Boris, trapped in an air pocket, screamed loud enough beneath the stones for the rescue workers to hear him and dig him out.

Alice's death made Joseph completely miserable, while confirming his deep sense of the world's inclinations. On the 16th of December that year Joe was traveling on a United Airlines DC8 from Chicago to New York, returning to his Uncle's home for Christmas. He held his damp little son on his knee. He would have to wait until they landed for a nappy change. The sealed jar with Alice's ashes was stowed beneath the seat. Joe sang to quiet the child, who whimpered as his ears felt the pressure, *Good King Wenceslas went out*. They would have to wait to land, the United Airlines jet had been ordered by traffic controllers to fly in a stacking pattern 5,000 feet above Preston, New Jersey, until the ok was given to proceed to Idlewild. At the same moment, a TWA plane was given orders to fly a similar holding pattern 6,000 feet above La Guardia airport. Their separate courses from the stacks over each airport would be several miles apart.

While radar controllers at both airfields stood mesmerized, watching their blue screens, they saw the images of the two aircraft merge into one, and continue for a little, then split into two again and fall out of sight. The DC8, burning and blazing, sliced the steeple off St. Augustine's Roman Catholic Church, then buried itself in the church's foundations, while pieces spun off crashing down into the street. Joseph was killed at the first mid-air impact, the words of the carol still wet on his lips. His ashes mixed with his wife's. Baby Boris was extricated from the wreckage, terrified. He would not stop screaming for twenty-four hours.

3.2

Water! Water! These were the last recorded words of Grandmother Sonia Wang, when that common substance entered rudely, without invitation, and filled her sleeping berth on the Zealand Express.

Meanwhile, fifty miles away her husband Claudius spent this Christmas Eve 1953, groaning and sweating beneath Miss Katrina's powerful hands. Sweating out the toxins of twelfth night celebration in the steamroom of the Auckland Salt Palm Spa and Curative Waters, the mercury climbed and their bodies, the massaged and the masseuse, released a spectrum of odors, mixing and combining in the saturated atmosphere. Miss Katrina jabbered to him in Danish the names of muscles, while Claudius' mind was divided between an irritated longing for Sonia's arrival later that night, her Christmas reunion with himself and baby Lilly, and strategizing a connection with Katrina for later in the week, to fill in time after Sonia had again returned to the tribal territory.

When Sonia's Mother Rachel was lost in the 1928 Florida hurricane (Hurricane Mable), little Sonia was found and cared for by a tribe of Seminole Indians living on the edge of the Everglades. This tribe had been one of the few never to have formally surrendered to the Great White Chiefs in Washington, and they were a proud people. They educated her in their ways, and she learned to distinguish the thousand voices of the swamp, and how to kill and cook and (this a boy's task which the odd little girl insisted on attempting) how to wrestle an alligator and calm it using special words *Teee-ho*, and regulated breathing and a particular rubbing motion on its belly. When she was removed by the authorities from the Indians at the age of 14 and sent to the famous Boston College for Young Ladies, a crevasse formed in her psychology which provided the perfect avenue for the march of her congenital madness.

She had a brilliant if somewhat erratic academic career and, living on a large trust fund, she enrolled in the jet set and combined her serious anthropological studies with a judicious amount of sophisticated play amongst the world's pretty people. She had already gone through two brief marriages when she met Claudius who had just led a successful climbing expedition in Patagonia.

During the noisy clashes of two highly articulated ego-structures which followed, Sonia's illnesses, typically of the stomach and female parts, became more frequent, with myste-

rious bleeding and sudden hospitalizations. No one in their circle
could see a future for them as a couple. It was with some surprise,
then, that they received the invitations, on etched aluminum, to
the wedding which was to take place in the aerodrome in Ghent,
after which the bride and groom were to fly off to New Zealand
where Sonia would spend some time living with the Maoris. The
bride looked stunning in her silk flying uniform, apple-faced,
radiant, three months pregnant, with her dimpled chin and her
brown hair cut short as a boy's.

New Zealand consists of a mountainous, slender, wasp-
waisted archipelago of two large and a good many smaller islands,
and it was at a point just at the buckle on the belt around that
waist that Lilly was born premature four months later. For 6 days
while she struggled for breath in the incubator, Claudius had to
empty his wife's loaded breasts which were too tender for the
machine. Sucking at the sweet juice he became aroused, and
exhausted Sonia grinned at him, in pain, excited, weeping. Later,
with the little girl strong and thriving, Sonia installed father and
daughter with a good old Irish nursemaid and servants in a grand
house in Auckland, went back to the Maoris, and commuted
every two weeks to play with baby Lilly, and to join her husband
in plentiful cocaine and tantric exercises when the child was
asleep. She loved him too much, as a New Woman she was
rationally indisposed to jealousy, but all of his little *affaires*
maddened her and she felt herself becoming obsessional. She
returned to the tribe gratefully. She had won their canny hearts
when she responded to their initial bare-bottomed insult first by
laughing enormously, like a four-year-old undone by a wonderfully funny scatological joke, and then by unbuttoning her corduroy
overalls and dropping them, and with her caramel silk pants
around her ankles, turning, bending, proffering her own bright
ass. The Maoris were delighted and took her to their hearts,
welcoming her even with her anthropologist's notebooks and
curiosity. They often gave her true information in place of the
elaborate jokes they were used to playing on important visiting
scientists.

Christmas Eve, after feasting on too much boiled meat,

Sonia rubbed noses with the tribespeople and bade them Happy Christmas and goodbye until after the holidays, then she boarded the train which was to travel the one hundred miles between Tangiwai and Auckland. She retired to her bunk, but could not fall into a restful sleep as her stomach rumbled over the black stew.

Twenty miles away, Mount Ruapehu, 9,000 feet, suddenly rumbled, woke, and began throwing out scalding mud, rock and water. This mass pushed over the landscape, collecting all that lay before it, thundering toward the bridge at Tangiwai that spanned the River Whangaehu. It wiped out the bridge without effort. *Boom*. As the train hurtled toward the river, Sonia in the upper bunk was slow motioning at a hypnogogic pow wow by a stand of live oak and evergreens where the Seminoles and Maoris came together, *bottoms up!*, making her cry with the poignant gesturing of the spoilt authochthonous.

The train hit the river. Sonia woke and opened her mouth, WA.

3.1

The infant Grandfather Claudius had been unkindly ripped into this wailing world and left as the only humunculi survivor of triplets. The other two neonates, identical boys, had survived almost to the end of their interuterine journey, swimming and sucking, but the dreadful shock which their Mother Venus had suffered when she realized that a great war was again unavoidable had rendered the placenta inefficient and so they perished. Venus held them, the two cold, still, dead babes, for the entire night before they were taken from her and disposed of. And so Claudius, who began by seeming simply an animated instance of the same type as his little dead brothers, each with a vestigial digit on the right hand, grew daily, burst the molds, his frame and features stretching out.

As a young man he moved in a fast set. He had some ability at climbing very high mountains and driving very fast cars, and he was big and hairy and graceful and the ladies loved him. He was an unintentional bigamist when he married Sonia Wang, caught by her radical style and her oddness. He moderated his risk-taking, just for a little, out of a wish to calm his hectic wife during her first pregnancy. He was initially indifferent to tiny, squalling baby Lilly, but as she grew he came to adore her. Claudius respected his wife's anthropological studies, and determined to enjoy Auckland's resources.

At the news of Sonia's death, Grandfather Claudius Lippershey took little Lilly and flew to New Zealand, so much comradely death on mountains and race tracks had not prepared him for this. He made the funeral arrangements through agents.

He spent the next two years showing young Lilly the great world. Then he approached his own great test. Had he been given time to reflect, Claudius would have appreciated the catastrophe's ironic decoration. He had considered driving in the 1955 LeMans, there was a place for him on the Maserati team, and racing was his great stimulant. He had been delighted when the invitation came, the smell of absolute effort, danger, acceleration. He could taste it like metal in his mouth. It was with some reluctance, then, that he decided to go simply as a spectator, so that he could enjoy the event with his beloved daughter. The little girl had the same effect on him as had her glorious mad mother, storming his fortifications, unpicking the locks, catalyzing that which had been inert and then—and always with shocking force—moving into a blissful, radiant intimacy.

Lilly, at four, had an estatic savage's sense of ceremony. She galloped around the hot fairground, accelerated by the music, stirring up the fragrant dust. Now she had stepped out of her lace-trimmed pinafore and was drilling three children she had collected from the crowd. They were making up a dance, it was to combine elements from Seminole and Maori ritual and mimetic tokens of the race going on just on the other side of the barrier, where the cars were moving at 120 mph. And so the dancing children represented the cars, speed itself, the sun, the wind and other elements of the bright June day. Lilly was gesturing with a cornet baton of strawberry icecream, pinkly spotting her own smooth apricot hide and spraying the confection over the landscape and her fellows.

In the serious play of the day, World Champion Fangio was competing, and it was anticipated that with new cars and top drivers new speed records would be established. Fangio, in his silver Mercedes No. 3, was being seriously challenged by Mike Hawthorn in a new type Jaguar. They were building up enormous speed, and taking the turns at 150 miles per hour. The audience watched, Claudius among them, full of excited attention. Then sudden as a whim of Zeus, disaster. One of the Mercedes cars slewed from the track, bounced over the mound of earth that stood as a safety bank, rocketed through the massed crowd of horrified spectators, and finally exploded killing nearly 100 and injuring many others. It took less time to happen than it does to read about.

Claudius was decapitated by the hurtling metal. The last thought of his severed head was *Sonia, Lilly!* Two of the children with whom Lilly had been dancing were similarly sundered, one blonde head still slobbered at its icecream. They found Lilly wandering demented through the fairground, striped with red blood and pink icecream. The child was mute.

2.2/1

Forty weeks before Gabriel was born, his Mama Lilly Lippershey opened her mouth and uttered her first words in 24 years. These shrieks were either *GOD! GOD! GOD!* or *CLAUDE! CLAUDE! CLAUDE!* as she and Boris Adpo accomplished her deflowering. Neither one of them could swear to what the words were, or what they meant, as the cries poured like broken glass from a bird's mouth into the air of the empty swimming pool. From that moment on she was capable of speech with only a slight roughness in the timbre of her voice to indicate former abnormality. She began to argue with her lover.

And so they were two swimmers together, Lilly was long, tawny skinned with broad square shoulders and a cloud of gold wire hair, she stroked and kicked powerfully. (Slightly) or (soon to be) mad Boris was the first man to bridge her formidable defences and to storm past the silent beauty with his loud brilliant babble. The 900 year comet flashed over them as hairy Boris puffed and snorted, he kissed her private raspberry birth mark and her cleft chin, *push push push*. They toiled through the night, and by cockcrow the karmic merging of the two catastrophic lines was achieved and Gabriel, bicellular, was begun.

She was enroute to Australia, an economist working with the problem of primary and secondary effects of the ongoing desertification of areas of the planet.

It is not by saying *"honey honey"* that sweetness comes to the mouth.

She was careful during the pregnancy, avoided drugs, but could not give up her passion for chocolate.

And so Gabriel was a desert baby, born at day break, when the sky was flooded with green and rose. The midwife tore away the membrane of the caul and the little fellow hollered at the loud, rushing world.

Gabriel glided from couch to table, blotting each with chocolate, some Auntie had give him a chocolate bear. Lilly reached down and hugged him and licked at the chocolate on his right cheek with a quick dart of the tongue. *I'm like a Mother Cat and you're my Kitten*. Gabriel gave her a social grin, he was not complicit with her in that game as he would have been a few weeks earlier. *Oh Gabe, growing up so fast*, Lilly was at her desk, measuring the take-up index of the non-superficial cells of the cactus *Jossoli penex penniculae*, largest verticullus cactus of Australia. He clambered up her, pulled her hair, started to fiddle with the titrating equipment, got chocolate on the papers, *down you go, down you go little chocolate man*.

On the night they first met he told the mute beauty stories, and then she danced for him, and after Lilly's dance he was aroused, and Papa Boris Adpo bounded around the laughing woman in the style of the Priapic satyr. Naked except for a pair of unmatched socks, red and green, his thick, shapely body was heavily furred with a rusty, curly pelf. He was shaking his silver head and grinning, yodelling *Oh Lilly Lilly Lilly Loo-oo-oo*. He rubbed his cleft chin.

Big nosed, dusky, left-handed, slant-eyed Boris mimed the Hawaiian love dance and the Tewa's cat's cradle replicas of suspension bridges. He repeated the upper northern Afghani courting yodel, darting close to the spinning blonde, a kiss *smack smack*, the narrative of a postmodernist, full of emblems and insistently pluralist. *I luff yoo my yellow papaya* he droned. It was Boris's sense that the world was speeding up. This was the peak of his manic phase. Each time he went mad, he began by falling head over heels for another woman and he agitated with the sprightliness of the new lover. And each time he began to recover, he would re-enter his old life with a deep and unrelenting depressive format, eschewing the formerly beloved and writing new computer programs that testified to his freshly incremented sense of things. He was on the consultant board of a secret organization which formed the information revolution's branch of the Masonic Empire. Lilly helped him toward the painful understanding that his satyrism and manias flowed from his earliest experiences with his Mama's inturned dugs, which had been political. *Help me.*

It was on the day that Gabriel was born that Boris became convinced that their phone was being tapped. He was glad to travel with Lilly and the tiny baby to Australia where Lilly had planned some field research. *When is paranoia not illness, but the appropriate response to the post-modern world?* This was a toast over Chilean wine on the polar flight.

Boris was allergic to cats, strawberries and monosodium glutamate.

At Field Station 3, they could hear the fire before they could see it, it was roaring, dragon-tempered. They could see the columns of smoke which seemed to hold up the heavens, of course, and the odd lurid salmon color of the midday sky. Then rounding the corner a complete wall of emerald flame was visible, very loud, it leaped the fire-break, on past the wet earth and hesitated a moment, dragon breathing, at the edge of the compound. And then smack, thump, there comes the dragon, huffing right here beside Lilly, who rolls her eyes and tries to form some kind of prayer. Her voice is gone again. Her thoughts winkle out. . . . *Gabriel!*

When Lilly died Boris packed up his gear and Gabe's, and made a run for it. They had traveled through fourteen countries when the authorities caught up with them and moved them to the reservation. And it was only a short time later, in a freak earth shift near the Four Corners, that Boris embraced his destiny, fire, earth and water.

1.

Smiler and Gabriel are out for a walk, a boy and his dog. They tack back and forth between the blind concrete wall of the lab and the Italian "black" cypresses which line the two miles of electrified inner perimeter. The garden is laid out according to a neo-Heroclitean conception, The Theatre of Rational Nations. This is a quite complicated gardening conceit which uses traditional relationships of lawn, shrubbery, blooms, trees, paths, junctions, statuary, and topiary to display an ideal concord among a set of happy nation states. Gabriel darts between the legs of a naked and innocent pink marble Monsieur Citizen, identified in brass as representing France, who is muscularly engaged in enthusiastically bussing the blue basalt shoulder blade of a perplexed Ms. West Africa. Smiler follows closely after, limping, they are playing tag. They are watched by the three real-time observers, and by the benign stony patriotic instantiations; and also by a verdigris-clad little fountain which features a boy, just a bit older than Gabriel and with the same sweet oval-topped, heart-bottomed face, pissing into a pool; and by Nurse who has come out to stroll on the grass and lift her face to the sun and watch the child and his dog playing, although she is not on duty.

The regulations require a minimum of three naked-eye real-time observers at all times, a minimum of three observers at all times, and it is still a mystery as to how the probabilities could have conspired to leave Gabriel unregarded. As the reports showed afterward: #1, who was closest, was bending over Smiler to examine the left front paw which he had suddenly begun to favor; and #2, who was manning *(sic)* the inner perimeter gatehouse platform was lifting his eyes skyward to inspect a small vertical takeoff air-taxi vehicle which was passing overhead, and #3 went suddenly operationally blind and deaf because the boy looked so *ordinary,* the garden was so *peaceful* that his scanning attention simply cut out and he relived, word by word, every irreversible detail of breakfast with his wife this morning, in their small kitchen full of slanted early light, during which she had told him that she *had had enough of his coldness, his depressions, his rudeness,* which she detailed, *and that she felt as though he were someone foreign and unknown when he was lying in bed beside her or on top of her, and that she was planning to take their daughter Amanda and leave for Texas, and that as soon as possible she would get a divorce.*

And then they all looked back to that green napkin of grass between the urinating fountains and the magnolia bush, and *no, what?, no, he was gone.*

And then all hell breaks loose. And then the drill commences, the entire staff is mobilized and the siren does its banshee, flaying the aural space, *yaw yaw yaw yaw yaw.* They look at each other with terrible surmise. *Did you see the air-taxi, it might be the Rooskies!* And at headquarters where this garden suddenly empty of its treasure is being watched on a bank of twenty screens, scientists have their bio-feedback exercises for the regulation of dangerously high blood pressure on their lips like mantras, and the heart pills under their tongues like miniature, fallen, eucharist.

Gabriel Gabriel Gabriel. #1 is on the satellite phone to Washington, and also putting out a message over the world grid. For all the talk of the Rooskies, Project Gabriel has strong internationalisticki components; the worst-case scenario involves the initial collapse of communications, so they are tended assiduously by their special information technicians, or "geisha." #2 is opening the gates for the jeeps, checking their i.d. #3 is amok, running mindlessly back and forth, forgetting his drill, *straighten up, soldier,* shouting into his walkie-talkie and burning the ears of the technicians who are still inside the lab. He tries to push the button to clear his inner screen of the image of Amanda pinioned by the holocaust because of her Daddy's error. It will not turn off. And the Nurse, who had after all not been on duty and had no reason to reproach herself, reckoned now that the little lad had been missing for twenty minutes, she was calling *Gabriel my honey, my coney,* and was weeping and babbling dreadfully.

One of the jeeps has already established a mobile emergency headquarters and set up another siren horn, and there are two helicopters coming in to land on the pad, making a terrific local wind which bends the cypresses almost in half and blows dust into the officials' faces and sprays the watery spout back against the green boy *(where is your twin?)*, and then in a chink of quiet between the rival sirens and the whirlipigs, *achoo achooo achoo!*

Smiler's sneezing! And at first they think it must be the dust stirred up by the aircraft teasing his delicate nose, but wait, no, he is helping and nosing at the entrance to the monumental cuckoo clock constructed of seashells which is the gift of Tahiti to Happy Switzerland, *but surely the entrance is too small for the child, no, no, he's double-jointed, no, wait, yes!*

Gabriel crawls out, he is laughing and crying, he calls out very loudly *olli olli orfen free!* He puts his arm around the sneezing dog, *you're it!*

Gabriel remembers just a little of his Mama, an iced cake in the shape of a swan; some game in which she bounced him on her lap, singing in her rough voice, *trot trot to Boston, trot trot to Lynne, watch out little boy so you don't fall in,* and the lap opened and he would hurtle downwards *boom,* safe.

And he can remember Dada more clearly, but the tone is sour, Dada playing with him, wrestling, but Gabriel could tell, giant Dada wasn't really trying. Mama gone, and Dada crying in the kitchen.

Dour faces up against the one-way glass opened their lips and spoke to one another, *To design an ends/means disposal, in our opinion, might precipitate the very event we all hope to avoid.*

Smiler sneezed and Gabriel giggled and released him. And his Nurse had him on her lap, and was telling him this story about how the animals were trying to make a house, build a house. *And the Raccoon brought the nails, and the Camel brought the hammer, and the Coyotes came and worked on the foundation, and the Elephants and the Mongoose came, and the Lemur and the Crocodile mixed mortar, and some played music while the others worked. The Okapi and the Timber Wolf came hand in hand, and the house finished up full of strange doors and windows and chimneys in all styles, and parts of it fell down and lay in ruins while the others went on building, and along the road comes an old Mule, and she says, Ah doan wanna hurt yer feelings, honey, but when Ah looks at dat mess, Ah jes needs to laugh or cry, so Ah'll laugh, and she was laughing so hard that she didn't look where she was going, and she stepped on a safety pin that lay in the middle of the road, and the pin bent and the story ent.*

blonde at first, red later, turned brown, and now she was as dark as her mother. *Me too.*

I used to eat bacon
water is bacon
meat is not clean
potatoes when you are hungry
coffee when you taste
milk once a week
beer once daily
Do you want to die? well, so-something-or-other. We'll a better *feeling?*
How often is all her soul feel. Her soul is here

Dear Mother and Dad, We arrived in Amsterdam safe and well, and although Joe had a little cold during a trouble various and were all fine. The city is splendid, small enough to comprehend with a coherent rhythmic structure laced on economic vanish. How are you both? Will you be able to get away to the lake early this summer or are you Dad, going to be teaching summer school again? Have you heard anything from Sally? I've written to her but no word as yet. I hope Aunt Kate is better now. Just the doctors said what's the matter with her? Is it anything serious? The proprietor of the hotel has taken to the soul keeps giving her chocolates every time we go out, so we wander around the city always with a snappy faced boy he my little girl. There is an immense sense of community here after the fierceness of New York. The people are terribly nice clean the buildings shining, ornamental and the colorful former creatures. History is lying around in great lumps everywhere. Graham and Ray join me in sending love. xx xxx

THE JEWISH BRIDE
For all its richness and splendor, the picture of painting is never an end in itself with Rembrandt, but a means of embodying his innermost thoughts. Such is the case with the *Jewish Bride* in the Rijksmuseum, Amsterdam. After countless attempts to explain this picture, its exact meaning